The
Do-Re-Mi

The
Do-Re-Mi

Ken Kuhlken

Poisoned Pen Press

Copyright © 2006 by Ken Kuhlken

First Edition 2006

10 9 8 7 6 5 4 3 2 1

Library of Congress Catalog Card Number: 2006902894

ISBN: 1-59058-337-X (978-1-59058-337-1) Hardcover

Poisoned Pen Press
6962 E. First Ave., Ste. 103
Scottsdale, AZ 85251
www.poisonedpenpress.com
info@poisonedpenpress.com

Printed in the United States of America

For Pam, so you can see how the world looked before you'd lived long enough to make it better.

Acknowledgments

A thousand thanks to the Zarp brothers, the whole Torrey family including Quiggles and Flowers; to Havens and Bev, Lucas and Carol Field, Bob Williams, Laura Munger, Ron Martina and Patricia wherever you are; to the Niman brothers, Karl Hartman, Alan and Laura (for letting Alan out of the house) Russell; to Dan Thrapp, Ron Argo, the Wednesday evening mob, and no doubt a bunch of people I'll remember as soon as this note is out of my hands. Special thanks to my amazing kids Darcy, Darren and Nicholas Mentone, Cody Kuhlken, and Zoë the wonder girl, for your patience and love; to Karen Hasman for giving me time, to Gene Riehl, for ideas and answers, and to Barbara Peters and her crew at Poisoned Pen Press for superior advice and help. Deepest thanks to Pam. You all helped create my story.

Chapter One

Pop wanted me to practice law. USC admitted me to their Juris Doctorate program.

So I asked Pop, "Are lawyers crooks to begin with or does being a lawyer make them crooks?"

The sun was falling fast toward the Rubicons across Lake Tahoe from our cottage. Pop stood over the steaks he was grilling. Mama had gone inside for mosquito repellent.

For the past half hour, Pop and I had discussed the *San Francisco Chronicle*'s latest revelations about President Nixon's Watergate blunder.

Pop used the *Chronicle* to fan smoke out of his face. "Nobody's anything to begin with," he said. "Lawyers can go bad, but you're not that kind of man."

Pop was usually right. That time, he was dead wrong.

Later that summer, on the last Wednesday in August, 1972, I drove north on Highway 101, into the redwoods. The two-lane highway was cluttered with hippie vans, sputtering VWs, and family wagons descending upon the town of Evergreen.

Hippies claimed Evergreen was the closest place on earth to Eden. I wouldn't have disputed their claim. The air was crisp with a mild salty tang and the seductive fragrance of redwoods. Because of the mountains that horseshoed around the valley, leaving one side open to the breezes off the Pacific, twenty miles west, Evergreen was an ecosystem apart, with balmy winters and summers cooled by mists and night rains that blew away at dawn, over the Trinity Wilderness.

Most of us crowding the highway had come for Big Dan Mills' Jamboree. I believed that weekend would change my life. I only hoped it would change for the better.

The jamboree was a folk festival. Over the past three years, it had become a major event, even while half the people who used to talk politics in coffee houses had turned to dropping LSD and spacing out on electric guitars.

My brother Alvaro had convinced Big Dan to invite me to perform. I would be on stage Sunday, just before the finale. In my daydreams, it was my chance to turn pro, to meet record producers and earn a shot at playing clubs like the Troubadour in Hollywood. At least, I might land a booking agent and give myself a solid reason to forget USC, where I was supposed to start law school in twenty days.

As I passed a sign marking twelve miles to Evergreen, I was trying to decide what to play. I wished to God I had written even two good songs. But so far, the only tunes or lyrics that came to mind when I picked up my guitar were those I had heard. Besides, I didn't feel wise enough about the world to write honest yet meaningful words. Pop said the songs would come after I had experienced more.

Most of the people whose songs I played were coming to the jamboree. Lightnin' Hopkins, my favorite living bluesman, was coming. Ramblin' Jack Elliot, who had been pals with Woody Guthrie, would be talking about Woody and playing Woody's songs. Tom Paxton was coming, and Dino Valenti. Richard Fariña was dead, but his wife Mimi was on the bill. I wouldn't risk her displeasure by doing any of Fariña's songs. Buffy St. Marie was coming, which meant I wouldn't play the Peter Le Farge numbers I knew. They were about Indians, which was her territory, not mine.

Rumors had circulated that Bob Dylan meant to show up, forsake his rock and roll ways, turn back to standing alone with his acoustic guitar and harmonica, and rekindle the folk scene.

Maybe a Steven Foster number would work, I thought. Maybe "Beautiful Dreamer," one of Mama's favorites.

Alvaro could help me choose. I hoped to find my brother tonight. I hadn't seen him much in the past few years, since he left for Vietnam. And I was anxious to show him my new guitar, a Gibson Hummingbird, my twenty-second birthday present from Pop. I had lusted after a Hummingbird since Alvaro taught me to play.

I believed our family was blessed. Mama appeared to be healing. And as far as we knew, Alvaro had stayed out of trouble for months now.

Ten miles south of Evergreen, I slowed to observe three kids who could pass for cupids. They and a man stood with bowed heads around a simple cross of redwood branches in a ditch beside the highway. Grieving for a Mexican friend, I thought. Along the roads of Mexico, people marked the site of each fatal crash with a cross or shrine.

The man slouched beside the cross. He had strawberry blond hair, long, wavy and braided. The kids' white ringlets hung to their shoulders. They all were tan, and shirtless though the sun had disappeared behind the redwood forest a half hour ago.

I raced through an S curve and into a cacophony of sputters and rumbles. I stood on the brakes when a platoon of outlaw bikers fishtailed onto the highway from the dirt parking lot of a tavern called the Crossroads.

In the dusk, I couldn't read their colors. Cossacks, I thought. Alvaro had confessed to brawling in an Evergreen saloon. He had argued about the Vietnam issue with a biker. The biker ran with a gang called Cossacks.

Highball Trail began just south of the Crossroads and went east along the bank of Whiskey River. In a letter, Alvaro had mentioned the river's name, and added, "Tell Mama it's only water."

I drove into the forest while dusk turned to dark so fast the road seemed to dip and carry me underground. Along the trail, second growth redwoods made way for ancient trees as wide as logging trucks and tall as Jack's beanstalk. Their fragrance was like a potion. It left me giddy and able to imagine the world had become a safe and wondrous place, where evil could no longer reside.

Since I had failed to replace a burnt out dashboard light, I bounded over ruts and fallen branches trying to sense the passing miles. The road narrowed into a trail more suitable for horses than cars. I stopped, crawled into the back and found my flashlight in the crate of camping gear. According to the odometer and Alvaro's directions, the Mexican flag would greet me 1.3 miles ahead.

Night had come. Only drips of moon or starlight leaked through the trees. As I drove on, redwood branches scratched like fingernails along both sides of my wagon. I swerved and dodged, but ruts grabbed the wheels and yanked them sideways. The muffler scraped granite and showered the forest with sparks. I imagined a forest fire beginning here and consuming the face of the earth. Then I wondered why dread had possessed me.

Two miles ahead, I found a clearing and parked. I shut down the motor, sat still and listened for a human sound. I heard the river whoosh over rocks, and what sounded like a pair of baritone cuckoos. Jays squawked ornery lullabies. I shouted for Alvaro. The birds flew off.

Whiskey River and its flood plain allowed enough break from the redwoods to let starlight fall on the water, which frothed along the banks and churned in mid-stream. Fallen limbs and gnarly stumps flashed past. Across the river was a grove of trees like aspens except flowers grew from their branches. The flowers a shaft of moonlight exposed were red, yellow, and blue, like a vision of heaven that came to me when I got beaned by a wild pitcher's fastball. Even through the redwood fragrance, in the upriver breeze, I caught whiffs of jasmine and of somebody's marijuana garden. Not Alvaro's, I hoped.

Most of the ground between the trail and the bank was too soft to walk without sinking to my knees, but it made a good bed. I threw down a tarp and sleeping bag upon which I lay and dispelled dread with happy thoughts. I imagined myself on a stage packed with my favorite performers. I scrunched up against Mimi Fariña while I watched the booking agent who had just signed me up wave a high sign. And I wondered how disappointed Pop would be when I told him I was going on the coffee house circuit instead of to USC.

I didn't hate the idea of practicing law. But it was Pop's dream for me, not my own. Pop had left USC during the 1920s when his sister came down with rheumatic fever. To pay the bills, he worked days as a bank guard. Nights he played his clarinet in a dance band, which folded when the Great Depression struck. Then Pop joined the L.A.P.D.

Life had taught him to admire good lawyers. And he said I had the right stuff, courage and a passion for justice. But I had no passion for a life of courts and criminals. I wanted to sing, play guitar, and someday write songs that would encourage people to act more loving, kind and faithful. Like Mama, I was a dreamer. Not a fighter like Pop or Alvaro.

When I had told Pop about the jamboree, he gazed at me over his pipe and pondered. "You're a little rough," he said, "but that's your charm. The gravelly voice and your size gives you authority. People listen to you." I swelled with pride to think that Pop, who was no flatterer, thought of me that way. Then he added, "But the music business will break your heart."

The first gunshot woke me. The next report could've been a thunderclap. The last four sounded like maracas. For minutes I sat and listened, but the forest had gone mute.

I worried about Alvaro. In our family, if the phone rang at 3:00 a.m., we feared for Alvaro. If a police car drove up the street, we wondered what he had done. Alvaro was wild. Besides, amongst the tools he had brought on what he called Operation Clean was a rifle. He told us he meant to feed himself with the rifle and his fishing gear.

I worried myself to sleep. In the morning, I stumbled to the river and splashed my face with crystalline water.

I was tossing my gear in the Chevy when I peered down the road and spotted my brother's marker. The Mexican flag waved from a branch that overhung the road, twenty feet up. Last night, I hadn't looked that high, though I should have remembered Alvaro's monkey-like skill at climbing trees.

I parked just past the flag on a rocky patch between two redwoods and started along a single-file path. Walking toward the twang of guitar strings, I wondered what disturbance or nightmare had woke Alvaro before six. At home, we needed to use bribery or threats to lure him out of bed.

His camp was a quarter mile up the path. As I neared, he started playing and singing a *corrido* ballad he had made up while in Vietnam. It told of when he got wounded and missed his rotation on point and so his best *amigo* took over and died that day.

In the center of the clearing, Alvaro squatted Indio-style, finger picking the guitar he had bought in Paracho, Michoacan. He was the musical genius in our family. His right hand danced on the strings while the fingers of his left hand ran up and down the fret-board. He was perched on a redwood stump so wide an orchestra could have joined him. The clearing was bordered by a ring of second growth redwood small enough to allow daylight into the camp. Mexican string bags of groceries, clothes and utensils hung like *piñatas* from the branches. Behind Alvaro stood an army surplus bivouac tent that could accommodate a dozen cots. The Browning 30.06 hung by a strap from a notch in a flagpole beside the tent's entrance.

Alvaro handled his Paracho guitar like a relic. He laid it into a hard-shell case before he sprang off the stump, his arms wide to greet me. His embrace felt as if he meant to weld me there. When he let go, he jumped back and flashed the grin that was a primary weapon in his arsenal of charms. He had used it to hustle *turistas* in Mazatlan after his widowed *borracho* papa got sentenced to eight years in a Sinaloa prison. No doubt that grin had helped him hitch rides a thousand miles north and over the mountains to Tijuana. He survived in Tijuana by stealing and hustling and on the graces of *putas* he charmed, until he made enemies of vicious older street kids and decided to jump the border.

His charms helped him win his place in our family, and later they boosted his career as lead guitar and featured singer in a heartthrob Tijuana rock band. As the house band at the Aloha Club on Avenida Revolución, the district that drew Mexico's best rockers, he was becoming a star. Then he got nabbed at the *frontera* with fifty bottles of the methamphetamine pills we called blackbirds.

Today, though, he looked clean and sober enough. His *Indio* eyes with their long black lashes never blinked while he asked about Pop and Mama. They closed for a minute when I told him Mama was still in danger of slipping back into her catatonia.

I handed him the hundred-dollar bill Pop had sent.

"Keep it, *hermano*," he said. "You the man just graduated college. What'd I do to deserve Pop's money?"

I pressed the bill into his T-shirt pocket. "You're being good."

His eyes flicked away. He strode to the fire-pit, stirred coals, then stretched toward a woodpile beside the pit. He grabbed a long branch and snapped it over his knee, into three parts. He stacked them on the fire. "*Huevos* for breakfast. I got canned *chiles* but no *chorizo. Quieres cafe?*"

"In the biggest mug you've got."

I sat on the big stump between his guitar and a cassette recorder. The lid was open. The tape inside was by Phil Ochs, to whom Alvaro would introduce me in a day or two.

My brother had met Phil Ochs at a peace rally. He got introduced as a Vietnam hero turned against the war. Ochs asked him to tell his combat stories, and afterward they kept in touch. It was Ochs who got Alvaro the jamboree gig.

I considered Reverend King wiser than Chairman Mao, whom Ochs admired. I didn't like Ochs' songs that praised armed revolution. But Alvaro was no pacifist. He called Ochs gutsy for singing what he believed even though it could get him killed.

And once when I criticized Ochs, Alvaro said, "Hey, you've got to like the guy who wrote 'There But For Fortune,' no?" With that, I couldn't argue.

Still I wondered about the fascination that made my brother lead off both letters he'd sent me from Evergreen with quotes from Phil Ochs songs.

The coffee pot hung from a spit above the fire. Alvaro used a hot pad. He always took care of his hands. He poured a mug full and passed it to me. "Yeah, you can tell Pop I'm being good. I did the cold turkey thing. One day I didn't get out of my sleeping bag, just hung in there all scrunched and sweating, waiting for the mole people to attack." He shot me a glance that meant, You just got all you need to know, little brother. "How long you here for?"

"Only the weekend."

"Then it's off to begin your climb to the Supreme Court, right? When do you play at the festival?"

"We. You're going to back me. Sunday at four."

Alvaro shrugged. "Pop's not coming, right?"

"He won't leave Mama yet."

"I miss her," he said. "So, soon as you get to USC, you're going to bury your nose in the books, *entiendes*?" He fixed on me a gaze that meant, Or else.

We laughed together at the irony of the prodigal lecturing the dutiful son, and Alvaro prophesied, "With a brother like me, we better get a lawyer in the family but quick."

As his last words faded, he turned and peered at the path I had walked. For a minute or more, he stood frozen, his right hand raised as if to signal a platoon. We both heard a twig snap.

I whispered, "What—"

Alvaro sprang past me, leaped toward the tent and grabbed his rifle.

Chapter Two

I had watched Alvaro pelt a mountain lion with a slingshot, just for the sport of escaping from a riled mountain lion. I'd heard his confessions about robbing pimps when he was six years old. He had earned three bronze stars in Vietnam though he viewed the war as a feud the locals ought to settle on their own. Alvaro was brave but not *loco*. He wasn't going to stand and fight six armed men with badges.

He only grabbed the Browning and ran. He never raised it or turned, yet the two lead deputies fired. A bullet ripped through the tent, while my brother dashed into the forest. Four deputies chased him, tripping and slashing with arms and pistols through the underbrush.

Off in the forest, Alvaro yowled. I waited in horror, one eye on the guns leveled at me, the other eye cocked in the direction my brother had gone. I didn't breathe until I heard the far away shouts of deputies questioning which way he had run.

The sheriff stayed behind. I'm six feet, two inches, yet the badge and nametag on his chest were level with my chin. W. Willis. I gazed up at mold gray eyes, a nose that looked like a plum somebody had stepped on, and a mouth crimped into a look as sour as though he were about to tackle a skunk. He had narrow shoulders and a wide belly, like a bear.

Beside him, a deputy moved toward me, step-jumping side-to-side as though to dodge enemy fire, rage in his lean face. And like the sheriff, the deputy gripped a revolver with both hands, straight-armed and pointed at me. His gun-barrel traced circles in the air, even after he stopped two yards in front of me. "On your face! Spread eagle!" He sounded like somebody getting strangled.

I obeyed. The deputy holstered his revolver, dropped to his knees, wrenched my hands together and cuffed them. He adjusted the cuffs tight as tourniquets. Before he had finished patting me down, my fingers burned, then tingled and went numb.

While the sheriff bowed his pistachio-shaped head, inspecting my wallet, he consulted with the deputy, whose name was Brady Barker.

Part of me doubted this scene was real. In that forest of giant redwoods and white-barked trees with zigzag branches and leaves like doilies, and flowers whose colors changed as the sun climbed higher, everything seemed dreamier than my dreams. Still, I wracked my brain for words that might prove Alvaro wasn't dangerous, that no matter if they found his plot of weed or whatever they had come intending to find, they didn't need to shoot him. But I only managed to sputter, "Alvaro won't shoot anybody."

Willis folded my wallet, stuffed it into his shirt pocket and hovered over me. "Clifford Hickey." His voice was high as a chirp. "You and the Mexican are what?"

"Brothers."

Deputy Barker rasped, "You don't look like any Mexican's brother."

The sheriff said, "Just give him Miranda, Brady."

"What'd I do?" I demanded.

The sheriff only mumbled as though talking to himself. "Conspired to murder Jimmy Marris."

I choked on the air. The word "murder" echoed inside me. I felt as if I had slipped and tumbled off a cliff. And I recognized "murder" meant the deputies chasing Alvaro would shoot on sight, or at least not risk as much as a turned ankle to bring him in alive.

While Barker recited my rights, he stabbed my tailbone with his boot-heel whenever a comma would've been appropriate, until the sheriff said, "Brady, save it for the one we figure killed your boy."

I listened for Alvaro. Every minute without a clue that they had captured him raised my hopes. He had been a speedy halfback at Mission Bay High, and a woodsman during our summers exploring the mountains around Lake Tahoe. In Vietnam, he had learned a guerilla's tactics. He might slip away.

Willis squatted beside my head, a small tape recorder in his jumbo hand. "You best give us the Mexican. Maybe you tried to stop him from killing Jimmy. We don't know you. Maybe you a good boy. But the Mexican ain't. We know the Mexican." He pushed the record button. "Talk."

I didn't.

In the caged back seat of the cruiser, parked at the junction of Highball Trail and the path to Alvaro's camp, I bent and twisted my wrists and hands, seeking to allow enough blood past the cuffs to keep my hands alive. I had asked them to loosen the cuffs. Twice. They had ignored me, twice.

Willis and Brady came and went, waiting for their *compadres* to drag Alvaro's carcass out of the forest, and for the dog team Willis had requested by radio to arrive.

Somebody had murdered a boy named Jimmy Marris.

I tried to reason. Alvaro must have killed in the war, although he claimed firefights and skirmishes involved such a delirium of bullets, rockets, and grenades, nobody could ascertain who shot whom.

And no doubt any human could murder in a rage. But Alvaro didn't rage. To survive as a Mexican street kid, he had learned to keep his head, to think when most of us would only react.

One summer during our high school years, while we were living at our cabin on Tahoe's north shore, an Incline Village girl jilted her rich boyfriend on account of Alvaro. The rich kid gathered his posse and jumped my brother outside the King's Beach Burger Barn. They stomped his face, broke his nose, cracked a rib and a finger bone. Alvaro could have rallied King's Beach boys, a far tougher crowd than Incline's spoiled brats. Instead, my brother shrugged off the beating and even warned me to leave them alone. He said, "No reason for me to fight, *hermano*. I already won. I got Melinda." She adored him for two years, until she graduated and flew off to Vassar.

I couldn't imagine Alvaro murdering anyone, unless somebody harmed Mama or Pop. Then, he would pursue the offender even to Mars, and deliver him to hell.

While I sat still in the cage listening for my brother, a pickup skidded to a stop beside the cruisers. A pack of red tick hounds bounded off the bed and up the path toward Alvaro's camp, dragging their handlers.

Five minutes later, Willis and Barker came trudging out of the forest. They each flung open a front door, then climbed into the cruiser and slammed the door. They had argued, I supposed, because they shot each other dark glances, while Willis drove.

He careened up the road, flying over ruts, sliding around bends, spewing a rooster tail of black dust. On the highway, he raced top end using lights and siren. Not a word passed between the sheriff and deputy. Every mile or so Barker craned around and bared his gleaming fangs, and his wolf eyes promised that he would piss on my grave.

"Was the murder victim your son?" I asked.

The deputy only stiffened and shifted his eyes away.

Willis said, "Shut up, boy."

On Manhattan Avenue, the willow-shaded, two-lane main drag of Evergreen, Willis slowed and switched off the whirling light and siren. School kids and hippies perched on benches outside the Dairy Queen and Foster's Freeze. Pickups from primered Model A's to shiny new Dodge Power Wagons, and clusters of chopped Harleys, filled the parking lot of the Napa Auto Parts, Sears Catalog Outlet and Safeway mall. Every building I noticed on Manhattan Avenue and the dozen residential side streets was sided in redwood, as if that was all the building codes allowed. Even the station and jail were redwood. As we pulled into the lot behind the station, I said, "You're taking me to the magistrate, right?"

Willis spoke his first civil words toward me. "Magistrate's got a business. He don't sit till closing time."

Brady Barker ordered me out of the cruiser, shoved me toward and through the station back entrance, into a room split by a pass-way and quartered into three usable cells and another serving as a storeroom. Willis pushed a buzzer. A bald and buck-toothed jailer stepped out of a room beyond the cell block. He wore a napkin as a bib. I smelled hot grease and onions.

Willis pointed at the cell on the east side, next to the store-room. The jailer unlocked the gate and ushered me in, while Barker strode out of the cell block and through a narrow hall to the big room with desks and the reception counter at the far end by the Manhattan Avenue door. As the gate shut behind me, I asked the sheriff to kindly remove the cuffs.

"Brady's got the key," Willis said. "I'll send him in directly." He yawned, turned and left through the doorway we had entered. The jailer strolled back to the kitchen.

Each cell was furnished with two sets of bunk beds, a toilet, and a sink. An old-timer sat using the toilet in my cell. A small *Indio* squatted against the wall, beneath the high window. The concrete floor chilled my feet through the soles of my sneakers.

From behind the bars across the pass-way, a tiny man, about the size of a fourth grader, stared at me with rabbit eyes set into an oblong head so small I guessed it could slip between the bars. Something like a maple leaf was drawn or tattooed low on his forehead, so the stem touched the bridge of his nose. His sleek black hair was in a single braid like Chinese coolies in frontier days. He wore a scraggly goatee. Gripping the bars with two hands, a heavy ring on each of his fingers, he studied me like a mad scientist attempting to read my brain waves. After a minute, he said, "If the pigs don't toast your ass, I will."

I stared, wondering if I were still asleep by the river, only dreaming of murders, mean sheriffs and tiny demons. "Huh?" I said. "Why do you want to toast me?"

He laughed, like the bark of a Dachshund. Then he turned from the bars and joined his gang, four other bikers in a circle on the floor. They were throwing dice. They all wore greasy jeans and sleeveless Levi jackets lettered "Cossacks." One of them stood and leveled at me a look that reminded me of a kid in my high school who, at any real or imagined insult, would go berserk and launch a vicious attack and not relent until he got restrained by at least four or five of us. Then, he would brush himself off and grin.

This Cossack stood only a head taller than the little man. He was shaped like a barrel. He looked young as if only the stiff beard with one gray streak kept him from getting carded. His cheeks were round, his eyes glistened, maybe from allergies.

"So, Hound Dog," the little man said, "any ideas how we ought to terminate Pretty Boy?"

Hound Dog only sniggered and continued leering at me.

In the other cell across the pass-way, two hippies paced and one sat cross-legged on the floor, eyes closed and hands folded at what yoga people call heart center.

The old-timer on the toilet pulled up his dirty khaki trousers. His matted hair was the same dark blond as mine. Out of his gaping mouth issued a litany of complaints. "Mexicans. Hippies pound nails for minimum. Communists. Miss a single paycheck, women give you lip. Don't that beat all?"

I sat on the floor against the wall to the storeroom, beside the *Indio*. His name was Joaquin. For an hour, while he and I traded stories in Spanish, whenever the tiny biker caught me glancing his way, he bared his teeth and mouthed, "Dead!"

I guessed the murdered boy, Jimmy Marris, had been a Cossack.

Joaquin was Mayan. His stories of the journey from his Mexican state of Tabasco to Evergreen and of his arrest for recruiting other cherry pickers to join Cesar Chavez's UFW allowed moments when I forgot to worry about Alvaro, the tiny Cossack, or my numb hands that still were cuffed and maybe dying. Thoughts of a ruined hand sickened me. My dreams required good hands.

During that hour I called for the jailer three times. Each time, when he looked over from the chair where he sat reading comics, I raised my cuffed hands in the air and said, "Just loosen them is all I'm asking." The first two times, he left for a minute, then returned and nodded at me. The third time, he didn't bother.

A bondsman came and visited the hippies. One of them told him, "Go talk to Quig, maybe he'll spring us."

A few minutes after the bondsman left, Sheriff Willis came and spoke to the bucktoothed jailer. Then the jailer opened my cell, pointed to the old-timer and held the gate while he stumbled out. The jailer led him up the hall to the front. When he returned, he opened the cell across from mine.

He pointed to Hound Dog, who held his wild eyes on me while he left the cell and followed the jailer down the hall. The jailer returned for another. When the tiny man left the cage, instead of turning toward the front, he came straight across and put his nose, sharp as a pyramid, between the bars. "Watch your back, Pretty Boy." He looked me up and down and shook his head as he walked away, barking his laugh.

I stood clinging to the bars, stricken by a kind of fear I had only known a few times. It had first struck when I was about five and watching a movie called "The Bad Seed," in which a little girl murders her innocent family. A few years later, it caught me while Mama and I sat in church. A visiting preacher was describing with cruel relish the elect basking in eternal joy and the others who writhed and shrieked in the pit of hell. Mama's hand turned ice cold.

The last time I'd felt the same dread, I was working nights in a foster placement for delinquent boys. Some of them had killed people. But Reginald, a sixteen-year-old, was there only for minor offenses and because he had no other family, yet he was the evil one, who ground out a cigarette in a retarded boy's eye. When the little boy screamed, I came on the run, and Reginald flashed a grin whose demonic glee chills me even now, whenever I think back.

I watched the tiny man saunter down the hall and out the front door. I was still clinging to the bars when Deputy Barker appeared, handed keys to the jailer and fired a glance of disgust my way.

After the jailer removed my cuffs, the fingers of my left hand tingled as they returned to life. On my right hand, nothing. I could only move the thumb.

The jailer led me to an interrogation room across the hallway from the kitchen. Sheriff Willis was sitting across a table, next to a rosy-cheeked blond fellow not many years older than me. He introduced himself as agent Per Knudsen of the Bureau of Narcotics and Dangerous Drugs. He motioned for me to sit and asked the jailer to shut the door.

Knudsen loosened the collar on his dress shirt, folded his hands behind his head and leaned back into them. "Tell us about Alvaro." So they hadn't yet found my brother. I smiled.

"Locals say he came to the woods to grow weed. True?"

I laid my hands on the middle of the table. "You guys knock me down and cuff me tight enough to do this." I showed them my bluish wrists with red grooves like bracelets. "You tell me nothing. But you suppose I'll help you catch and frame my brother. Strange."

Willis covered his mouth and yawned. Knudsen kept staring at my hands. "If anybody abused you, it wasn't me. Look, the victim, Jimmy Marris, was Deputy Barker's sister's only kid. Somebody snuffs a boy you taught to hunt and fish and all, you'd exhibit a little meanness. Right, Clifford?"

"I guess."

"You would, if you're human. So I'd advise you to thank Sheriff Willis. If Brady had of caught you on his own, it's possible your hands wouldn't be of much concern anymore. So, now we've registered your complaint, would you like me to lay out the reasons we're betting the shooter is your...is it half brother or step brother?"

"Brother," I said.

He shrugged. "Look, Jimmy was shot with a Browning 30.06, like the model Alvaro bought shells for, here in town, on June two of this year. Second, what I hear from the sheriff, when he came calling, Alvaro went for the gun. You were there. Tell me if I'm wrong in saying he didn't pause to reflect. Didn't skip a beat. Just snatched up the murder weapon and ran. Why'd your brother do that, Clifford?"

"Murder weapon says who?"

"We'll get to that. Anybody tell you why Alvaro's camp was the sheriff's first stop, after the body washed up?"

"Nope." I glanced at Willis. He was nibbling the back of his hand as though trying to extract a sliver.

Knudsen said, "Look, I hear Alvaro's been around only a couple months but he already earned himself a rep and a record. Tried to pick up a local girl and got into a brawl with some townies over same. Sheriff, you talked to Alvaro that night. What was your impression?"

"He's a mean one," Willis said. After he wiped something off the back of his hand, he folded his arms.

"Want to tell Clifford who was the girl, and who were the boys?"

Willis and I locked eyes. "Jimmy's girlfriend," he said. "The boys was Jimmy and a couple of his pals."

Knudsen stood, stretched and leaned against the wall. "One scenario, Jimmy might've come out to the woods looking for Alvaro, brought along a pal. Alvaro might've got spooked, thought self defense was called for. Who could blame him, after a hitch in some Vietnam jungle? So, Clifford, your family rich?"

I gave him the stare such a question deserved.

"Why I'm asking," he said, "your brother left a fat wallet behind. Fat as a pusher's."

"Or a guy who found a couple nuggets."

He lifted his open hands. "Hey, it'll be a damned shame, your brother getting shot down, which he most certainly will if he won't stop running, when all he's got to do is come in and cop a plea. Maybe he walks."

"Yeah, maybe," I said. "If I run into him, I'll tell him these sheriffs are the kind of guys he can trust with his life."

"Clifford, you're going to feel responsible if the deputies have to kill your brother. That sort of guilt can be tough to live with." He assumed a dark grimace and waited for his words to sink in. "Now, how about coffee or a soda while you're making up your mind?"

"No thanks."

The sheriff bolted up and marched out of the room. Knudsen observed, "The way this town's going south, people want a scapegoat. I'm betting—if they don't nab your brother—it'll be *you*."

Chapter Three

Alone in the interrogation room, for the first time I imagined the worst. Alvaro bleeding to death in a forest arroyo. My stomach cramped as though I had eaten rattlesnakes and forgotten to kill them first.

When boot-steps sounded in the hall, I decided to remind these lawmen they had best be quite sure, and have exhausted every other possibility, before they risked harming Alvaro—because they were not only messing with him, but with Pop, who had brought down far tougher *hombres* than they, and with Mama who had the ear of God.

Lighter steps sounded. The door creaked open. Agent Knudsen stepped in and tossed me a paper sack. Inside were my wallet, keys, loose change, everything Barker had confiscated. Knudsen motioned with his arm toward the door. "As we walk out of here, don't even look at anybody."

I minded my manners and watched my feet shuffle all the way down the hall and out the Manhattan Avenue door. On the sidewalk in the golden light, Knudsen said, "One reason why the sheriff and deputy hate your guts is, they know you're going to a fancy law school, and your dad was a hotshot big city cop and then a private detective. When they busted your brother for fighting in the bar and some deputy called him a wetback, he told them about your family."

"Barker called him a wetback?"

"I don't know which deputy it was. Look, even though your dad being ex-police and your law school might impress other people, to the sheriff, all law school makes you and big city police work makes your dad is snooty sons of bitches. And the only reason he's cutting you loose is that one piece of evidence indicates Alvaro did the shooting on his own."

He waited for my reaction, but I gave him none. "From the turnout where tire tracks indicate Jimmy's truck was parked, the sheriff's men found boot prints leading to the river that match prints all around Alvaro's camp, including some taken from the woods he ran into when they showed up this morning. Only difference is, the ones leading to the river are deeper, indicating the guy who wore them carried extra weight.

"But these locals—I know them some, and I doubt they'll stop with Alvaro. If there's a single thread to tie you to Alvaro last night, they'll find it, and down you go."

Knudsen slipped a card out of his coat pocket and passed it to me. The dollar-a-thousand kind. It only gave his name, "Department of Justice, Bureau of Narcotics and Dangerous Drugs," and a phone number.

"Sticking around for the jamboree?" he asked.

I almost slipped and told him I was on the bill and that I needed to get to my Hummingbird before a deputy or some other lowlife broke or stole it. But Pop had often warned me against trusting strangers with any information I didn't need to give. "Maybe," I said.

"Ought to be a good show, until the hippies and bikers go to war while some dipstick's singing about brotherly love. You know what's wrong with the world?"

"People."

He laughed and patted me on the shoulder. "I was going to say ignorance. Look, if you run into Brady Barker, duck and hide until he's long gone. And when you find your brother, call me, will you? If my service answers, she can reach me even when I'm in the air."

I didn't answer. He said, "I'd take you to your car but as soon as the sheriff and his boys suspect you and me are chums, I lose their cooperation."

With a shrug of apology, he ambled away.

Jimi Hendrix' guitar screamed from a neighborhood park a block west of the jail. I walked the other way, looking for a pay phone even while I wondered if calling Pop would be wrong. He had troubles of his own, with Mama home from the sanitarium for less than a month.

I leaned against the wall of a meat market that smelled like bologna and decided that since Pop couldn't get here before nightfall anyway and since he wouldn't do much investigating until morning, I shouldn't bother him yet. If I spent a few hours snooping and turned up nothing that could make the sheriff call his troops off Alvaro, I'd call Pop early this evening. He could still arrive by dawn.

I walked past the jail, toward the park. And I thought about when Alvaro and I came here for last summer's jamboree, only weeks after his discharge, a few months after he returned from Vietnam. We arrived a week early because another soldier had told Alvaro that veins of gold rippled through the Trinity Mountains and on any stream a diligent seeker could pan dust and legitimately hope for nuggets.

We spent a week in the forest, picking wild apples and berries, basking in gentle sunlight and the sweet air hippies claimed drew toxins out through our pores. We fished for trout, learned to use the gold pan, and calculated that if we banked the gold we extracted and invested wisely, after fifty years we could buy each of our dozen grandchildren a peanut. We decided our fortunes lay elsewhere. Which gave me reason to wonder if I'd misread Alvaro, if his wallet might truly be fat with drug money.

After last year's jamboree, we returned to San Diego where I would finish college and Alvaro would join a new band that played clubs both sides of the *frontera*. He'd been with them six months when the drummer and bassist went racing around Tijuana, loaded on tequila. The drummer's foot must've slipped off the brake onto the gas pedal. His sports car didn't stop until it

ran under the trailer of a semi on a bridge that crossed the concrete Tijuana River. The car only stopped when it hit the semi's
rear axle, after the trailer had sliced off the musicians' heads.

This year, Evergreen was a different town. Last summer, in
the town park that sloped down to a stream bordered in berry
vines, beneath the redwoods and madrones, hippies played
guitars, mandolins, bongos, harmonicas, autoharps. All day and
evening, they sang protests. Against war. Against racial and social
injustice. About returning to innocence, powered by love. They
seemed to think love was easy.

Since then, the bikers had driven the hippies from the park,
and the few hippies in sight, going into and out of a feed store,
wore long knives sheathed onto their belts. They walked stiff
and shot threatening glances around.

At least twenty bikers perched on the park's benches or
sprawled on the grass drinking beers delivered by their tattooed
girlfriends. Every man wore a sidearm. Half of them sported
bandoliers. Now Led Zeppelin screeched out of the stereo of a
pickup one of them had driven into the middle of park.

Between last summer and this one, it looked as if the Lord
of the Flies had prevailed.

A hippie with sunken cheeks and a dent in his forehead shuffled
along the sidewalk, watching the street for a potential ride. He
didn't bother to hitch with townies in their pickups or sedans, but
as I neared him a Ford Econoline with a rusted sunburst paint job
approached. He waved his thumb. The van pulled to the curb.
Before he jumped in, I asked, "Is there a gun shop around?"

"McNees," he said.

McNees was a builders' and outdoor emporium, in the redwood
mall between Safeway and the Sears Catalog Store. A salesgirl
welcomed me. She directed me to the gun section where Hal,
a cheery fellow my age, answered my query. He estimated that
over the past year, he had sold twenty Browning 30.06 rifles.

The model that had murdered Jimmy Marris, and that Alvaro had grabbed before he ran.

I said, "You've got a list, I bet."

"It's in the files."

"Mind if I take a quick look?"

"Soon as you show me your badge," he said.

From McNees Emporium, I walked toward Foster's Freeze, where I meant to hire a hippie to drive me to my Chevy. Unless the sheriffs had stolen my camping gear, instead of investigating I could pack a bedroll and hike into the forest in hopes of finding Alvaro. At first, that seemed like a bold and worthy action, until I reasoned that finding him wouldn't help. Alvaro was at least as able a woodsman as me, and cagier. Besides, he was a trained and experienced warrior. As an outlaw, he was safer on his own. All I could offer was to look for evidence pointing another direction.

I was no detective. But the man who raised me was a detective. He was also a gifted storyteller when the mood struck, or a lesson he wanted us to learn called for a story, or when we begged him to tell one. From Pop, I had gathered some ideas about detecting.

As I passed Babe's Cafe, through the cramp in my stomach, I recognized another discomfort as hunger. A hand-printed card in the cafe window advertised rainbow trout, for which Alvaro and I would have been fishing today if nobody had shot Jimmy Marris. I saw no reason not to eat while investigating.

Mid-afternoon, the cafe was deserted except for a cook and waitress. I sat in a booth with a juke box selector, beneath a mural of a giant blue ox.

The waitress was a stocky teen with bushy black eyebrows, peace sign earrings, a badge labeled "Steph," and hairy legs. After she handed my order through the cutaway to the kitchen, while she stood behind the counter polishing flatware, I asked how long she had lived in Evergreen.

"Forever." She sighed, probably meaning the minute she turned eighteen, *adios* Evergreen.

I said, "Last summer, Evergreen was a utopia."

"What's that?"

"The trippiest place around."

"It was getting trippy all right, till the Cossacks showed up. I mean, before them, you still had the shitheads like my dad and uncle who never gave the hippies a chance. I mean, if the hippies don't work, my ol' man calls them bums. If they get a job, he calls them scabs 'cause they work cheap and drive wages down. And he thinks a little weed's going to kill us."

"You think it won't?" I said. "Even after it's turned your town into a war zone?"

Gaping as though I had spoken nonsense, she walked around the counter, sat down across the table from me, folded her arms on the table and reclined her breasts upon them. "Weed's groovy. If the Cossacks smoked instead of doing crystal and booze, they wouldn't be such pricks. Anyway, the hippies only grow weed to sell 'cause nobody'll give them a real job."

The bell dinged. She delivered my trout, home fries, and salad. Back to polishing flatware, she leaned over the counter and gave me a history lesson. "See, the Cossacks are out of the East Bay, and they were big in dealing meth till the Hell's Angels chased them out. They're basically chickenshit, you know. See, Little Vic is their honcho. You know why he's so little? Lola told me."

"Who's Lola?"

"Vic's girl. Well, one of his girls anyway. She says his ol' man used to whop him on the head with monkey wrenches and stuff when he was a baby. Anyhow, he's got this cousin who was living at Big Dan's ranch. So first Little Vic and then the rest of his losers came up here.

"See, they tried to do one of those protection rackets like the mafia does on TV. They tried to shake down the hippies who were growing weed. But the hippies got together and told them to fuck off." She glanced around, no doubt to determine if anybody had caught her profanity. "Anyway, that's when the Cossacks started poaching. Last year at harvest time. They got so rich, they took off for a couple months and kicked back down in Mexico.

"Lots of people think bikers are these cool rebels. But I'll tell you, they're no cooler than the rednecks. All the pigs really care about is money."

I remembered one of Pop's crime solving theories—if it isn't about sex, it's about money.

"You'd think the rednecks would hassle the Cossacks," Steph said, "but no way. The rednecks think they can get rid of the Cossacks and hippies both by hassling the hippies. If the hippies split, the bikers will follow, they say, 'cause there won't be any weed to steal and they're too lazy to grow it."

"How about the sheriff?"

"You mean Willis Willis?" She chuckled. "What about that dufus?"

"Is he in cahoots with the rednecks?" I asked.

"Sure."

"He jailed some bikers."

"Yeah, when they stomp somebody in a bar, he busts them for drunk and lets them out the next morning. Doesn't even search them for dope. Gives them their guns back."

When she finished polishing, she returned to my booth, sat and leaned forward, chin on her arm. "My mom says Evergreen's cursed. Maybe she's right. I mean, that crazy boozer Hound Dog killed Sara only about a week ago." The girl's eyes swelled and turned a shade grayer. "She was like my big sister, even got me this job. God, she only wanted to live in harmony with nature and raise her kids in a happy place, and teach them to love everybody. Then this psycho biker goes and zooms out right in front of her, and when she jumps on the brakes the wheels lock, and she goes into the ditch. God..." She pinched her eyes closed and rubbed them. "And the shitheads think weed's worse than booze."

"Hound Dog was drunk?"

"He's always drunk. He's one of those loopy Vietnam vets that can't handle being back in the world."

Wagging her head, she returned to her work and mourned in silence. I couldn't eat even half the trout or any of the fries. My stomach roiled from the thought that of all the lowlifes on earth, the one I needed to expose was probably the little man who had spooked me as if he were Godzilla, and his psycho sidekick.

Before I left, I asked her if the ditch where Sara died was along 101, a quarter mile south of the Crossroads.

"Yeah," she said. "And killing Sara didn't even make them lay low for a week. Just the other day, a Cossack they call Boomer went after some guys from Quig's 'cause he said they stole some parts off his Harley."

Quig's, I remembered from last year, was Evergreen's other major hippie commune, besides Big Dan's.

"And Boomer fired off his shotgun and a kid named Cisco lost an eye. And then last night, a Mexican shot Ava's boyfriend."

My jaw locked. Through clenched teeth, I said, "Ava's a friend of yours?"

"Kinda. What's the matter?"

I shook my head. "Where can I find her?"

"Why?"

"The Mexican's my brother."

"Oh…man. Sorry. I mean, you could find her at Quig's, I guess. Or at the jamboree. She'll be the pretty one in a flour sack dress, handing out tracts. Ava's a Jesus freak."

"You knew Jimmy?"

"A little."

"My brother didn't kill him."

"Then who did? Bikers, right?"

"Why would they kill him?"

She hissed. "Maybe some gutless prick who liked Ava paid them fifty bucks to waste him. Or maybe Jimmy smudged the paint on somebody's chopper."

Hearing that Jimmy Marris' girlfriend was a Jesus freak allowed me some hope, as I knew something of how those folks' minds worked.

Before the killings of Martin Luther King and Bobby Kennedy and the crushing of protest at the Democrats' convention, millions of hopeful kids had changed into apathetic hippies. And then the Charlie Manson murders poisoned the last morsels of innocence from the hippie mystique and sent hundreds of thousands of hippies running to crusades and churches. At my Christian college, I had known dozens of Jesus freaks.

Outside Foster's Freeze, I bartered with a hippie named Simon, a coal-black fellow tall as a flagpole, to drive me to my car. His chin was longer than his nose. He wore thick wire-framed glasses. He probably suffered from eye-strain. On the back seat of his VW microbus were volumes of Blake, Whitman, Burroughs, Poe, Brautigan, Ginsberg, Whitman, Basho, Snyder, Angelou, Cleaver. He leaned over the steering wheel and appeared to have to squint to make out the road while we crept south along the 101 and into the forest on Highball Trail.

When I asked if he knew Jimmy Marris, he turned and peered as though through a microscope. A smart, observant source among the hippies I could use. So I told him about Alvaro and me, about our troubles. Afterward, he drove a mile in silence and finally asked, "You get high?"

"Not much," I admitted.

"Whose side are you on?"

"What's that mean?"

"Haven't you noticed there's a feud going on?"

"I'm on Alvaro's side," I said.

"Yeah, well check this out—the man's out to bring down Alvaro even if somebody else wasted Jimmy. They'd sooner shoot your brother anyway, 'cause somewhere out there…" He saluted toward the east. "…he's got a righteous plantation. Five hundred plants, half ton of bud."

The idea of Alvaro growing weed distressed both my mind and heart, because it meant he'd broken a promise to Mama and Pop. "You know for a fact that Alvaro was growing?" I demanded.

"Hey, you want me to stick to facts, I can't tell you much of anything, about anything."

"It's rumor then?"

"More like common knowledge."

I pondered for a mile or so, then asked, "You know Jimmy?"

"Some. I met him when he partied coupla times out at Quig's, where I stay. Ava brought him out there. You know Ava?"

"Not yet."

"She was cool until Saint Bob got to her."

"Saint Bob?"

Simon turned such a scowl on me, I pictured Saint Bob as some Rasputin who evangelized girls into a frenzy, then boffed them.

"Jimmy, though," Simon said. "Quig didn't trust him. He asked too many questions, like what's the best soil to plant weed, what kind of light, how deep in the forest is best. Acted like a junior narc. Or a poacher."

"Or he was growing?"

"Hear this, man—Evergreen's like Oz, or D.C. Nobody knows who anybody really *is*. Scratch a biker, or a redneck, or a hippie, maybe you'll find he's FBI. Or CIA. Some ugly chick could be Hunter Thompson in drag. Your brother might be KGB. I don't know. You don't know. Right?"

I said, "Take a guess, then."

"Say Jimmy was growing, what's it mean?"

"You tell me."

"Means if your brother didn't blow the kid away, if you find the guy that did, he'll be riding a chopper."

Steph had pointed a finger at the Cossacks, Simon seconded her opinion, and who more likely than bikers whose occupation was poaching to kill a guy at night in the forest.

Agent Knudsen had claimed that footprints implicated Alvaro. But that morning my brother had been wearing his military boots, which he'd gotten used to in Vietnam. And bikers, who also favored boots, could buy the same kind for three dollars at an army surplus store.

I needed to go after Little Vic and his Cossacks. While dwelling on that prospect, I forgot to breathe.

Simon delivered me to my Chevy. Even while I was jumping out, he started his U-turn. By the time I hit the ground, his microbus was smoking down the road like a getaway car.

Somebody, probably the sheriffs, had jimmied the driver's side wind-wing of my Chevy. My stuff was strewn around but none of it was gone. I opened the case to my Hummingbird and unwrapped the cotton baby blanket I used to protect the guitar from nicks and bruises. I sat on a stump, cradled the guitar on my knee, fingered chords and wished my right hand back to life. I even mumbled a short prayer and asked for healing. Nothing changed. I managed to strum by wedging a flat pick between two of my numb fingers. After a few beats it slipped out and fell to the ground.

While I packed the guitar away, I commanded myself not to mope until Alvaro was safe.

I wanted to gather his belongings and to snoop around the forest, look for the boot tracks leading to the river and for clues the sheriff's team had overlooked or ignored. But the two black and whites parked near my wagon convinced me to wait until morning. The deputies might be deep in the forest hunting for Alvaro, or they might be on their way back to the cars, for a shift change or a dinner break. They might appear any second. I preferred to avoid lawmen.

My Chevy was a three-speed stick on the column. Thanks to my bum hand, I couldn't grab and shift but had to shove the lever up and down using my wrist. I used second gear most of the 4.5 miles along Highball Trial, to the 101, where the northbound lane was still a parade of folks on their way to the jamboree.

I wasn't anxious to go into the Crossroads, but somebody in there might know facts about Alvaro, the Cossacks, or even Jimmy Marris.

Only two Harleys and a few pickups were parked in the gravel lot. I pulled in beside the Harleys, pinched my eyes closed, sucked a few breaths and climbed out. After I locked up as best I could with a broken wind wing latch, I marched inside. The less I paused to worry or imagine, the better.

Chapter Four

I stood just inside for a minute, scouting the layout and waiting for my eyes to adjust. The only lights were neon, displays for Oly and Bud and a glowing sign on which a bear tiptoed into a pond beneath a waterfall. "Hamms, from the land of sky blue waters." The jukebox played Merle Haggard's song about Muskogee, Oklahoma, where folks didn't smoke marijuana or trip on LSD, unlike the folks who'd descended upon Evergreen.

A clean-cut fellow sat with two bikers beside the rear window. One of the bikers was Hound Dog. He was leaning back and had his feet on the table, until he saw me. When he sat up straight, his boots socked the floor. The clean-cut guy went to join several older men playing cards in the farthest corner.

A big redhead stood behind the bar rinsing mugs. She was my height, not including her mop of Orphan Annie red hair, and she had such a pair of biceps and robust spirit, I said, "Let me guess. Paul Bunyan was your grandad." She giggled. Her smile was the guileless, dangerous kind that could make a guy trust her before he ought to.

I hopped onto a stool. "You don't wear a name tag."

Her lip twitched and she snuck a glance over my shoulder in the Cossacks' direction. She looked far too sweet to be any outlaw biker's girl. Maybe they had told her to watch out for Alvaro's brother.

"Cherry," she said.

"Pretty name."

"You want a drink?"

"Bar scotch. On the rocks."

She didn't move. I knew why. I heard the boot-steps approaching and wheeled.

I expected Hound Dog, but in the lead was a guy as bony as Death. He fingered the bullets in a bandolier that angled across his chest. He had silvery hair in a long ponytail and sunken eyes ringed in dark shadows. His voice didn't fit. It was toney and mellow. "Yo, Citizen. Me and Dog'd like a word with you. Out front."

Hound Dog made a half-smile that showed the gap where two front teeth had gone missing. He tried to ease between me and the stool on my right and slip a hand around behind me. I might've grabbed it, but on account of my bum hand, I only could block it down and turn to meet his eyes, like Alvaro and I had learned during our years studying Tae Kwon Do. In the eyes, you can see the next move coming.

But now the bony guy was shaking his head, and poking my ribs with a revolver barrel. "Be nice, Hickey."

I stood. He backed away and waved his free hand like a maitre d'. I passed him and shuffled outside. As he stepped out, he slipped his revolver into the holster on his belt. "Pretty Boy," he said, "didn't all that college teach you how to listen? Vic sure enough told you to run for your life."

From the corner of my eye, I glimpsed Hound Dog reach into the bed of the pickup next to us. My fists pounded the sides of my legs.

"Nervous?" the bony guy asked.

I noticed Hound Dog circling behind me, and shifted around just as he swung a tire iron. He must've aimed for the small of my back. He caught me in the side of my belly, just below the ribs. I doubled over. My knees buckled.

"Aw, Hickey," the bony guy said. "Stand up, show some guts. And then get your weak self down the road before Vic comes. Who knows, he might tell me, 'Shoot that citizen.'"

After I heaved, mostly bile, I labored to my feet and stumbled a few steps to lean on the pickup. Hound Dog growled, "Hands off the Dodge, Pretty Boy. Your ride's the pea-green station wagon. Ain't they a pair," he said to the bony guy. "A swishy in a station wagon."

The bony guy laid his hand on the butt of his revolver. With his other hand, he pointed south.

I staggered to the Chevy, groped for the keys, unlocked and fell into the driver's seat. After a struggle to close the door and make the key find the ignition, I backed around and used the first break in traffic to pull into the northbound lane.

Relief and outrage tugged me back and forth. As I neared every roadside gift shop and gas station, I wanted to pull over, run to the phone and call Pop. But pride made me hold the wheel straight. A ten-year-old boy can pardon himself for needing his father. Any older, even the thought is shameful.

While the sky faded to steel gray, I drove back to Evergreen and turned onto Manhattan Avenue. By then I had decided where to go. Taverns ought to be the most likely places to find people who don't mind talking, I reasoned. But this time I would try to pick one with a gentler clientele, such as Louella's Lounge in downtown Evergreen. I parked a half block away on a dark street rather than announce my whereabouts to sheriffs or Cossacks.

Louella's, with Duke Ellington turned down low and wall-murals of plump, mostly bare renaissance ladies, was the perfect atmosphere for Scotch. Besides, I needed a pain killer.

Even before I finished dragging myself onto a bar stool, I saw the bartender tossing a signal at somebody. Then a gentleman came out of a booth and walked over. He looked like several of my college literature profs. Middle aged, amiable, stoop shouldered. As he neared me, he offered his hand. "Clifford Hickey?"

I nodded and gave him my left, which seemed to confuse him. He recovered and sat on the next stool. "This is awkward," he said. "You see, first a Bureau of Narcotics agent and then a sheriff requested that I call them if you should come here."

"Barker or Willis?"

He smiled. "Now, you look like a decent fellow. Still, I'm going to make those calls. I'd suggest that you buy a six pack and drink it elsewhere. I'll charge the Safeway price on the beer."

I slid off the stool and walked out. By the time I reached the pay phone at the corner by the meat market, I had rationalized that calling Pop wasn't out of fear of Little Vic or Hound Dog, but only for Alvaro's sake.

I let the phone ring at least twenty times, in case Pop and Mama were on the deck or on the beach close enough to hear. At last, I hung up and walked to the street lamp, took out my wallet and rummaged through the junk until I found my list of phone numbers.

At our neighbor Harry Poverman's number, his maid answered. "Gloria," I said, "Clifford here. Could you look around and see if you can spot Pop or Mama?"

She knew that Mama hadn't gone any farther than the cedar grove between our house and Harry's and the beach a few hundred yards each way in the month since she left the sanitarium.

I gave Gloria the pay phone number, squatted against the wall and waited, trying to ignore my throbbing side and hand and wishing I had let the man at Louella's sell me a pint of liquor.

As the gray sky blackened, I watched locals and a few hippies strolling past the park toward the river bridge. I inhaled the redwood scented air cut with a bite of sea breeze and felt a little peace and a moment of trust that Alvaro was safe, Mama was recovering, and the truth about the murdered boy would soon come out. I got so entranced, I jumped when the phone rang.

Gloria told me not only had she searched through the grove and on the beach without finding Mama, but she had looked behind our cabin and noticed that Pop's Cadillac was gone.

Since Pop let Gloria borrow the Cadillac in exchange for her running errands, I couldn't imagine where my folks would've driven, except back to the sanitarium. And though I realized other explanations might come, the chance that Mama had sunk back into catatonia made me decide the last thing Pop needed was another problem.

So I dug through my wallet for Agent Knudsen's business card. Maybe I could convince him to reason with the sheriff. An answering service picked up. I would've told her to get Knudsen word that the Cossacks killed Jimmy Marris, according to a waitress, a smart hippie, and me, since I could guess no other reason the bikers would try to run me out of Evergreen. But the woman said, "Sorry, I can only take your name and number."

"What if I don't have a number?" I snapped. "He said you could get a message to him even if he's flying."

"Only your name and number. Agent Knudsen generally takes calls between nine and ten a.m."

"Oh, swell. Look, tell him Clifford Hickey's waiting for him at the McNees campground, east of Evergreen. And tell him I know who killed Jimmy Marris."

Simon had directed me to the campground, through town and east on River Road, along the north fork of Whiskey River three miles past the jamboree grounds.

McNees Park was a recreation area for loggers, open to campers for the duration of the jamboree, thanks to an arrangement Big Dan Mills had made with Paul McNees. Simon had added, "When a Wobbly and a lumber baron cooperate, inquiring minds want to know why?"

Big Dan Mills was a folk singer who for twenty years had lived out of his car, coast to coast along the college and coffee house circuit, until The Rattlers' folk rock version of his song "Nobody's Slave" hung on the Top 40 chart all through 1967. Then Big Dan had proved true to his rep as an old-time, card-carrying Wobbly socialist, disciple of Mother Jones and Woody Guthrie. He'd invested his royalties on a hundred acres of cherry and apple orchards fronting Whiskey River. There he established the first of the Evergreen communes. He and his people bottled and sold apple and cherry cider and founded the Cider Mills Jamboree.

In 1969, the first jamboree lured a thousand folks to Evergreen. Among them were an heiress and dropouts from prosperous careers who returned, bought land, and began Quig's and the three smaller communes.

McNees Park looked as crowded as Brooklyn, with a tent, car, or van between every cedar and redwood, and bonfires enough so I imagined herds of deer charging toward Oregon, fleeing as from an inferno. I made camp in a nook beneath a craggy madrone, tramped through darkening woods inhaling the fragrance of fermenting cherries while I collected branches and twigs. I sat beside what Alvaro called *un fuego indio*, a modest fire, wondering if my brother had found a hideaway and if the man-hunters had given up at dark.

From sites all around, twanging banjos and slide guitars, trilling mandolins and warbling harmonicas joined in weird fusions. Tiny long-haired boys and girls wearing beads and flowers ran around squealing and dangled from the branches of trees. Passersby noticed me sitting alone and invited me to join their crowd. I declined and attempted to review what Steph and Simon had told me and what I had observed. According to Pop, detectives needed time to sit still or stroll and listen for inspiration.

And I attempted to convince myself that Alvaro hadn't shot any deputies, and maybe the search had been called off. And I kept wishing life back into my right hand. Still it hung from my wrist like an empty glove. I thought of going to a doctor but decided that could wait until Alvaro was safe.

As the last of my sticks burnt, I rolled out my mat and sleeping bag, crawled in, and lay reviewing my decision not to call Pop. If I did phone and tell him about Alvaro, I imagined half his heart would command him to speed to Evergreen, while the other half would order him not to leave Mama. As I fell asleep, I hoped I could wade this morass on my own.

When gunshots woke me, at first I believed they were real. Then, remembering the previous night, I interpreted these shots as the soundtrack of a dream that carried me back to yesterday, before the world turned against us. But the whoops, and the revs of two big V-8s, changed my mind. I rolled behind my Chevy, sat up, untangled my arms, and watched two six-wheel pickups skid in tandem along the road that jagged through the campground. More cracks and booms sounded. A dozen from pistols, two or three from a shotgun.

Before the six-wheelers reached my campsite, they cut back toward the entrance. The louts whooped, whistled, skidded out to the highway, and rumbled into the distance.

Campers shouted after them. Kids screamed. My neighbor sat on a stump between our camps, lit his pipe and offered me a hit. Because I declined, he presumed the intruders had scared me. "Just drunken loggers," he said. "When I'm king, dope's legal and booze is a capital offense."

I didn't tell him that whoever they were—between gunshots, one of them had yelled, "Come out and play, Clifford Hickey."

Daylight woke me. While woodpeckers tapped, squirrels chirped, kids chased up the road and campfires crackled, I tossed my things into the Chevy and idled out of the campground. A mile west, I pulled into the jamboree grounds, a meadow between Big Dan Mills' commune and the weedy lot where last summer a community garden had thrived. Concessionaires were already setting up their booths. A crew was at work on the main stage. I stood in what passed for a line and watched for any Jesus freak who might be Ava.

The gate opened at 8:00 a.m. I paid fifteen dollars for the three-day pass and entered. A sign over the gate read "Private Property. Anyone carrying a gun, knife or chain will be ejected. Anyone found with a concealed weapon will be prosecuted."

Folks were already spreading blankets, staking claim to plots of ground near the stage. After circling and crisscrossing the meadow in search of a pretty girl passing out Christian tracts, I sat beside the river and noted the changes a year had wrought. To the east, Big Dan's commune had transformed from a rustic site to a rural ghetto. Two dozen A-frame shacks, teepees and yurts surrounded Big Dan's log house and the geodesic dome meeting hall. West toward Evergreen, brown weeds and nettles covered the field where last year tall corn, pole beans, tomatoes and watermelons thrived, and where graceful hippie girls stood by the roadside, waving at cars and lavishing whoever stopped with sacks of produce and flowers.

I remembered a willowy girl named Bluefeather who invited us to meet her and some girlfriends later at a swimming hole. We did, and seven or eight of them showed and frolicked in the pool and all around, dancing and leaping from one smooth rock to the next, while Alvaro and I mostly stayed submerged, to hide our throbbing priapism. A year later, I remembered the scene with fond and vivid precision. On the drive to Evergreen, I had hoped for another encounter with long-legged, creamy Bluefeather.

The river was higher than last summer, its ice blue water slow through the shallows where by nine, naked boys and girls and their topless parents paddled and splashed. I noticed among them the three cupids and the father who had clustered around the roadside shrine a half mile south of the Crossroads. I felt sure they were the husband or lover and kids of Steph's friend Sara, who had crashed in a ditch after swerving to miss Hound Dog. The dad cradled the smallest cupid in the crook of his arm. The older ones held hands. Their free hands pounded the river as if they meant to break it.

Beyond the river, atop a wooded hill, sunlight flashed off the chrome of motorcycles parked beside an old barn. Last summer, Alvaro and I had camped on that hill and made our beds beneath the black pines. Locals called it Sugar Hill, after some prostitute who camped and worked there long ago.

Again I wandered, watching for Ava the Christian, past concessions and posters with the schedule and photos of Lightnin' Hopkins, Ramblin' Jack Elliot, and the headliner, Phil Ochs. Seeing Ochs' name made me think of Alvaro, and the visions of my brother dead or imprisoned came faster and gorier. All I could do to dispel them for a minute was turn to fears that I would go through life with a useless right hand. Then self-pity nagged at me with thoughts that the murder and my ruined hand had robbed me of my chance to play with people who would be my idols, if idols were allowed in our family. Between all that, I attempted to order the little I knew about Jimmy Marris and Evergreen.

I needed to consider other suspects, besides the Cossacks. According to Simon, a commune leader named Quig thought Jimmy was a snitch. For all I knew, Quig might treat snitches like Charles Manson had treated deserters from his gang. My high school friend Nancy had barely escaped from Manson's Death Valley camp after she discovered the graves of two girls who had tried to flee.

Or any of the hippie marijuana farmers might've decided Marris was likely to snitch on him. No matter if a guy's van was papered with "Make Love, Not War" and such, he needed to protect his income.

Unless Ava could persuade me Jimmy was no snitch, I would find someone, maybe Steph, to give me a list of marijuana farmers. And Hal the cheery gun salesman at McNees Emporium might check my list against the names of people who had purchased Browning 30.06s.

Or, I thought, the murderer could be one of the loggers who had terrorized the campground. Or he might be a nerd or gimp Jimmy Marris had picked on since second grade. Or he could be Marris' best pal, who'd gotten whiskey drunk and turned savage because Jimmy had met the pal's sweetheart in some hayloft. Or the shooter could be this Ava, gone *loco* because Jimmy had done her wrong. I remembered a story by Stephen Crane and the line "there are usually somewhere between a dozen and forty women involved in every murder."

I needed more details about Evergreen, and about Jimmy, reasons he might go to the woods at night. So I followed a trio of high school boys with hair that made me wonder if they were Marines, except one of them had Elvis sideburns. Beyond the main stage, as we neared the concessions, I fell into step beside them and asked, "You guys from Evergreen?"

"What of it?" the wiry one grumbled. A braided leather headband rested on his ears.

"So you knew Jimmy Marris."

The tallest one scratched his head. "Who're you?"

"Clifford Hickey."

"Hickey?" The kid who was dressed like a square dancer sniggered. "Hey, whoa. Ain't that the murderer's name?"

As if on a cue, the three closed in, the sideburned kid raising his fists. The square dancer spit a gob of tobacco that splashed beside my canvas shoe.

I dug in, fists at my waist, while the boys attacked me with curses, then turned and shuffled away. A fellow with a badge and a *Security* cap had stopped a few yards from us to observe. Compared to most hippies, this one looked like Sampson, taller and heftier than me. Not many hippies spoke in Texas drawls like his. He was talking to another bouncer who soon strolled off, while the Texan kept an eye on me. As I approached, he brushed wavy hair back off his shoulder.

I asked, "Want to help me figure who killed Jimmy Marris?"

He shrugged his hands. "Man, I'm from the city, only rolled in coupla hours ago. Somebody got murdered?"

I nodded, walked on and wondered if looking for suspects other than Cossacks was a waste of precious time. And, I thought, my best source to the lowdown on the bikers might be a deserter. I started watching for a tattooed girl among the hippies, in case a Cossack groupie had defected.

I was going with the crowd toward the stage, a little comforted that the security guards were outsiders and probably neutral. They might rescue me from the lynch mob that could result from my having the name Hickey or from my trying to befriend local girls. According to Willis, Alvaro's troubles in Evergreen had begun when he turned his charm on the wrong girl. Maybe on this Ava.

On the main stage, Big Dan Mills stood fine-tuning his jumbo Gibson. In cowboy boots he stood about six five and looked as strong as any logger. His beard was steel gray. His laugh was deep and kindly, as he kicked off the festival with a Woody Guthrie tune everybody knew, a singalong:

> Thousands of folks back east they say
> are leaving home most every day
> and beating the hot old dusty way
> to the California line…
>
> The police at the port of entry say
> 'You're number fourteen thousand for today
> and if you ain't got the Do-Re-Mi, boys…

By now the grounds swarmed with grimy dopers, grad students with John Lennon specs and sketch pads, and families who lived in flower-painted, rusty school buses and made their living hawking tie-dyed shirts and earrings of bent wire. I weaved through the crowd toward the rope that partitioned the festival from Big Dan's commune. Hippies, I reasoned, would talk more freely than locals. If the hippies didn't talk, I might consider their reluctance a clue and continue snooping in their direction.

Two skinny boys who looked scraggly as runaways stooped under the rope from Big Dan's. Their big sisters followed them. I recognized one of the sisters from last summer. One of the water nymphs. Bluefeather's partner in standing by the road and blessing passersby with sacks of corn, tomatoes, and peppers from the community garden. I remembered in particular her blissful smile, but at first she didn't appear to remember me. When I introduced myself, I didn't give my last name. I asked if we could talk about Jimmy. The frown she assumed made her look old enough to be the skinny boys' mother. She tapped her foot on the dirt, glanced everywhere but at me, and claimed she hardly knew Jimmy Marris.

"Any idea who killed him?" I asked.

"The guy you were with last year."

"Guess again."

"Cossacks."

"Why so?"

"Because that's what Cossacks do."

She wheeled like a propositioned virgin. I would've chased after her and asked if she knew anybody who had run with the Cossacks and ditched them, or if she could lead me to Ava. But a choir of Harley engines revved. Across the river and up the hill, dust whirled as the choppers rumbled out of their camp. I watched them zigzag the road that switchbacked down Sugar Hill. At the base, they gathered into a pack, fishtailed along the dirt road, crossed the river on a wooden bridge and turned onto the highway. I lost sight of them behind the vans and buses in the parking area.

On my way back toward the main stage, I considered opening lines, ways to ingratiate myself before questioning people. Pop's most effective methods were bribery and intimidation. I only had fifty dollars. And Pop could act tougher than I could.

A line of children snaked out from a booth where the students from the Salvador Dali Montessori School sold organic cherry snow cones. As I dodged to avoid the line, I caught a glimpse of reddish blond hair so long and shiny, I stopped for a better look. The splendid hair topped a lithe figure in brown muslin the color of a monk's robe. The girl held a stack of yellow pamphlets. She was advising a shirtless boy with a crooked leg and a cane that Bend in the River Community Church held Bible studies daily. Her head was bowed, her voice faltered. Probably from grief, I thought. Still, I heard something else, a sweet humility I had rarely heard except when Mama spoke. As the boy limped off and she turned my way, the woe in her silvery eyes and in the curve of her mouth slowly widened into a smile.

Chapter Five

"Here's something to read between shows," Ava said.

I took the pamphlet. On the front was a bold title, *True Freedom*, and a handwritten verse. "I am the resurrection and the life. Whoever believes in me will not perish but will have eternal life." I imagined her up all night while her pretty hand copied that promise onto hundreds of pamphlets.

"Can we talk?" I motioned toward the river.

Her wide eyes narrowed. A girl like Ava, with hair so thick and wavy and a splash of freckles on her cheeks and lips so soft and wide, might have to field such propositions ten times each day. But I guessed as a Jesus freak she would think, What if he wants me to lead him to Christ?

She nodded and led the way, around the candied apple and cider stand, toward a small stage in a corner of the meadow where a banjo clinic was beginning. In the open, I walked alongside her.

"Are you interested in Jesus?" she asked.

"You bet."

We sat on a grassy mound. Her muslin dress, belted with a rope, had large pockets. From one of them, she pulled a Bible, which she laid on the grass between us. "I'm not sure what you want. Prayer maybe?"

"That'd be good."

"Okay. About...?"

"My brother. He's in big trouble."

"What kind of trouble?"

"He got accused of murder."

Her shoulders drew closer together. Her arms crossed over her breasts and she grasped one shoulder with each hand. Her eyes kept blinking while she stared above the forest as though on the lookout for an airplane or a storm. "Is your brother named Alvaro?"

"Uh huh."

Ava stared at me as if trying to fathom why God made such beasts as us Hickeys. Then she closed her eyes and rubbed them. She glanced at me, then back at the sky. "Do you know who I am?"

"I hear you were Jimmy Marris' girlfriend."

She made a face like somebody remembering happy times long ago. "It's been two weeks since we broke up." She lifted a wrist and brushed her cheek with it.

"Did you know my brother?"

"I met him one time, and that's all." She flashed a defiant glare, as if I had accused her of something. "What do you want?"

"Truth."

"You're not just trying...?"

I waited, but she only closed her eyes and stared at the dirt. So I said, "Trying to save Alvaro? Maybe, but the fact is, when I showed up yesterday at my brother's camp, I'm sure he didn't even know about Jimmy. If he'd shot somebody, I'd see a clue. He's my only brother. We were going to fish and come to the jamboree. I'm even scheduled to play a couple songs, so was Alvaro. But the sheriffs came and next thing, my brother's on the run and I'm in jail. They think Alvaro killed Jimmy over a girl.

"Maybe you," I said, then watched her eyelids quiver as if straining not to blink. "But they're only guessing. Somebody found Jimmy downriver from Alvaro's camp, and Alvaro owned a 30.06 like the killer used. That's all. But I've known him since I was seven."

She caught her breath and reached for her Bible, laid it on her lap and folded her hands atop it. "Who do *you* think killed Jimmy?"

Rather than risk swaying her judgment, I shook my head. "Maybe you'll help me figure it out?"

She turned toward a platform where an old fellow in a beret was demonstrating styles of bluegrass banjo. After a minute she turned back and stared at me.

She had one of those stares that make you feel naked. "Tell me about Jimmy?" I said.

She rubbed her eyes. "I hope he's with Jesus. He got saved last year, but he…people say he was too smart for his own good. He did math for fun, and hard crossword puzzles, and he read about science and politics and philosophy, on his own. Some kids called him a geek, but he wasn't a loner like a lot of smart people. He wanted everybody to love him. And most people did."

She wiped her cheek. "I don't know if he's in heaven. When we broke up, he was reading that *Communist Manifesto* some girl from Eugene gave him when he was up there checking out the university. Girls wouldn't leave him alone, even my friends sometimes. They—" She stopped when cheers and whistles erupted at the end of Big Dan's set. Her gaze rose to the sky.

"What'd Jimmy look like?" I asked.

"Like you," she said. "Blue eyes and skin a little darker than yours, kind of olive. His hair was browner than yours and he wasn't as big. He was a hurdler on the track team and he could almost fly.

"In summers, his skin got pretty dark. He told everybody he was Sicilian, 'cause he didn't want to be the only black kid in Evergreen."

"His mom's Brady Barker's sister, right? So Jimmy's dad's black?"

When Ava shook her head, her wavy hair rippled. "Jimmy didn't know for sure. His mom was a nurse in the Korean War. Jimmy said she married his dad a few days before he got killed by rocket fire. She claims his dad was white, but Jimmy saw a couple pictures of a guy who looked like him, only way darker. Anyway, who cares?"

If I had carried a note pad, I would've scribbled—Motive? Racial? Political? Sexual? Racial because Evergreen might harbor the northwest chapter of the KKK. Political because in those days, even at a liberal San Diego college, an organizer for the American Communist Party got beaten into a coma. Sexual because sex inspired most everything that money didn't.

From down along the path that led past the concessions toward the main stage, a pack of bikers came swaggering. I had hoped the Cossacks couldn't abide folk music. I shifted, sat with my back to them and asked, "Did Jimmy hang out with any bikers?"

I wondered if the disgust that crooked her soft lips was on account of my question or the sight of Cossacks. "No," she snapped.

"Did he piss any of them off, or get in their way?"

The way she shook her head and gripped her Bible, I believed she was considering a lie. I said, "A waitress at Babe's Cafe told me—"

"Steph."

"Yeah, and she told me the locals are scared of the bikers so they blame Evergreen's descent from paradise to a combat zone on the hippies. Because the hippies planted the weed the bikers came to steal."

"The Cossacks are parasites, okay," she said. "Ask me something else."

Even now, if I painted a Christmas mural, Ava would become the Virgin. Her face was all curves, the arched eyebrows, the wide mouth and chin. The silver light from her eyes made me stutter. Still, I wondered if she were afraid of the Cossacks, or in cahoots with them, or what. "Besides Quig," I said, "who else thought he was a snitch?"

"If Steph told you so much, why do you need me?" She tried to glare, then softened. "Everybody from the communes thought he was a snitch, okay. That's kind of why we broke up. I told him God had sent me to Quig's, as a witness to the hippies. He said God was a drug."

"How about the race thing? Any big brother or dad who might've wanted to get rid of a black guy on account of something he did to a white girl?"

"You mean me?" Again she tried to harden her face, but in seconds she let the pose go. "He only told me about his dad because he said I ought to know what he was made of, just in case we slipped up." Probably without meaning to, she had let go of the Bible and folded her hands on her belly.

Ava didn't have to speak to tell stories. From her firm posture and clenching fingers I saw her heart was sore and perplexed, but not yet broken. Her eyes flooded and spilled a slurry of silver tears, while on the main stage a gospel quartet sang:

> One fine morning
> when this life is over,
> I'll fly away...

Ava stood and pocketed her Bible. "I'm going to watch."

I wished I could lead her in the other direction, to someplace the Cossacks wouldn't be. But she looked determined.

Though she hadn't invited me along, I followed her through the aisle of refreshments, tapes, tie-dyed clothes, Mexican tapestries, Navajo jewelry, and the rest. She gave no sign that she'd prefer I would leave her alone.

The gospel quartet was on the main stage. Their banner read "Faith, Hope, Charity & Mavis." The crowd had thinned after Big Dan's appearance, gone off to stroll the meadow, to swim across the river and harvest wild cherries or explore the flowery woods, or to attend one of the workshops where musicians demonstrated tunings and other techniques along with playing their songs. Ava found us a seat on the grass ten yards from the stage on the left side, not far enough from a trio of tattooed girls. One of them tossed me a smirk and strutted off, no doubt to tell her master that Hickey fool was still around.

The quartet sang:

May the circle be unbroken
By and by, Lord, by and by.
There's a better home a waiting
In the sky, Lord, in the sky.

Little Vic led the pack of five Cossacks who came striding along the edge of the clearing. They cut through the crowd toward us, stepping on blankets.

Vic swaggered over to us and stood with his legs spread and tiny fists knocking heavy golden rings together. The sun flashed like a laser off his golden earring. While the gang half-surrounded us, he leered at Ava and licked his tongue between his lips. "Baby, you need a real man."

Ava's eyes had turned to bullets. "Get lost, Vic."

"Don't talk shit to me, baby." Outdoors, his voice had a trill that only made it more menacing. "I'm just asking, why not come to me instead of this trash? I mean you go ahead and fuck a poodle, it's no skin off my white ass. But this faggot, him and his wetback brother smoked Jimmy. And if he don't get down the road or snuffed by some patriot first, I'm gonna have to smoke him."

"Go away, Vic."

"Bitch, you ever seen me take orders?"

By now, I was up and ready to charge whichever Cossack attacked first. A loud whistle sounded and the Texan bouncer came loping, followed by three other fellows in jamboree T-shirts and *Security* baseball caps.

Without a glance at the bikers or Ava, as though I were the obvious villain, the Texan stepped between me and Little Vic and dropped two heavy paws on my shoulders. "Partner, give me your pass and get along outta here."

Bikers laughed. Vic said, "See you in hell, Pretty Boy."

Ava looped her arm in mine. As we reached the path, she said, "You're not so pretty."

"That's a matter of taste," I grumbled, and got rewarded by her gripping my arm a little firmer. A minute later, as we neared the concessions, we heard shouts and turned to watch a platoon of security hippies surround the Cossacks.

I said, "Jimmy didn't know bikers, but apparently you do?"

"Who said Jimmy didn't know any bikers?"

"I thought you did."

"I said he didn't hang out with them. Okay?" Then, as though giving me a secret I had no right to know and would find myself ashamed at having pestered out of her, she said, "My sister's Vic's girl." She let go of my arm and marched toward the exit.

The Cossacks' Harleys were parked in a line with their front tires under the rope and sawhorse barricade that was supposed to discourage freeloaders from entering the jamboree. The way Ava stopped and stared death rays at them, I imagined her kicking the first one over and watching the whole line domino.

Chapter Six

We drove east in my Chevy to a turnoff next to a river bridge and walked down the bank to a place Ava knew where the river narrowed and swirled into shade. Buffy St. Marie's pretty warble in the distance harmonized with cooing birds in the shoreline's bushy pines.

Ava slipped out of her sandals and dipped her feet in the water. We listened to the roar of Harleys leaving the festival and fading, going west. Ava's arms folded over her chest. "Lord, thanks again for Jimmy's life. If he gave up on you, please forgive him. Take him to eternal joy. And Father, please send angels to help us find the killer, and bless Jimmy's poor mom." She looked up at me. "And protect Alvaro," she added, without much fervor.

To spend an August day with such a girl on the bank of Whiskey River might've ranked as a highlight of my twenty-two years, if my brother hadn't been wanted for murder, and if I'd felt certain that Ava was honest. "Christian" and "honest" weren't synonyms, I had learned. I watched her muslin dress flutter in the breeze, her fingers become a spider on a mirror, and her chin tilt forward onto her breastbone.

"You know Jimmy's mom pretty well?" I asked.

"Some."

"How about taking me to her?"

Shading her eyes with one hand, she squinted at me. I said, "If I go by myself to talk with Jimmy's mom, why's she going to

talk to me? But if she thinks I'm a visiting evangelist or something, maybe she'll talk."

"About what?"

"How about what Jimmy was doing in the forest night before
last?"

"Maybe he wasn't in the forest until the killer took him there."

I waited, hoping she would let go of a secret. But she stood,
bent, and picked up a handful of stones and pitched them one
by one into the river. "Okay. Let's go."

Ava suggested we take her car in case the Cossacks were out looking for me. Her car was in the jamboree lot, an old Plymouth
held together with bobby pins and duct tape. I rode shotgun,
ready to duck at the sight or sound of a Harley.

Jimmy's mom lived on Burgundy Lane, one of the residential
streets off Manhattan Avenue. The homes nearest Manhattan
were large and bright, their hedges clipped, lawns emerald green,
tulip beds weeded. A quarter mile north, where Delene Marris
lived, the houses looked like servants' quarters on weed-choked
lots. The Marris cottage was barn red splotched with white,
recently scraped and primered. A bird feeder hung from the roof
of the porch. The lawn was the yellow of hay.

We parked at the curb. For a minute, Ava sat still behind the
wheel, quieting her heart, I supposed. Then she climbed out
and rounded the car. A next door neighbor stopped pushing
her child in a rope swing to watch us, and an old fellow across
the street leaned on a rake and stared.

Ava knocked, waited, and knocked again before the door
opened. Through the screen door, I saw a spindly woman whose
short bleached-blond hair showed an inch of dark roots. She had
deep, haunted eyes like her brother Brady, and the same sharp
features as his. She might've once been a looker. "Hi, honey," she
rasped, and pushed open the screen. "Who's your friend?"

"Clifford. Just a guy from church," she said. I hoped she
only used "just" so Delene wouldn't think she had found a new

boyfriend already. "We were praying for you and decided we should come see how you're doing."

"Well…" Delene held her small hand out to me.

She led us into a living room furnished like a budget motel, in straight lines and dark blue fabrics against powder blue walls and frilly white curtains. A single mom with a lousy income attempting to create a gracious home, I supposed.

Ava and I took the couch. Delene sat stiff in the matching chair. On the coffee table lay a fat paperback, *Havana Heat*, and a *TV Guide* serving as a coaster for a Coors bottle half full of ashes and butts.

"Funeral's Monday," Delene said. "You wanta ride in the limo with me and Brady?"

A little moan escaped from Ava and her shoulders hunched toward her ears. "Even though I broke up with Jimmy?"

"Honey, anybody would give him the boot, the way he was behaving. Ever since he got that damn scholarship letter to Whitman College. What kind of deal is it, they give you a scholarship but you still hafta pay out a fortune? The time he pays for this dormitory and the cafeteria, it's gonna cost more than I make in a year, not counting tips. You know, that kinda deal's what soured him. What turned him into thinking like a communist."

Only minutes ago, we had passed banners emblazoned with Phil Ochs' name and photo. So when she said "communist" I remembered the poems of Chairman Mao on the back cover of a Phil Ochs album.

"Aw," Ava said, "jJust because he was reading some books doesn't make him—"

Delene said, "Not books dammit. I'm talking about the union. Big Dan folksinger and that Chavez and their communist union. Last two days of Jimmy's life, he was out in the cherry orchards, signing up pickers for the communists. The way I figure, the Mexican killed him for money."

"Whose money?"

"Somebody that wants to get rid of the union. Every lousy thing's about money."

"Mom," Ava said, "it wasn't only the money. When Jimmy got saddest was when he worried about leaving you."

"Me?"

"The way he saw, you two were a team. He wasn't sure either of you'd be worth much without the other."

"Jimmy thought that? Girl, he would've been ten times better without me." Delene turned to me and stiffened her jaw, probably to keep it from quivering. "Jimmy got it all, like the genes all dove in the pool and hit the mark one time, so Jimmy got the smarts and the goodness that our family never put together before. Like Brady says, family's what counts in the long haul. It's family that's going to carry on, make us all somebody. Or nobody."

The image of Brady Barker as philosopher was odd but not amusing. My right hand lay like a sausage on my knee. Ava glanced up at Jimmy's mom, who had crinkled her brow.

"Brady's sterile," Delene said. "That's one of the reasons Susie left him. And look at me, you think any man that could father a boy like Jimmy would get the hots over a sight like me. Not on your life. Me and Brady are the last of the Barkers."

Ava leaned forward, reached out and began, "Come on, Mom, you're—"

Delene interrupted by taking Ava's hand. "No way around it, honey. Jimmy was our hope. Now we're good as extinct. And don't go telling me God'll make things right. God's no damn use to me now."

Ava petted the woman's hand, while I sat confounded between sadness over the fate of Delene and Jimmy Marris and questions like had Alvaro as well as Jimmy gotten mixed up in radical politics? If so, might they have worked together? But those questions could wait until I was alone. Now, I needed to find a way to swindle Delene into reminiscing about the last days of her son.

Brakes squeaked, the rat tat of an old motor with loose valves shut down, a creaking door slammed, and boots tromped the gravel path. Through the window I saw Brady Barker climb out of a '59 Chevy convertible. As he climbed the porch, he called out, "Brought lunch, Sis."

He walked in carrying two Foster's Freeze sacks. By the time he saw me, I was on my feet. He panted through his teeth while he placed the sacks on the floor. Waving a thumb at me, he snarled, "Who'd this cocksucker tell you he is?"

"Jesus, Brady…" Delene said.

Ava came and stood beside me. "I brought him here."

"He's your friend, little girl, then you got till the count of one to scoot your ass out of our house."

"It's *my* house," Delene said.

"Sis, you're talking to the brother and accomplice of the Mexican that murdered Jimmy."

She covered her eyes, then dropped her right hand and grabbed the Coors bottle from the table. Her face had transformed from pale and slack to a horror mask, round-eyed and taut as if the sharp bones were attempting to break through the skin. When she hurled the bottle, I ducked so it only clipped my ear and the base of my skull. It bounced off the bookcase stacked with old magazines and cracked the lower right pane of a French window. "I talked my heart out," she screamed.

Barker pointed at me then at the door.

Keeping my distance while I passed him, I walked out. As I stepped off the porch onto the gravel, the deputy growled, "Hey."

I walked a few more paces and turned. Ava was on the porch. She looked around and paused in mid-stride, one leg forward and bent. Delene was in the shadow of the doorway. Barker stopped an arm's length from me.

"Hickey," he said, "you think if you disappear anybody around here's gonna look real hard? Or you think some USC law professor's gonna come investigate? Or you think your old man being a retired rent-a-cop puts the fear in anybody?"

His eyes sparked, then dropped to stare at my hand. "What I'm saying is, you want to live to grow up, run home to your mama and daddy. And tell them to give up the wetback for dead.

"See, your Alvaro makes it out of the mountains, I'm going to chase him through the valley. He crosses the valley, I'll chase him over the plains. He gets to the water, I'll chase him across the ocean. I'm like that TV cop on the trail of Richard Kimball, only I'm smarter than him and the wetback's dumber than Kimball. Way dumber. Why just this morning he broke into a cabin in Little Falls, stole food and a Colt handgun. You hear?"

"I hear."

"You going to run home like I say?"

I smiled to keep my teeth from grinding, and shook my head. In his eyes, I saw a punch coming. Maybe he would've let it fly. Maybe not. Ava pushed me out of his reach.

In the Plymouth, I waited for Ava to break out of her guilt over violating Delene Marris' trust in her, and to bawl me out for causing it. But she drove on in silence, without telling me her destination.

The trail that led down from the Cossacks' camp atop Sugar Hill intersected the River Road just west of the garden. A Harley was stopped at the intersection. A woman passenger, behind the tiny driver, leaned against the sissy bar. As Ava turned left onto River Road, the Harley skidded a U-turn and fishtailed back toward the Cossack camp.

"Lola and Vic," Ava said. "You didn't duck fast enough. He's probably going to get Boomer or somebody. God, Clifford, it might take a miracle just to get you out of Evergreen alive."

I had been thinking the same way, wondering who would kill me first, Vic, one of his slaves, or Brady Barker.

She raced the old car past the jamboree, nearly sideswiping a flowered school bus that was lumbering onto the road, while a guy with a scratchy voice like Dave Van Ronk belted a Phil Ochs song:

> "We're the cops of the world, boys,
> We're the cops of the world…"

Alvaro used to sing that protest song in the shower after he came back from Vietnam.

Ava said, "I thought we could go to my church and ask Pastor Bob for guidance, but Vic might catch us there. We need to go someplace the Cossacks don't dare come."

Saint Bob, I thought, but kept silent, as Ava must've thought more highly of the Pastor than Simon did.

Two miles past the jamboree, she turned into the commune owned by the stock analyst people called Quig. The gatekeeper, a slight, pale fellow with a bush of chalk-white kinky hair, sat flipping peanuts overhead and trying to catch them in his mouth. His shaggy dog snarled and woofed at us.

I had heard about Quig, last summer and in a letter from Alvaro. His real name was Charles Quigley. The home where he lived when he wasn't on lecture tours, treks through the Himalayas, or photo safaris, overlooked Whiskey River. His stone house was the biggest residence in the commune he owned and supported.

The commune was bordered on one side by the river, on one side by River Road, and on the other two sides by woods of spruce as shapely as Christmas trees and stands of redwood rising up above the spruce like skyscrapers out of a one-story housing tract.

The commune's two dozen or so structures included yurts, miniature A-frames on stilts, rusted camping trailers, army tent-houses, and a Quonset. With nearly all Quig's people at the jamboree, the grounds were deserted. Ava wove along a car path between the structures and parked out of sight from the road in a clearing behind Quig's residence. She helped me out of the car and led me down the river bank to a sandy beach.

Motorcycles roared past on River Road. It might've been their noise in league with my numb hand that gave me a shiver and made me feel useless, not half the man it would take to save Alvaro. Once again, I reconsidered calling Pop.

Since Gloria hadn't found Pop or Mama yesterday, I worried he might've taken her back to the asylum. If she were locked up, he would be freer to come save Alvaro. And Barker's zeal to take down my brother had convinced me that to keep playing detective on my own was to play games with Alvaro's life. The detective in the family wasn't Clifford, but Tom Hickey. Besides, if anything was wrong with him or Mama, I wanted to know. And Pop would rather have another problem to solve, or another thousand problems, than lose Alvaro.

If, once again, Pop didn't answer, I could phone Harry Poverman at his casino and ask him to send out a search party. All my life, we had spent at least the summers at our cabin on the shore of Lake Tahoe, on the acre that was worth a million or more, in the cabin Incline snobs wanted condemned. After Alvaro and I graduated from Mission Bay High, Pop gave up his P.I. business in San Diego and took over as Chief of Security for the South Shore casino our neighbor Harry Poverman owned. And every day since Claire, Harry's wife and Mama's best friend, took a bullet meant for her husband, Pop walked Mama along the beach past the Poverman estate and tried to lure her onto the lake in a speed boat or to ride one of the horses. He kept hoping a rush of excitement might one day jolt some life back into her.

Ava picked up my limp hand and gazed at my face. The sunny river appeared in her eyes. "Let's go see my uncle Mitch. He's a doctor."

I asked her to stop by the jamboree. Mid-afternoon, the heat was getting so cruel, I worried about my Hummingbird, which I had left in my Chevy. I needed to loosen the springs or the tension might yank the bridge off the box.

As Ava's Plymouth rattled into the jamboree parking lot, Big Dan was reminding the crowd that tomorrow, Phil Ochs would join them to sing his own compositions and lead a tribute to Woody Guthrie.

At first I thought the change in my car was a mirage, some prismatic effect of sunlight. The Texan and an Asian guard stood beside it, chatting.

After I realized it was no mirage, as I stumbled toward my Chevy, Ava caught up, wrapped her arm around my waist and snuggled her head against my shoulder. I guessed she knew my desire for comforting had just grown to boundless.

The Texan said, "I bet this is yours. I shoulda figured. Man, we couldn't see taking on thirty of 'em."

"About ten, actually," the Asian guard said.

"Whatever. So I radioed, got hold of the sheriff, but his boys are occupied, out chasing a murderer."

"They didn't touch the glass," the Asian guard said. "It looked more like they were doing an art project than trying to wreck your wagon. Six or eight ball peen hammers. Five minutes is all it took."

I leaned over the hood, burning my elbow on the metal and feeling some foreign spirit or substance come to a boil inside me.

Master Yi, with whom my brother and I had studied Tae Kwon Do, taught us not to fight unless we were ready to die, or to kill. I was ready.

Chapter Seven

After we saw my car, Ava changed our plans. She asked me to drive into town, report to the sheriffs what the Cossacks had done, then go Babe's and wait for her. Don't leave the cafe. Give her an hour. She wouldn't say why.

The Cossacks had customized every inch of the doors, roof, fenders, and hood of my Chevy with dents like a golf ball's dimples, each about a quarter inch deep. When Ava drove off, west toward Evergreen, I sat on the hood listening to Lightnin' Hopkins. He groaned a blues I had played but never honestly felt until now. It was about sinking as low as low went.

Pop had driven Chevys until Harry Poverman gave him a Cadillac. He maintained his cars like new. To smooth the body and repaint my Chevy would cost more than its new car price in 1955 plus the repairs ever since. But it ran the same as ever. On the way to town, I watched for Harleys. Any Cossack, I meant to run over or off the road. His choice.

Whatever Ava thought telling Willis about the hammering of my car would accomplish, I didn't foresee anything but grief coming out of a visit with the sheriff for any reason. Instead, I pulled into the shopping mall, parked in front of McNees Emporium, walked in and marched to the gun counter.

I had grown up mistrusting guns, with Pop's stories of folks who might be alive if they or their husband hadn't owned a gun. If Pop ever kept one in our home, it was hidden. The .38 he had owned since his days as a rookie Los Angeles cop stayed in his office until he needed it.

I had never before used a pistol or wanted to. I replayed the past forty hours since I came to Evergreen, feeling light and hopeful, excited to visit my brother and to play on the same stage with masters. Now that I'd gotten jailed, crippled and threatened with death, I felt in the grip of some proud demon that wouldn't let me skulk away and live in shame.

In McNees Emporium, the handguns were in a locked glass case. I pointed to a .38 like Pop's. "How much for this one and a box of cartridges?"

Hal the gun clerk beaded his eyes and stared. No doubt he wondered if I meant to rob the store. "Hunting?"

"Target practice. Beer cans and such."

"Uh huh. Eighty-seven for the gun, eight for the bullets. Half now, the rest when you come to pick it up in ten days."

I croaked, "Ten days."

"State law. You want to shoot your beer cans today, there's no waiting period on rifles, and with a rifle you might hit 'em."

At the pay phone inside Babe's, I looked up the number of the Crossroads, dialed it, and got lucky. The redhead answered.

"Cherry," I said. "Clifford Hickey here. The guy who had to leave abruptly."

"Oh, hi. So you're the Mexican Hickey's brother or what?"

"You know Alvaro?"

"He stopped in a couple times, to ask the boss if he could use a musician. The boss told him to get lost and told me don't serve him. Mister Hoppe thinks Mexicans are dirty or something."

"But he lets Cossacks drink there?"

"They're white."

"Are you from around here?" I asked, and paid full attention to her rambling answers, using the formula Pop had taught Alvaro and me for scoring points with women. Ask most anything, then hush up and listen.

When she'd told me all she wanted to, I said, "The Cossacks killed Jimmy Marris. They must've framed Alvaro. And the deputies who are stalking him through the forest—the sheriff told them shoot to kill."

"That's not right."

"All I need is a private audience with one Cossack," I said. "Preferably Hound Dog, the one who clobbered me with a tire iron. So I'm wondering, since he's a drunk, maybe he comes there alone sometimes."

Her voice dropped to a whisper. "Here's an idea. Hound Dog, he was always clogging the john. So Mister Hoppe tells him, 'I see you going in there, I'm throwing a grenade in after you.' So Hound Dog tried pissing off the deck, but Hoppe went out and knocked him over the rail. So now he goes down to the edge of the woods."

"Your boss has got some guts," I said.

"Aw, it's not guts. Just that him and Little Vic are tight. They both used to ride with the Rebels."

She told me what time the Cossacks usually arrived. I thanked her and said she must be an angel. Then I let her go and phoned our number in Incline. Nobody answered, so I called Harry Poverman's number, telling myself I only needed to know where Pop and Mama had gone, and that they were okay. If Gloria couldn't find them, I would call Harry at his casino and ask him to send out a search party. He had the resources.

Harry had lived the American dream. As a teenager in Detroit, during Prohibition, he had driven for a gang that ran liquor down from Canada. While the others passed along their loot to women and bookies, he invested in enterprises we chose not to discuss and used the profit to open a nightclub and set up roulette and craps tables in back. In 1946, he moved west, came to the lake and built Harry's South Shore Casino.

I grew up in the lowliest cabin along the beach in Incline, between Harry's estate and the mansion of the Blackwoods, a family of Tahoe pioneers. Claire Blackwood was a young widow when she and Mama became like sisters. Claire was elegant, tall, strong and educated, while people thought Mama simple-minded.

My evil grandfather had used Mama for sport, and made her retreat so far inside, she found God there. She hadn't attended even a day of school. Still, Claire thought Mama was wise. She adored Mama so dearly, Pop said one reason Claire married Harry Poverman was to live next door to us.

The month Alvaro returned from Vietnam, while Harry and Claire were sailing, one of two bullets fired from a hill near Meeks Bay, from an Italian WWII surplus MC carbine like the one Oswald shot at President Kennedy, nicked off Harry's shoulder and severed Claire's jugular vein.

Though Mama hadn't spoken more than a few words since the awful news came, every afternoon she and Pop crossed the meadow between our shack and Harry's estate. She liked to feed and brush the horses. And, Gloria told me, they were with the horses now.

While Gloria went to fetch Pop, I reminded myself I was only calling to check on him and Mama. I might tell him about Alvaro, I rationalized, just to get his advice. Or maybe he would know how to pressure Willis with a phone call.

He sounded winded. "How's the music, so far?"

"Good," I said. "But Alvaro's in a jam. They think he murdered a kid."

Pop breathed hard into the phone. I imagined him springing out of his chair.

"They think he fought the kid in a bar," I said. "The kid went to Alvaro's camp to settle, they're saying, and Alvaro shot him and dumped him in the river."

Still I heard him breathing hard. I told him Alvaro was probably hiding in the Trinity Wilderness. Then I asked about Mama.

"Better," Pop said. "Now what are we going to do about your brother?"

I had hoped he would tell me, not ask. "Find the real murderer, I guess. I turned up a few leads. Maybe you could stay near the phone, though. I've got an appointment that might solve the whole mess. If it doesn't, I'll call and read you my notes, get your advice."

"When you call," he said, "have some comforting words for Wendy. She knows something's up with her boys."

"How did she know?"

"Got word from God."

I didn't tell him I might be crippled or need surgery on my hand, and the car he had pampered for eighteen years looked like something the Marines used for target practice, and both a miniature psycho and a deputy sheriff had threatened to waste me.

My mind is peculiar. I can imagine better than I can remember. Like I imagine Pop calling Harry Poverman.

I see him telling Harry about Alvaro's mess. I hear him saying, "I'd be on my way to Evergreen if Wendy could handle the ride. Yesterday, she asked me to drive her around the lake. We got ten miles. Then she started that humming she does when she's about to go under."

"Where the hell is Evergreen?" Harry says.

"Up by Eureka."

"Right. I got a couple pals retired up that way. This hick sheriff got a name?"

"I'll find out, call you back."

"Hey, you go watch out for Wendy. I'm getting on the line up north soon as I hang up on you."

Asking favors of Harry or anybody isn't Pop's way. Besides, Harry's pals leaning on the sheriff could backfire, he knows. But Alvaro on the run justifies unorthodox methods.

I see Pop return to where he'd left Mama, in the pen behind Harry's stable, with nut-brown Gloria clutching her hand.

In a couple years, Mama will be fifty, but she looks more like a girl with her trim figure and creamy Danish skin, soft lips and eyes still trustful and bright, no matter what evils she has endured. She asks, "Clifford's okay?"

Pop says, "Yeah. Sure." He thanks Gloria, takes Mama's hand and leads her out the gate and onto the path through the cedar grove. They walk to the deck on the lake side of our homemade cabin, which the township of Incline would've condemned years before if Harry hadn't advised them to take their snooty mugs elsewhere. "Wine?" Pop asks.

"The small glass."

He returns with her wine and a tumbler of Dewar's on the rocks. She's in her favorite chair, which Pop had made out of cedar planks. She sits peering across the lake at the Rubicons, through the mist that rises from the cold water on days as hot as this.

Pop lays his hand on her shoulder and shakes his head while telling himself he can't leave her, not even for Alvaro.

He knows he can take Mama back to the sanitarium. If they don't want to babysit, he can exaggerate her symptoms. Except he can't make himself leave her. Not when's she's still teetering on the edge of catatonia. Pop has watched people die, seen friends tortured and mutilated, witnessed the suffering and degradation of men and women he loved or admired, but nothing chills or haunts him like the sight of Mama's body with the spirit gone missing.

Besides, he can't leave her while his heart pains are coming too hard and often to let him feel assured of living through the day. Not while his only fervent wish about death is that he can see Wendy's face or feel her hand on him while he does it.

He watches a catamaran tacking into the wind, fills his lungs with what Mark Twain called the air the angels breathe, and wonders if he should've told his boys about his lousy heart.

Chasing a murderer might kill him, he knows. But he isn't about to let his boys down. As precious as his life still feels, Alvaro's life is far more precious than his own. So he tells Mama my story.

I had hoped Steph would come into Babe's. If I told her how the Cossacks had wrecked my car, she might direct me to a hippie with a gun for rent. But the waitress was the old gal with a hearing aid. I ordered a pastrami sandwich and water.

My right hand lay on the table, worthless as a stump. Out the window at the curb sat the ball-peened Chevy, which Pop used to wash every week and wax every month. A dragon in my state of mind would be spewing flames.

I was eating my sandwich and had just chomped my lip when Ava pulled up across the street. The sight of her quenched a small fraction of my wrath. She walked with short steps, like a ballerina on pointe. I imagined long, downy legs beneath the peasant dress. Her hair cascaded over one shoulder and down her breast. In those days, hippie girls often gave up the half of their beauty that makeup, creams and perfumes bestowed upon other girls, for the sake of going natural. But Ava looked so good, I would've bet no salon or spa could improve her. Her skin was supple, the freckles on the crests of her cheeks like tiny gems, her unpainted lips a deep magenta.

She sat across the booth from me, sighed and drew her shoulders up, folded her hands on the table. "I went to see Lola."

I stared, having one of the spells when my brain felt as numb as my hand.

"My sister," she said. "Vic's girl. I went to ask if the Cossacks have had their fun with you or if next time, you know."

I asked, "Do you think if we knew why Vic is so anxious to get rid of me we'd know who killed Jimmy?"

"Maybe."

"Did you ask her what's Vic's problem with me?"

"Uh huh. She laughed and said, you know, 'Buzz off.' Now do you want to hear what I think?"

"You bet."

"Jimmy's dead. He's not in danger anymore. Your brother's okay. He's not too worried, or he wouldn't be robbing cabins."

"Maybe the robber wasn't Alvaro."

"Anyway, the guy in mortal danger around here is you. Vic is talking up how cool Jimmy was—I don't know where he gets off, they weren't friends. But never mind, Lola says Vic figures if you got killed in a fight or something, the sheriffs would call it self defense. I mean, everybody knows the sheriffs are scared of the Cossacks. And Vic says the sheriffs would consider it a favor if the Cossacks got rid of you."

"Vic let her tell you all that?"

"He wasn't there. I got lucky. Lola's having asthma, so she didn't go on the run down to Clearlake."

Ava's uncle Mitch had an office attached to his home, a redwood two-story that covered most of its half-acre lot on Daiquiri Street. The uncle looked stiff and wan as any mortician. He appeared to adore Ava and despise me. Still he wedged me into his schedule, examined my hand and determined that a ligament had torn clean through. He prescribed X-rays at a Eureka clinic. He bandaged my wrist and hand and rigged them into a sling.

"How long before it works again?" I asked.

"Get the X-ray," he said.

Outside in the sunshine, I doctored my lungs with the scent of the colossal redwood in Mitch's front yard, while I set my next goals. First, since it seemed Ava had decided to help, I would send her to learn what Jimmy had been up to Wednesday night. While she was busy, I would find a gun.

We sat on the running board of her car. I proposed that she go out snooping. She agreed on the condition that while she looked around for Jimmy's friends, I would lie low at Quig's.

I said, "The Cossacks are gone to Clearlake."

"I didn't say all of them went."

As we pulled into Quig's, I began to notice the heat. Weather hadn't made my list of concerns the past couple days. But now I felt wilted, and I noticed heat waves rising off the dirt and glistening up from the river.

Dogs and chickens clustered in most every parcel of shade. Evergreen was starting to feel more like Death Valley than Eden. No birds cawed or peeped. The only creature who braved the sun was a fellow standing in the vegetable garden beside the parched corn stalks. He looked stiff and ragged as a scarecrow. Aside from him, the only people in sight were two girls holding infants, sitting cross-legged on the shaded grass beneath a giant madrone, beside the sandy playground.

Ava pulled up at her dwelling, a yurt two doors toward the river from the community toilet and bath house. She had bought the place in exchange for an autoharp she got in trade for a rug she wove. I knew yurts were the Mongolian version of teepees, made for climates of strong winds and bitter cold. Ava's was shaped like a circus tent with a hole at the top of the ceiling and a fire-ring in the middle of the floor. The floor was tarpaulins, her bed a futon. Mobiles of origami designs fluttered whenever one of us moved, like a physics lesson on the delicate activity of air. A stool sat in front of a hand loom with the beginning of a tapestry, a wavy pattern in sunset pastels.

The place lacked chairs. She pointed at the futon. "Lie down if you want."

I flopped down beside a Bible commentary on St. Paul's epistle to the Romans. She sat on the stool, folded her hands, studied me and frowned. "You look sick."

"A little discouraged, is all."

"Does your hand work any better with the bandage?"

I lifted it and tried to wiggle the index and bird-flipping fingers. "Nope."

"Clifford, things could turn out okay. Maybe we'll find a way to clear your brother. Maybe you can still play on Sunday."

"Yeah, if I can figure how to hold a flat pick between my teeth, hold the guitar up to my mouth, and sing at the same time."

Her smile, which made dimples on both sides of her mouth, lifted my spirits more than a smile ought to. "Okay," she said, "so what else should I ask people, besides where did Jimmy go the night he died?"

"Get them talking, pay attention, people will blab and let things slip. Remember everything anybody says about Jimmy. Take notes."

"Okay. Make yourself at home. Sleep. If you want to read, hang that flashlight from the mobile there." She pointed to an Eveready on the floor beside the bed and hitched a thumb toward the mobile. "In the Chattagua hall there's a fridge that's always got Kool-Aid."

"I'll be fine. You'll come back in a couple hours?"

She leaned closer. You can kiss me, I thought. Instead she touched my chin with her cool fingers.

Moving the Bible commentary, I sprawled on my back until her car sputtered away, then gave myself another minute to appreciate the futon and the mint and sandalwood scents and wondered if God had realized the depth of trouble he was brewing for men when he made most girls so damned pretty. Reveries about Ava's humble voice and moist lips tempted me to keep my word and stay here. But, laying my hand on the wound from Hound Dog's tire iron, I pushed myself up and walked out.

On my way to befriend the gatekeeper and ask if he owned a handgun, I noticed a long, ebony leg draped off the side of a chaise lounge beside the rustiest of several rusty trailers, in an oak stand along the riverbank. The trailer was an old, melon-shaped 12' model, the wheels replaced with a foundation of concrete blocks. The attached veranda was woven from saplings.

Simon reclined in the lawn chair amid a dissipating cloud of smoke. A book, up close to his face, held him captive. Even when I squatted beside him he ignored me. The book was Kierkegaard's *Fear and Trembling*, a meditation on the story of Abraham and Isaac. A requirement at my Christian college for philosophy minors like I had been.

Simon turned the page, then closed the book, cocked his head, and looked me over.

I said, "Remember my Chevy, nice green paint job? Check out how the Cossacks customized it."

Rising like a sleepwalker, he shaded his eyes from the glare and gazed over my pointed finger at the ball-peened wreck beside Ava's yurt. "You'll need a ton of Bondo."

"A gun's what I'll need," I said, and told him my plan.

He paced to the riverbank, leaned over the water and stared like a predator scouting fish. He craned his head around, sized me up, laughed and turned back to the river. At last he walked over to where I stood in the shade. "Who all are you going to shoot?"

"Maybe nobody. If it's anybody, it'll be a Cossack."

Simon watched a tall girl, naked except for the towel her hair was wrapped in, stroll out of the bathhouse and down a path. After she entered a teepee, he said, "Here's the deal, if I can cut it. Thirty bucks now, like you said. Five hundred more if it shoots anybody and you want me and its owner to clam up."

"And I get to keep it until morning?"

"Let's see what can I do." He went for his keys, jumped into his microbus, fired it up and sputtered away.

Walking to the river, I thought, God help me. I sat in a dugout place on the riverbank, felt the snakes in my belly hiss and writhe, and played a game I had invented while trying to prep myself for law school. I argued a case I called Clifford the Hero vs. Clifford the Chickenheart. I represented Clifford the Hero. Chickenheart didn't require counsel. He argued, Heaven? You only hope there's a heaven. You *know* how you'll miss Mama, Pop, Alvaro. Even if your music dreams don't fly, you'll miss your chance of finding and winning a wife, maybe one like Ava, miss playing your songs, writing your stories, miss taking care of Mama and Pop as they grow old.

Before I could argue on the hero side, I needed to ask myself what made heroes plunge into danger? How did Pop and a band of Indians once rush into battle against Nazis and the Mexican army? How did Alvaro trek through the jungle dodging traps and land mines without letting terror melt his brain?

They just quit thinking and did it, I surmised. But I wondered what allows somebody addicted to thinking to quit when his brain's firing commands to find an escape. Maybe Pop had been tired of life or fed up with worrying. Maybe Alvaro, as a Tijuana street kid, learned to survive by turning off his brain whenever he needed to act.

Maybe other guys believe they have no choice, or think they're invincible, or delude themselves with visions of glory, fame, or adoration.

None of those ways fit Clifford Hickey, who loved life and peace and imagined happy futures. If I had once thought myself invincible, the past couple days had taught me otherwise.

Chapter Eight

When Simon returned, he climbed out of his microbus empty handed, walked around, and opened the tailgate. The pistol lay atop the engine compartment, wrapped in an olive drab towel. It was a small black model like you'd see a floozy holding on the cover of an old mystery novel. The maker's name plate was gone and the serial numbers were invisible beneath a riot of scratches.

"Looks like the gun has a history," I said, and gave Simon thirty dollars. I picked up the gun with my left hand. It weighed about half as much as Pop's .38, the only other pistol I had held.

Simon handed me a kitchen-match box heavy with bullets.

"Twenty-five caliber," he said. "I wouldn't plan on hurting anybody from more than about twenty feet."

I needed to see if I could work even a small pistol left-handed. I asked Simon for a ride to some remote place where gunshots wouldn't draw return fire from a weed farmer. Simon agreed to show me such a place.

The gatekeeper's bush of kinky hair had changed from white to midnight black. Simon must've noticed me gaping. He said, "Twins. This one does Clairol."

We turned east on River Road and chugged past McNees Park and the Bend in the River Church. Simon hitched a finger toward the church. "Home of Saint Bob, your typical junkie con from the Haight who found out Jesus is not only the savior but also a meal ticket. Have you asked that crook who he thinks popped Jimmy?"

"Should I?"

"It's your game."

Simon's way of tossing crumbs made me wonder if he was attempting to lead me away from the truth. Maybe if I held the gun to his head, something I needed would spill out of him.

Beyond the covered bridge that cast its shadow over a log loading ramp, we crashed over ruts up a logging road, five miles into a razed forest of saplings that drooped as though in shame. Simon pulled off the trail and stopped beside the remains of a party site. The beer cans and bottles could supply a battalion of sharpshooters with targets.

While Simon sat in his microbus reading Kierkegaard, I shot left-handed from ten paces, fifteen, then thirty. I used the back of my right hand to brace the gun underneath. That skewed my balance, but when I used the left hand alone, it trembled. The longer I practiced, the more my hand shuddered. After firing two clips, twenty shots that knocked down three cans, I pocketed the gun.

On our way out of the forest, I pointed to a footpath through a grove of second growth fir, which I imagined would lead to some hippie's secret garden. I said, "The forest service ought to tack up a sign warning hikers not to eat the foliage unless they want to get high."

His scowl made me wonder if he had agreed to and abetted my plan because if it failed, Evergreen would be infested with one less snoop.

Back at Quig's, as he dropped me off at my mutilated Chevy, Simon handed me a joint.

"No, thanks," I said. "All it would do is make me paranoid."

"Or it might help you be still," he said. "You've got to be still to hear the voice that told Abraham, 'Take your son up to the mountain and stab him.'"

Fear and Trembling is an essay on Abraham and Isaac. I assumed Simon meant to inform me that if father Abraham had missed, ignored, or disobeyed the voice of God, he might've lost out on his destiny.

As I pulled out of Quig's past the gatekeeper's shaggy dog that choked itself from lunging at my car and me, I thought about destiny. I wondered if I had one and if I did, whether it involved getting shot and dumped into Whiskey River. My plan began to seem *loco*. But Pop had acted *loco*. He had rushed in to fight Nazis and mobsters. And at least a dozen times he'd told us, "Once you've decided, turning back is the most dangerous thing you can do."

A quarter mile east of the Crossroads, behind a wall of redwoods, I sat in my car and held the pistol with both hands, wondering what had become of the rage that had made me willing to shoot people. I no longer wanted to even risk shooting anybody. Besides, I was taller and heavier than Hound Dog, and no doubt stronger, from sports training and from surfing.

Still, I wedged the gun under my belt, tripped down the gravel road and mumbled words like, "It's okay, Clifford. You're cool. Nothing to fear."

A hundred yards from the saloon, a trail crossed a vacant lot to the river. I hustled along the trail, slid down the bank and plodded downriver on rocks and mud. The sun was already behind the forest. Its rays came at me in pastel shades of green and rose. Gusts of sea breeze fluttered leaves, needles, and cones.

A hammering woodpecker startled me. A brown trout swam figure eights an inch below the surface. Mosquitoes swarmed and squads of them at once attacked my neck and forehead. Last year, I hadn't seen a mosquito, and one of the nymphs at the swimming hole told us the pests never came near Evergreen because the sea breezes carried them east to the mountains. But here they were, like a plague of locusts, I thought.

I sat near the river, out of sight from the saloon deck and parking lot, listened for motorcycles and worried lest Cherry might've sold me out to the Cossacks.

If night fell and the bikers didn't show or if they roared past the Crossroads without stopping, I would take that as a sign to make a safer plan.

I gnashed my teeth, chewed grass, swatted mosquitos, and tried to occupy my brain remembering the melodies and lyrics to some old Quaker songs that usually could quiet my mind.

But thoughts of Ava kept interrupting. I felt like a creep for lying to her, going off on a *loco* mission when I had promised to wait for her at Quig's. "Quit thinking, Clifford," I mumbled every minute or so, only I used various nicknames. Bonehead. Jerk. Fool. Still, I felt as able to become a werewolf as I did to quit thinking.

In twilight I peered across the river and down the highway at the cross I first saw when arriving in Evergreen, where the three cupids and their dad had clustered. I wondered, would anybody place a shrine marking the spot where Hound Dog killed me.

As dark fell, fog rolled in from the ocean, twenty miles west. I shivered as though time had warped and delivered me to winter. Black fog seeped through my pores, nose, and ears. I reminded myself of Friedrich Nietzsche's opinion that courage was the will to overcome fear. And I remembered our Tae Kwon Do master's promise that having earned our black belts proved we possessed indomitable spirits.

Even through the fog, I heard the rumble of a dozen Harleys when they were still a mile away. To me, they were as loud as a fleet of Cobra helicopters firing rockets. I climbed the river bank, and drew the pistol from under my belt.

They cruised at about one m.p.h., it seemed. Maybe they were looking into the forest, searching for me. Maybe Simon was a Cossack snitch. Maybe Little Vic had planted Simon at Quig's to snoop out the locations of marijuana farms, and after he dropped me off, he sped to a phone and called some roadside bar where he knew the bikers would stop. Maybe he had given them a laugh about the chump with his tiny gun who thought he was a match for them.

As the choppers swung off the highway, revved, and bumped across the gravel, I imagined Vic yelling, "Come out and play, Pretty Boy." I reached for the pistol and held it beside my face.

They parked in a straight line against the railroad ties that marked the walkway. I counted eleven of them, five with tattooed girls perched behind them. As they dismounted, the girls shook their hair loose and unsnapped the fronts of their leather jackets or Levi vests, exposing their halters. The men looked around, alert as guerillas and with savage expressions. A loud biker said, "That farmer in the Dodge that wouldn't let Frag go by, we oughta rode circles around him."

"Shut up, Hound Dog," another guy said, "shut up and get in there and tell Daisy Mae to start pourin'."

I guessed the hand that shot up from behind other bikers and gave the finger belonged to Hound Dog.

Little Vic led his pack into the Crossroads. I wheezed a breath and stared at the gun until my night vision sharpened and I could inspect it. I pulled out the clip, shoved it in again, checked the safety, and crammed the barrel under my belt.

As I tiptoed across the road, my Converse shoes on the gravel sounded like avalanches. "Sneakers, hell," I whispered. Cowboy boots with full-heel taps might've made less noise. I considered going barefoot. But I might have to run from the Cossacks into the forest, through burred vines and lava spills and across the snow-capped mountains.

I stationed myself behind a tall pine at the edge of the woods about twenty yards from the steps that led down off the saloon deck, upon which nobody sat drinking. I thanked God for the plague of mosquitoes. I crouched, peered around the tree, and slapped at the pests with my good hand. When my legs started to tingle, I stood and stretched and shook blood into them.

About a half hour passed before the Crossroads' rear door flew open. My heart triple-timed. A couple men who looked like weekend hippies with holey jeans and leather bands around their business-cut hair came outside and leaned against the rail. One of them fired up a joint.

While they smoked, I watched the door, imagining that Hound Dog would appear and stroll across the meadow and piss on the base of my pine while I couldn't jump him, with the smokers there to witness. But as usual, my imagination failed to prophesy the truth. One of the men flicked the roach into the meadow where it sizzled in a patch of stagnant water, and they shuffled back inside.

Somebody opened a screened window. The jukebox was loud with John Fogarty's complaint about getting stuck in Lodi. Hound Dog slammed the door open and stumbled out. He tripped over something on the deck but righted himself before he reached the steps. Going down them he used the rail for balance.

I grabbed the ski mask and pulled it on. Once the eye and nose holes were straight, I watched Hound Dog crossing the meadow, heading for the tree to the left of mine. I felt for the ripped T-shirt hanging out of my left hip pocket, then reached around for the nylon cord in my right pocket.

Tonight, Hound Dog looked peaceful. He yawned, then cleared his throat and spat a big wad. He was the kind of pisser who unlatches his belt and drops his jeans.

After a long, deep, and silent breath and exhale, I rushed around the pine and attacked from the rear, ducking my shoulder to waist high and curling my head out of the way. By the time I landed a cross body tackle he was reacting to the noise, starting his turn toward me, with his right hand still occupied. It didn't keep the stream of piss from shooting up like water out of a loose hose.

After glancing off the tree, he fell hard, face first. I shoved his face into the pine needle mulch and held it there with my right elbow.

My good hand found a pressure point on his neck and jabbed with my thumb. Though I had felt the effect the move had on my own neck, that was during Tae Kwon Do class. This was the world. So when the biker quit thrashing and went limp, after I caught my first breath since before my attack, I thanked the spirit of Master Yi.

I grabbed the ripped T-shirt, worked one end of it under Hound Dog's down-turned face and to where I could grab both ends in the same hand and pull. After fumbling and cussing, I managed to gag him and use my good hand and the other elbow to tie a knot. Then I pulled his arms around back and cinched his wrists together with a short length of nylon cord.

He was twice as heavy as I expected, until the black-out passed. Even when he came to, he was groggy, and still limp. But he knew what a gun looked like, and what even a little one could do from up close.

I held the pistol at the top of his spine and shoved it upward. With that encouragement, he rose to his knees, then to his feet, and started walking the way I pointed.

Whenever he tried to pull up his jeans, I shoved him. A guy with his pants half down might be less dangerous. He couldn't walk fast, but still we arrived at the gravel road and marched along it, deeper into the forest. In about ten minutes, we passed my Chevy, which was mostly hidden from the road. While he walked, he tried to shout but made no sense and little noise. A hundred or so steps past my car, I marched him off the road and between cedars and undergrowth to the bank of the river. I slammed him against a crooked cedar and kicked him in the groin to dissuade him from trying to break and run while I lashed him to the tree using the rest of my nylon cord.

That done, I untied the gag. His cussing didn't show much imagination. But the name he threw at me dozens of times was a good choice for making a savage out of a guy like me who cherished his mother. I shouted, "Hold on, partner. All you've got to do is tell me which Cossack killed Jimmy Marris and why, and I'm gone."

He laughed and added "Hickey" to his curses.

I threw a side kick on his belly. It knocked the wind out of him but didn't erase his smile. I backhanded him in one ear and clobbered him with a roundhouse punch on the other ear. His laugh became a bray.

When I noticed his boner, I gave up and left him there. He filled the woods with noise while I plodded back toward my Chevy.

Chapter Nine

Rather than drive through territory where Cossacks would be scouring the woods for Hound Dog by now, I drove deeper into the forest, remembering Alvaro's directions: "If you get to the second bridge, you've come too far."

At the second bridge, I crossed the river. On the south side, the gravel road was smoother, and every few hundred yards I passed a house. One of them was an A-frame near which two of the cupids I had seen by the cross beside the highway and again at the jamboree attempted to play catch with a Frisbee beneath a round silver moon and bright stars.

At the 101, I turned south.

The detour I chose, a country road that delivered me to the coast access loop, killed an hour.

In Evergreen, I saw Delene Marris staggering around a corner, probably walking home from Louella's. I made the turn, pulled over across the street and offered her a ride. Maybe, from a woman deranged from liquor and grief, I could learn something that would make the day less than a perfect failure.

She stopped and peered through the dark. When she recognized me, she reared back and screeched, "Hey, you louse, if your brother ain't a killer, why's the FBI keep tabs on him all summer?"

"FBI?"

"Get lost, Hickey."

"Did your brother tell you?"

She staggered off muttering curses. I let out the clutch so my Chevy crawled along beside her until she wheeled and shouted, "You don't believe me, go ask the Swede."

Knudsen, I thought.

I let her walk on alone, shifted into reverse and thought, Yep, he's watching Alvaro on account of some business with Phil Ochs.

◇◇◇

I picture Mama reading *A Tale of Two Cities,* which Pop and I had recommended. Pop is studying maps of the Shasta Wilderness, trying to deduce where Alvaro might've gone. He catches the phone before the second ring. "Clifford?"

"I'm a lousy detective," I say.

"What'd you learn?"

"Some bikers and a deputy sheriff act like Alvaro came from hell to spoil their fun, and since I'm his brother, I'm just as dangerous. And it looks like the FBI's been keeping tabs on Alvaro. That's all."

"We're on our way," he says. "How far is Evergreen up the 101 from Highway 20?"

"You can't leave Mama," I tell him. "Sure, things are getting too complicated for my second-rate mind, but all I need is advice."

"How far?"

"Eighty miles or so."

"I'll be there by half past six."

"No, Pop. Just tell me what to do. You can't leave Mama."

"I won't."

A half hour later, they cross Donner Summit and speed down the grade toward the Sacramento Valley and the Mendocino Forest. They're in the 1970 Cadillac Eldorado Harry Poverman had bought Pop as a retirement gift when he left the job as Chief of Security at Harry's South Shore Casino. The Rat Pack

Cadillac, people call it, because Dean Martin and his cronies drove them.

Pop is wearing his favorite driving hat, a relic from the last year the San Diego Padres played in the AAA Pacific Coast League. He prefers minor league baseball, where the hungry players always hustle. The black-framed glasses, which he only uses for driving and watching movies or ball games or at church if he cares to see the preacher, magnify and darken his eyes to the blue of deep water. His face is so flushed, he looks sunburned. He drives left-handed while his right hand kneads the scruff of Mama's neck.

Mama sits still like most always, hands folded on her lap, her mouth slightly open as though prepared to speak, though she hasn't spoken a hundred words since last year. And now, with her stillness and grief, Mama looks all the more like Mary in Michelangelo's Pieta, only with cornflower blue eyes, milky skin, and golden hair.

Pop says, "There's a river in Evergreen, and motels along the riverbank. I phoned, but they're booked. How about you pray for a cancellation?" He looks over, winks, and runs a finger around her cheek.

Mama hasn't spoken all night.

At Quig's, washboard and kazoo music wafted out of what they called the Chattagua hall, along with singing, shouts, and laughter. A gang of small kids raced around playing hide-and-seek, ducking behind the teepees, lean-tos, and trailers.

I stashed the pistol in a hole I scooped out of the loam behind the rear tire of my Chevy. At the entrance to Ava's yurt, I whispered her name. I waited and called again, slightly louder. After the third time, she said, "Oh hell, come in."

She was cross-legged on her futon, reading scripture. I asked, "Good book?"

Without looking up, she muttered, "Well, you're alive anyway."

"I went down by the murder site," I said, which wasn't the whole truth but also was no lie.

"Crutch came to the gate," she said. "Quig had to go out and make a deal before Crutch would go away."

"Crutch who?"

She slammed her Bible closed and finally looked up. "Guess."

I slinked to a dark place, sat on the tarp, pulled my knees close, and rested my elbow in its sling on top of them. "What'd you mean about Quig making a deal?"

"He promised that if you showed up again he would grill you and unless you could prove Alvaro wasn't the killer he'd chase you out of the commune. I guess it was like a compromise, to save face. Quig's half politician. He asked me about you and I said you're probably crazy enough to kidnap and torture a Cossack. So when Crutch reports to Vic, he'll either decide there's no deal and come inside the compound to kill you or wait outside and kill you there. How will you get out of this one, Clifford?"

"Beats me," I said, then sat mute. So did Ava, for the whole ten minutes before she picked up a medicine bag and headed for the bathhouse.

I went to my Chevy, retrieved the gun from behind the tire, and climbed into the front through the rolled-down driver's side window. If I opened a door, the dome light would beam and might tell Quig I had returned. I climbed over the seat, wedged the pistol between the mattress and the side-panel, sprawled atop the sleeping bag, and watched out the window to see if Ava would go from the bathhouse to the Chattagua hall and report to Quig.

But she came straight back and ducked into the yurt. A minute later, the lantern darkened.

I slept, woke to the squawk of a saxophone, dozed until footsteps approached, then groped for the pistol. After the footsteps passed and faded, I slept until the first gray light.

Nobody was outside except the white-haired gatekeeper and his bloodthirsty dog, and a duo of topless nymphets practicing yoga beside the riverbank.

The flap to Ava's yurt was tied shut. I reached through a gap and untied the bottom, which allowed me to crawl in. I knelt beside Ava, watched her eyelids flick and her hand rise to wisp a cluster of hair off her cheek. Its mission accomplished, the hand fell beside her chin. I wondered, if I woke her with a kiss, would she clobber me? Instead I touched her shoulder with one finger.

She jerked and bolted up, wrapping the quilt around her.

"Morning."

"You…" She rubbed her eyes. "What?"

"Could you sneak me out of here?"

She raked her hands through her hair, coiled her legs under her, and stood straight up. She wore boxer shorts and a McNees Lumber T-shirt with the chainsaw-wielding beaver. In spite of the baggy shirt, I observed one of those waists so tiny you wonder how all the organs can fit, and full breasts that swelled and quivered with her breathing. "Go get in my car," she said.

I crawled outside. After fetching the pistol from my Chevy, I wrapped it in a bandana, then tiptoed along the path to Simon's trailer and laid it on his lounge chair. While I crept back toward Ava's car, one of the topless yoga girls turned and stared as if I, not her, were the exhibitionist.

The Plymouth was unlocked. I climbed in and lay on the floorboard in back, while Ava hustled off, probably to the bathhouse. When she returned, she climbed into the car and gazed over the seat at me. Her hair was brushed, and her eyes were bright as if she had polished them.

If I had waited for her to invite me up front, I would've been on the floor all the way to Babe's. So I sat up and slid over the seat after we passed the old community garden lot, directly below Sugar Hill. A tip of the sun cleared the peaks of the Trinity mountains. Ava glanced over at me, in a pout.

I said, "Thanks."

"Do me a favor, please."

"Sure, what?"

"Say the sinner's prayer right now, no matter if you've said it before. Because the Cossacks are going to kill you, and I want to be sure you're in heaven. Not like Jimmy."

Her comparing me to Jimmy could mean she thought of me as a boyfriend. The idea made my eyes water. She noticed, and her face softened. "Are you always crazy?"

"Not anymore," I said. "Pop's on his way."

She studied my face and smiled for the first time since yesterday noon. "Can Pop leap tall buildings?"

"Yeah." I checked my watch. "He said to meet him at 6:30. Five minutes one way or the other, he'll pull in. He's got a gift for time. We used to drive a lot between Tahoe and San Diego. Alvaro and I would pick a town hundreds of miles down the road. He'd tell us what time we'd get there, to the minute."

But at 6:10 we found Pop's mile-long silver-blue Eldorado parked at the curb outside Babe's. I said, "He must be a little overanxious."

Chapter Ten

They were in the first booth on the left, Mama facing the window. Pop was on the other side, turned with his back against the wall so nobody could sneak up behind him and he could see all around, a habit of his even in peaceful times or at home. He saw me and smiled. A second later, Mama gaped as though surprised to see me and lifted her arm and waved. Maybe not quite sure I was real.

The cafe was busy. Loggers slumped over coffee in most of the booths. As I held the glass door open and Ava walked in, Pop slid out and stood. He shook Ava's hand as if greeting a queen. "Tom Hickey."

I introduced her and asked Pop, "Did you tell Mama what's up?"

They both nodded. I said, "Jimmy Marris, the guy they think Alvaro shot, was Ava's boyfriend."

A little moan came from Mama. Pop sighed and shook his head, then stared at my bandaged hand. "Who did you hit?"

"A deputy handcuffed me tight and tweaked a nerve or something. No big deal."

Mama had swung her knees around. I helped her up and we hugged. When we separated, she kept hold of my good hand and offered her other hand to Ava. Their hands remained clasped at least a minute.

Pop lay his arm across my shoulders. "Alvaro's still on the loose. I stopped by the jail, talked to the night man. The sheriff's supposed to be there around eight. So will we." He turned to Ava. "Hungry?"

"Uh huh." From the smile she gave him, I supposed Pop had charmed her already. Once Claire Blackwood had told me, "Tom's eyes, his voice, his gestures, posture and everything about him testifies that he'd never hurt a woman, or let anybody else get away with it. He's a genuine man."

We slid into the booth, Ava then me, with our backs to the window. Now and then Pop glanced past us to the street. He watched Steph walk in, wearing her white uniform, drowsy and listing to the side. When she saw Ava, she beamed and reached over me to clutch Ava's arm. "You doin' okay?"

"Uh huh. God's helping me through it."

Steph leaned close to my ear and whispered, "You're screwed." As she wobbled toward the kitchen, she called over her shoulder, "Be right with you guys."

Because Pop stared at me and raised his eyebrows, I said, "These bikers, the Cossacks, somebody messed with one of them, and they're blaming me."

Pop fixed his gaze on my eyes. "Take it from the top."

"Yeah, well Alvaro was camped down the river from here, up a forest road from a saloon called the Crossroads, on the 101. Wednesday night I couldn't find him, so I slept in the car, a few miles off the highway. By the river. Late in the night I heard gunshots."

"How many?"

"Three. Maybe four."

"How close."

"Say a half mile. Far enough so I didn't lie awake worrying about them."

"What time?"

"Two or three, I guess. Then first thing in the morning, I found Alvaro's camp. I'd only been there a few minutes when the sheriff and his boys swarmed in.

"Alvaro grabs a rifle and takes off. They shove me around, lock me up, and in another cell there's Little Vic, stands four-foot-something." I didn't mention Hound Dog, hoping to avoid that topic. "Turns out Vic's king of the Cossacks. He threatens to smoke me, maybe on account of he thinks I killed Jimmy, and Ava's sister's his girl. Or maybe to get me out of town, and make sure Alvaro gets convicted or dead, so the truth won't come out.

"At the jamboree, they…Pop, the Chevy's pretty much junked. They ball-peened it. The Cossacks did. All over. Hundreds of times. It looks like the offspring of a dinosaur and a golf ball."

Pop flipped his hand, meaning a car didn't matter when Alvaro was in danger.

Steph arrived with her notepad. Ava ordered tea and oatmeal with peaches. Pop ordered two omelets, Mama's plain, his with ham and cheese. I chose the blueberry hotcakes. Steph moved to the booth straight across, where three loggers in McNees T-shirts sat still and grim, eavesdropping.

I said, "Ava can tell you what's happened to Evergreen."

We all turned to Ava. "Greed happened," she said. "The hippies planted marijuana all over the forest, so what could they expect besides some kind of mob to move in. Quig says the Cossacks are no better or no worse than like IBM or General Motors."

"Quig owns one of the communes," I added. "Last night he cut a deal with the Cossacks, to turn me over to them."

Ava said, "*If* he decides you tortured Hound Dog."

Pop looked back and forth between Ava and me. "Tortured?"

I said, "Somebody waylaid and interrogated this biker, is all."

The loggers across the room slapped money down on their check and sat still, listening. Pop watched them long enough so I guessed he was trying to catch their attention, but none of them looked his way. He turned to the jukebox selector on the table by the wall and dropped in a quarter. His first choice was "Mood Indigo," one of his favorite tunes to play when he moonlighted on clarinet with a jazz combo.

At 7:15, Pop turned south on the highway. Mama rode shotgun, resting or praying with her eyes closed. Ava and I were in back.

After a mile, Ava touched my knee, just long enough to imply she might forgive me for last night, if I behaved henceforth.

A plane zoomed low overhead. I told Pop it was probably the law scouring the woods for Alvaro.

"Who's investigating?" he asked.

"Besides the sheriffs," I said, "a guy who says he's Bureau of Narcotics. Agent Knudsen." I fished in my pocket for the business card Knudsen had given me. "He's the only one who told me anything he didn't have to."

"Such as?"

"He said they found footprints around the camp that matched the ones at the murder scene. But he could be a phony. I think Jimmy's mom told me he's FBI, and he's been keeping tabs on Alvaro."

"You *think* she told you he's FBI?"

"She was drunk, yelling at me. Does his card look for real to you? I mean, would a Fed's business card be that rinky-dink?"

"Could be," Pop said, "if he's FBI and the card's a cover. I hear Hoover's a tightwad who keeps account of paperclips. Did he show you any ID?"

"No."

"Did you ask for any?"

"No. I should've, right."

Pop filled, tamped, and lit his pipe and rolled his window all the way down. "So Ava, who'd Jimmy pal with? Bikers, hippies, jocks, fishermen?"

"He thought the bikers were rats," she said, "and the hippies he didn't understand, like hardly anybody who grows up poor can make sense of the hippies living on purpose that way. But some of them are smart, and Jimmy liked that. He could talk to them about politics and philosophical stuff. He was pretty tight with a black guy named Simon for a while, last year."

I groaned and notched another mark in the error column of my record. If I would've asked Ava that simple question, who were Jimmy's pals, I might've tried harder and found a way to loosen Simon's tongue. Instead of waylaying Hound Dog.

Ava had stopped talking when I groaned. Pop had cocked his head my way. I said, "I've been talking to Simon, but I didn't know he was tight with Jimmy."

While Ava told Pop that Jimmy was also tight with his mom and with his uncle Brady, the deputy sheriff, Pop handed me a pocket-sized notepad and a ballpoint. Ava listed and briefly characterized Jimmy's half dozen best friends.

I scribbled names and notes. Then I thought about Simon. Ava had told me Jimmy was half black. Besides jamboree musicians and a few hippies, blacks were rare as crocodiles around Evergreen. Simon had risked plenty more than the few dollars he asked for by involving himself with me. Yet I hadn't asked Ava or anybody about him.

I directed Pop onto Highball Trail. As we passed the Crossroads, Ava said, "That's the bar where *somebody* caught Hound Dog and took him out into the woods and tortured him."

"Not tortured," I insisted. "Tortured isn't the way I heard it."

Pop craned around to look at me. He didn't have to ask if I was guilty. He could read my face as well as I could read "Run Spot Run." He turned back to the road and asked, "How far to Alvaro's camp?"

"Four and a half miles."

"And the shooting happened near there?"

"About a half mile upstream, they say."

Pop's Eldorado floated over the bumps and sinkholes. With one hand resting on the ledge of her open window, Mama gazed into the forest, where wild plums and pears shone bright as Christmas bulbs. Mama beamed as if she had just discovered heaven.

Our first stop was Alvaro's camp. A blind person wouldn't miss the trail, since the road and clearing beside it were etched with the tracks from where police cruisers had spun U-turns.

I led the way. Pop covered the rear. The trail was scuffed by so many foot-tracks, Willis might have imported a brigade of Marines and marched them through it.

His campsite wasn't taped off. Either the sheriffs had gathered everything they considered evidence, or they figured they didn't need evidence, since they meant to shoot him on sight. I wondered, if he got desperate, would he use his rifle and make the charge that he was a killer come true.

The campsite looked like a pillaged garage sale. The string shopping bags, which on Thursday had hung from redwood limbs as Alvaro's version of a kitchen cabinet and a dresser, lay torn on the ground beside the strewn remnants of his underwear, plates and pans, toiletries, and canned goods. His Paracho guitar, rosewood with an ebony fingerboard inlaid with mother of pearl, lay next to its case, upside down on the strings.

After I packed the guitar into its case, I followed Pop into the tent. The sheriffs had sliced the canvas floor on three sides and peeled it back. Probably after they ransacked his pallet bed, books, and all, they cut the floor and heaved it to one side, in case he had buried treasure or corpses beneath it. Pop and I laid the floor back and spread Alvaro's things around as we looked them over. The first objects I searched for were roach clips, whiskey bottles, any evidence that Alvaro had gone back on his clean and sober promise. I would've shoved them into my pockets. Pop didn't need another something to grieve. He brushed aside a pile of books, Kurt Vonnegut paperbacks and a few comic mysteries.

While I gathered Alvaro's dozens of tapes—blues, rock, folk, mariachi—Pop thumbed through the magazines. A few of them he carried into better light near the entrance. "Tell me about Phil Ochs."

He passed me four magazines. *Playboy. Mother Jones. Rolling Stone. Guitar Player.* Each of them dog-eared to an article about Phil Ochs.

"A folk singer," I said. "Some of his songs are lyrical and sweet, but he gets mean when he sings about injustice. Or capitalism. Or Vietnam. He's got no problem with violent revolution, and he admires some communists, like Fidel and Mao. He's the headliner at the jamboree."

"Look at the dates on the magazines."

None of the issues were recent. The oldest dated back four years. Pop rapped his knuckles together. "Did you ever hear that Alvaro got mixed up in politics? Joined some outfit like Vietnam Vets Against the War?"

I thought a minute and shook my head. "But if he did, and if Jimmy Marris was mixed up in politics...what if the FBI knocked off Jimmy and framed Alvaro, to get rid of them both?"

"Not likely," Pop said. "But possible."

Mama was sitting on the big stump, in the only pool of sunlight the towering redwoods let in. Hands folded in her lap, she glanced around the campsite and shook her head, looking distressed as though Alvaro had thrown a wild party and left the cleanup to her. Ava stood nearby, feeding crumbs out of my brother's Tupperware breadbox to a party of squirrels. Pop asked her, "The little guys tell you anything?"

"I'm trying to make it out," she said, "but they talk so fast."

He asked her if Jimmy was involved in any kind of politics. Her face got defiant. "His mom thinks he was a communist, but he wasn't."

I looked around for Alvaro's tape player. When I gave up, I sat with Mama. Pop continued to snoop through debris, but all he considered worth pocketing was a pair of aviator sunglasses he found half buried in the mulch under a redwood tree. When he showed them to me, I said, "You wouldn't catch Alvaro wearing those things."

"Not unless he was riding a motorcycle." Pop checked his watch. "Better keep our appointment." He held Mama's arm while she hopped off the stump. He picked up Alvaro's guitar case. I carried a burlap bag of tapes and the magazines that featured Ochs, thinking I could scan them for clues about Alvaro. Ava and Mama walked ahead of us, up the trail to the car.

Pop walked beside me. "Any cabins, or other camps, upstream from here?"

"I don't think so, not on this side of the river. Maybe on the other side."

He gave me a deadpan look, which probably meant I should've checked out these details yesterday, instead of waylaying a biker. Then he chucked my arm. "You're all right, Clifford."

A little squeal issued out of Mama. She had stopped still and wrapped her arms across her chest. She was staring across the path where tall fir and cedar grew close together, manzanita and ferns tangled between them, and every piece of ground where sunlight fell was a bed of blazing wildflowers. "Somebody's out there," she whispered.

We looked and listened but detected nothing. Still Mama was spooked. And she saw and heard things other people couldn't. When Pop asked if she could point to them, her head began to shake back and forth so hard I worried it could injure her neck.

Pop wrapped his arm around her. We saw her fright becoming terror. She was biting her lip when Pop decided to get her out of the forest.

Chapter Eleven

Evergreen was bustling as if every homemaker, logger, hippie, Cossack, and jamboree visitor dedicated Saturday mornings to shopping. Along Manhattan Avenue, all the pickups had double gun racks, usually holding a rifle and a shotgun. The hippies wore hunting knives in sheaths. All five bikers crossing the street to the park carrying grocery sacks packed side-arms.

Pop said, "They should call this burg Tombstone. So, Clifford, after we meet with the sheriff, then what?"

"You tell me."

"Wouldn't be right, when you're in charge here."

Because I thought he was joking, I played along. "Yeah, but I'm open to suggestions."

"Once we get Wendy settled in, find somebody to sit with her, should we talk to the Agent Knudsen? And the kingpin hippies? Most always, the guy at the top knows it all."

"Big Dan Mills," I said. "We'll find him at the jamboree."

Ava said, "And Quig."

"Quig and Mills, then? And how about a chat with Little Ric?"

"Vic," I said.

He reached under his seat and brought out two guns, his .38 and one I had never seen, a big .45 automatic pistol like Sam Spade might've carried. For each of them, he had a shoulder holster. After handing the automatic to me, he reached again and pulled out a leather bag, from which he removed a clip.

"Nine shots," he said as he slapped it into my hand. "Keep it in your pocket."

He told me where the safety was and how to insert the clip. "But keep it on ice as long as you can. Try everything before you lay a finger on that monster. Before you grab it, you've got be willing to kill, and just because you can hit a target, doesn't mean you can shoot a man. A trained marksman can miss by a yard when time comes to shoot for real."

Though I had more than once been the target of Ava's frown, until now I hadn't seen her glower. She said, "Do you guys really need those things?"

"Sometimes, we do," Pop said.

Mama didn't seem to notice the gun transaction, but she appeared to know a jail when she saw one. We parked in a space near the front entrance. She folded her hands as though refusing to reach for the door handle.

While Pop slipped into his summer sport coat and exchanged his driving cap for a straw fedora, Ava said, "I'll stay here with Wendy. Maybe Clifford should too. They might have a warrant or something."

I shrugged and followed Pop inside. The front part of the sheriff's station was one long room. Even Willis didn't rate a private office, only a desk twice as big as the other four. He appeared cramped sitting behind it. With an elbow on the desk and his chin resting on his fist, he stared our way, watching like a batter for the pitch. He didn't stand until after the deputy at the counter, a lanky fellow with a red patch up the side of his face, made us sign our names on a register. Yesterday, at Alvaro's camp, I had noticed this deputy trip over most every log as he chased my brother into the forest. Now he said, "Believe I winged your Mexican boy."

I looked at Pop. His jaw had petrified. Both hands gripped his belt. But as we rounded the counter and approached the sheriff, who had stood to meet us, Pop made his face relax. He reached out for Willis' hand and shook as if the sheriff were a respected colleague.

Willis invited us to sit. He rounded the big desk to his swivel chair. "How 'bout you say what your kid here told you, save us time."

Pop reclined in his chair, reached into his coat pocket for his pipe, filled and lit it. Between puffs, he said, "First, would you mind giving me the basics? Where you found the dead boy, his condition, any ballistic reports and so on."

Willis reached into his trash can, retrieved a copy of the *Eureka Times-Standard* and passed it across the desk.

Pop took another puff. "Clifford says things would be different if his brother hadn't of ran. He figures you had adequate cause to bring Alvaro in—him camped in the vicinity and something about a fight over a girl—and he figures the coincidence of Alvaro's rifle being the same kind as the probable murder weapon cinched your suspicions. Even though I suspect more folks in Evergreen own a Browning 30.06 than don't, Alvaro's the fellow that ran off carrying one.

"So far as all that goes, we've got no complaint. But it looks to Clifford, all this circumstance makes you so sure my son did the killing, you don't care to waste your limited resources chasing wild geese. So you concentrate all you've got hunting Alvaro."

Willis shook his head as though he'd just labored through a pack of lies. "Your kid here tell about last night, down to the Crossroads, 'bout kidnapping and torturing a dangerous fella?"

Pop threw a poison look at me, which I hoped was feigned. I widened my eyes, leaned forward, and gaped my best imitation of wounded innocence.

"No, sir," Pop said. "He sure didn't. Dangerous, you say?"

"We count thirty-four Cossacks, more or less. They come and go. Your boy picked the worst."

"In what way?"

Willis clapped his big hands together and raised them over his head. Gradually they lowered onto the desk. "I don't see where it matters, long as you take my advice. Which is, considering all the factors, I'd get this boy of yours out of the county straightaway. We don't need the aggravation of deciding which biker to arrest for killing him. Besides," he drawled, "I'd hate to see any man lose two sons all in the same week."

Pop tamped his pipe, then relit and lofted a half dozen smoke rings. As though thinking out loud, he said, "I'm with you. Say I drive Clifford home where our doctor can check out his hand. As long as there's no permanent damage, no need for a lawsuit. I mean, who couldn't understand that deputy overreacting when he thinks he's got one of the punks that killed his nephew?"

The sheriff nodded.

"No fault of yours bringing the deputy along to Alvaro's camp. What else could you do? Small town, big trouble, you've got to be shorthanded.

"Now, if I read you right, since you're advising us to go home, you intend to call off the search for Alvaro, considering that he could be in Tibet by now. You're going to switch your efforts to collecting evidence, and, when the time comes, to building a solid case against whoever your county or federal prosecutor gets convinced shot the boy. Am I right?"

Willis was grinding his teeth.

"And," Pop said, "you'll want my word that when Alvaro shows up, I'll bring him in. Well, you've got it."

Willis mocked a chuckle and pointed a finger at me. "Your boy here lives long enough, learns to distort a man's words good as you do it, he might could make one slick lawyer."

Pop said, "Sheriff, if I offended you, I sure didn't mean to. What I did mean is, there's no way either Clifford or I can leave a place where men are out gunning for Alvaro, and where nobody but us, as far as we know, is looking for other suspects. On that subject, if you don't mind my asking, what do you hear from the Fed?"

"Ask the Fed. And while you've got his ear, remind him he owes me a call. He needs to know about the pair of heavies the mob your Mexican works for sent to give me a lecture on how to run my town."

That comment stumped me. But Pop didn't look surprised.

Willis whistled at the deputy. When he turned, the sheriff said, "Show these folks to the door."

The deputy walked around the counter to the door and held it open. "Thanks for your time," Pop said. As we stood, before I could say my goodbyes, he nudged me toward the door. On the way out, he patted the deputy's shoulder. "Remind your partners that a don't-shoot-to-kill policy could save them and Sheriff Willis a lifetime of poverty."

Outside, as soon as the door shut behind us, I said, "Heavies? Mob?"

"Maybe," Pop said, "I should've asked your advice before I mentioned Alvaro's fix to Harry. Should I go back and explain to the sheriff who those boys were?"

From his voice and expression, I started to think Pop really wanted me to call the plays. If he did, I feared, he was losing his mind.

We stood beside the Cadillac while Pop slipped out of his sport coat and cleaned his pipe by knocking it on the front bumper. "What all don't I know that I ought to? Anything else somebody's after you for?"

"Deputy Barker acts like he'd kill me for jaywalking."

Mama had gone to the back seat with Ava, who was drawing on my notepad, a caricature of a face like mine only with the cleft in my chin way deeper. Mama was watching her draw. She looked back and forth between me and the sketch and gave a nod of approval.

I climbed in front. We drove to Babe's so Pop could use the payphone. He called Agent Knudsen at the number on his card and talked the answering service into giving him an Evergreen number. He dialed it and reached the agent's lodging in Evergreen. The Riverside Lodge. Knudsen's room didn't answer. While he had the lodge on the phone, Pop asked if they had a room available. The clerk told him no, and furthermore, there wasn't a vacant room between Willits and Eureka. Pop offered her a week at Harry's Casino. She told him please call back in case of a cancellation.

In the car, he mentioned having noticed a sign advertising Scotch Glen Resort. I'd seen the sign, at the junction to the coast access loop. "Sounds like my kind of place," Pop said. "Let's check it out. If they don't have a room, could be there's a comfortable lobby where the gals could sit and think while you and I go root around the scene of the crime."

On our way up Manhattan Avenue, Pop slowed to observe a pack of a half dozen motorcycles as they neared the exit from the Safeway mall. Vic wasn't among them. In the lead was the dark-skinned guy Ava told us was Crutch. A spindly blonde sat behind him. Ava ducked but too late. The blonde had seen her and waved.

"Friend of yours?" Pop asked.

"My sister," Ava said.

We all, even Mama, watched the bikers, expecting them to follow us, but they still hadn't exited the parking lot when we lost sight of them. We turned north on the 101 then west on the coast access loop. Pop drove a few miles before Ava heard the motorcycle following and tapped my leg. We looked around. It was only a blip on the horizon.

"Just one," I said.

Pop checked the rear view mirror. "A scout. He's liable to go back for the rest. If they catch us someplace without witnesses, I expect they'll want to make a party out of it."

At the Scotch Glen Resort sign, Pop turned onto the dirt road. But at the first wide spot, he swung a U, drove back and stopped with the Cadillac nosing out just far enough so we could watch both ways on the county road. Mama rolled down her window and gazed into the flowery woods, but every minute or so she turned and looked at Ava, who was leaning on the back of our seat between Pop and me, her face only inches from mine. She said, "Here they come," about five seconds before the Cossacks entered my vision.

The muted rumble of two dozen Harleys gradually became a roar. Spots of light jumped like flares off the chrome. Fear told me to go under my seat for the Sam Spade gun, but I knew the smartest course was to trust Pop. He lit his pipe, blew smoke out the window, and watched their approach until they closed to a hundred yards away. He tamped out the fire on his pipe before he swung the steering wheel to the left and eased onto the county road.

Little Vic was riding out front. Crutch was few yards behind. The others rode three abreast. When they saw us and braked, most of them skidded broadside. They all recovered. They were stopped in the middle of the highway by the time we zoomed past.

Ava said, "They're not looking for a party. They mean business. There's not a single girl with them."

Before long the Cadillac was flying, at least 100 mph. I didn't have the leisure to check the speedometer while watching the bikers turn and chase us. Pop said, "If they're just out for fun, I suspect they'll do that ride around act from the Marlon Brando movie. But if they mean business like Ava says, if you're on their hit list, they'll lay back and bide their time. I could slow down, see what they've got in mind. How about it, Clifford?"

"Yeah."

He slowed to about fifty. After we'd turned onto the 101, about a mile before the Manhattan Road junction, the bikers disappeared. I caught my breath then tried to sound cool. "They probably pulled off at a fruit stand. Ava, why do you suppose they do their own shopping when they could make their girls do it?"

"If they sent the girls shopping they'd have to give them money. Vic says women can't be trusted with money."

"So why does your sister like a cheap misogynist?"

"Like him?" Ava hung her head. "Dope's what my sister likes. She says crystal meth is all that saved her from booze. That's how loopy it's made her."

Pop said, "Clifford, the sheriff's idea, you getting out of town. Are you willing to?"

"As soon as they pull the dogs off Alvaro." I saw Ava's frown and added, "And we catch whoever killed Jimmie Marris."

Following Ava's directions, we took Cognac Lane past a row of two-story redwood Victorians and their rose gardens. At the end of a mile-long block, the road teed into Moonshine Trail, a strip of blacktop along the middle fork of Whiskey River. Pop turned left and drove to the second of a half dozen motels.

The Riverside Lodge office was on the left, across the road from ten cottages with decks and chimneys that overlooked the river. I followed Pop into the office. The girl on duty sat at a stool behind a counter. She had broad shoulders and arms I imagined could curl a refrigerator. She glanced up from a fan magazine.

Pop said, "Any cancellations?"

"Nope. And folks ain't already cancelled ain't likely to. We got a forty-eight hour policy."

He asked if she could check other motels. She guaranteed him that every motel and boarding house between Garberville and Eureka was booked. "We been booked for this weekend since February. Hey, did you hear the news—Dylan's gonna show up at the jamboree, and them Canadian guys that he plays with. If I was you, I'd buy camping gear."

"Tell me," Pop said, "you've got a guest, Mister Knudsen. He reserved way back in February, did he?"

The clerk folded her mighty arms. "No rooms."

"Call Agent Knudsen for me, would you?"

She rang his cottage. No answer. Pop bummed stationery and started a message for Knudsen, then looked up at the clerk. "Knudsen's what? FBI?"

"I'll give him your note. You were the guy on the phone, I bet. And you're gonna fix me up with that room in Tahoe?"

Pop nodded and pointed to his name and number on the note.

On the way to the car, he told me, "I was out of line, asking all the questions. Next time, I leave it to you."

Ava and Mama were still in the car. When I mentioned the odds of renting a room between Mendocino and Oregon, Ava said, "Quig's isn't luxury, but I can probably find you a clean shack with a good bed."

Pop had gone to the backseat with Mama. He asked me to drive. Ava came up front. I followed Moonshine Trail to the dead-end, just west of the community garden and directly below Sugar Hill, a grassy slope splotched with dead sunflowers leading to a crest studded with black pine. It looked like the battlements of an evil kingdom.

A path rutted with motorcycle tracks led across a field to River Road. At nine a.m., the traffic crawled along River Road and into the parking lot. The grounds were already crowded as a refugee camp.

I worried that upon our arrival at the commune, Quig would interrogate me about the Hound Dog incident. Unless I could lie like the pro I wasn't, he might dash to a phone, call the Cossacks and evict me into their custody. But to deliver me to the bikers, Quig would have to stand against Pop. A challenge as arduous as debating Socrates.

The gatekeeper Ava called Whitey broke from a horseshoe game to peer into our car. Ava waved, he waved us through. Mama and Pop, sitting close together in back, gawked at the yurts, lean-tos, A-frames, tarp-covered geodesic domes and tents, and at the residents, blond men with Chinese pigtails, topless nymphs watering the garden, naked toddlers caked in river mud. The residents gawked at Pop's car. Last year, most of them would've gathered to welcome the newcomers, Cadillac or no. Now they held back, sullen and suspicious.

We parked beside Ava's yurt. I walked with Mama and Pop to the riverbank. We sat on the grass while Ava hustled around until she found a couple who agreed to rent their A-frame for ten dollars a night. For as long as we needed or until the October rains came, they would stay in a tent across the river. Ava walked us to the A-frame.

The couple was already packing to leave. They were scrawny people, and older than most hippies. Their home was ornamented with sketches of sailboats and jumping fish, seascapes, two rusted anchors, and knickknacks from Africa, Asia, and the South Seas. Pop introduced us, complimented the house, one downstairs room with a wood floor and a sleeping loft. He gave them fifty dollars. The man crammed the bills into his pocket as though fearful they would disappear. While the woman showed Mama and Pop around, he nudged me aside. "You're the dude that messed up Hound Dog?"

I said, "That's the rumor going around, like the one that says Bob Dylan's going to show up at the jamboree with The Band."

Pop had overheard. Touching my arm, he walked me outside and into the shade of a madrone. "Your mama feels good around Ava. We'll leave the girls here and see if we can get to the crime scene without playing Pied Piper to the motorcycle rats. That is, if Ava's willing."

She agreed. After Pop and I kissed Mama goodbye, I took Ava's hand, then leaned and pecked her cheek. She dropped my hand, lowered her head, and backed away. The last time our eyes met, while Pop and I were pulling away, she was shaking her head. I wondered whether she meant don't kiss me anymore or don't get killed.

Pop drove. I worried about Mama. Always, what she needed to recover from the episodes doctors referred to as catatonic or schizoaffective was peace for a long time, and home, which a teepee in a hippie commune wasn't.

But all I could do was try to help get her home soon. So I outlined everything I had done and heard since Wednesday's sunset. I began with the sight of the father and his three cupids beside the roadside shrine. About my search for the trail to Alvaro's camp and the night sleeping out beside the river, I detailed everything I could pry out of my memory and stressed my recollections of the gunshots.

I listed the events of Thursday morning, and tried to quote everything Alvaro said before the posse showed up. About most of what I had learned and done, I included even details that seemed irrelevant, just in case Pop found some meaning in them I didn't. I cataloged the jail's inmates, the hippies, Little Vic, the other Cossacks and the farm worker who got busted for unionizing. I recounted my interrogation by Willis and Knudsen and the warnings Knudsen issued when he followed me outside, that any thread of evidence connecting me to the murder, the sheriff could use to lock me away.

I passed along Steph's assessment that the cops were harassing the hippies largely because they feared the bikers and hoped if they chased off the hippies, the bikers would follow. I confessed my blundering attempts at questioning hippies and locals at the jamboree, and then recalled my only success, my first encounter with Ava, how I won at least some of her trust. "Unless she's a genius at lying," I said. "I guess she *could* be a pretty, shrewd bad guy."

Pop said, "I like that girl."

"She likes you. How is it all the girls fall for you? I mean, you're quite a dude, but you're pushing a hundred and you're not all that cute."

He glanced my way and winked. "It's a mystery all right."

After summarizing the praise and mild complaints Ava had offered about Jimmy—he was brilliant, ambitious, troubled on account of his absent black father and his mom's poverty—I gave a blow by blow account of my run-in with Brady Barker at his sister's house.

Pop grumbled, "Soon as we snoop around the crime scene and vicinity, we'll go have a talk with that deputy."

I mentioned Simon as my first contact with Quig's and the guy who had picked me up hitchhiking. He probably knew more than he allowed, I contended. Because, according to Ava, Simon and Jimmy had been tight, and Jimmy was half black and Simon lots more than half, and there were more Sasquatch than blacks around Evergreen. About Simon procuring the pistol and my subsequent adventure with Hound Dog, I didn't confess. If Pop wanted the truth about last night, he would ask. Besides, we had arrived at our turnoff.

We floated in the Caddy along Highball Trail looking out for camps and residences. Pop wanted to question every camper and resident within two or three miles of the campsite where I heard the murderer's gunshots.

"Who owns this land?"

"Government on this side." I pointed north. "Private property across the river." A month ago, on the phone, Alvaro had told me that the forest where he lived, between the south and the middle fork of Whiskey River, belonged to the state. It would turn into campgrounds, hiking trails, and a commercial tourist village once the lease details were agreed to by the state and developer Paul McNees.

Our first stop was at the site where Jimmy washed ashore, according to the sheriffs. We walked past the kite-flag tied onto a branch, the tire tracks, and the chaos of boot-prints leading up and down the bank. The only place that remained un-stomped was at the water's edge. Parallel to the water, on a gradual incline, the outline of a tall man was sketched in chalk on muddy grass, around an impression in the mud. Jimmy Marris had lain face down. His nose, brows, even his belt buckle had etched themselves so clearly, somebody could make a cast and resurrect him in a wax museum. I remembered Ava saying Jimmy looked like me. I sat on an outcropping and pressed my stomach to make the snakes settle down and behave. Pop said, "We ought to view the body and talk to the coroner, right?"

"Sure, I guess."

"Where's he located?"

"Probably Eureka." I imagined a morgue, the corpse, the smell. "Why do we need to see him?"

"I'd like to know how bloated Marris was."

"Why?"

He gave me a look that meant, Think about it. "If he isn't all that bloated, should we wonder if he might've got dumped here, not been in the river at all?"

I grumbled, "Why are you wasting time asking me questions? You're the detective."

"Retired," he said, and tiptoed along the riverbank, studying the ground.

I followed him. "Well I'm no detective at all."

"You could be."

"No way. Pop, I'm not you, and I don't intend to be."

"Sure," he said, "I know you want to make a living with your songs."

"And you think I can't?"

He stopped and stared at my face, then stepped to my side and hung his arm across my shoulders. "Not for a minute do I think that. You've got more talent than most. But…do you think I wanted to be a cop?"

"I know, you wanted to play music, same as I do. But the Depression knocked you out."

"And something might come along and send your dreams packing. The fact is, most of us can't be what we want to be."

"Why not?"

He frowned like a war reporter giving yesterday's body count. "Because life has a habit of making us be who we are."

Chapter Twelve

For a half hour Pop and I tried to make sense of the footprints that led away from the mud-cast of Jimmy Marris. We especially looked for deeper ones that might indicate men carrying the body from somewhere else and down the bank to where the sheriffs had found it. When we gave up, Pop asked, "Besides the gunshots, did you hear anything else peculiar?"

"I told you everything I remember."

"Yeah, it takes a cannon to wake you up."

Back at the car, we heard the Cessna. A few hundred feet up, it appeared in our vision gliding due west. Directly above us it coughed and stalled, before making an upward loop, then swooping down like a crop duster.

Pop stared in that direction long after the plane was gone. He said, "I bet that kamikaze's in radio contact with the sheriff. Keep an eye out for visitors."

"I'll bet it's Knudsen," I said.

Pop asked what was up ahead. I told him I had seen more camp trails along the dirt road beyond Alvaro's, though they looked overgrown. Up those trails we might find strange hermits with the solution to the murder or the answers to other great mysteries, or we might hike all day and see only wildlife and deserted campsites. But on the other side of the river were some houses.

Pop said, "Where you've got more people, you've got more cause to murder."

We crossed the bridge, a sturdy one, concrete with steel rails, supported by concrete pillars. It might've carried a railroad long ago. The river was several yards below the high water line but still it churned twice as foamy as the middle fork that ran through town. Pop let the Cadillac idle to the middle of the bridge, then he threw it into park and climbed out. We leaned over the rail and shaded our eyes from glare off the water.

Pop mused, "Willis estimates the body drifted a few hours and a couple miles before it washed up. Anything's going to float stronger and faster if it's in midstream. Along the bank it'll bump and snag. But he's saying Alvaro dragged the body to the edge and tossed him in. Then how would he get the body out to the middle unless he dove in and towed it? And if he's that calculating, why wouldn't he sink it? No, it's a case of mistaken identity, son. If they think Alvaro heaved the body out to midstream, they're confusing him with King Kong."

"What if the killer threw him off this bridge?"

Pop nodded long and slow. We watched the plane I believed was Knudsen's return and circle. I waved for him to come down and hoped he was using strong binoculars. I was more anxious to talk to him than to anybody, to demand he tell us what the FBI had against my brother. Or against Phil Ochs and his friends and associates, including Alvaro. The plane swooped out of sight.

"Worried?" Pop asked, and read my face for his answer. "Clifford, think like X would." Since my brother's middle name was Xavier, our nickname for him was X. "You're wanted, where do you run?"

"Mexico."

"And how do you get there? What's the fastest, safest way? Land, air, or water?"

"So he doubled back and headed for the ocean?"

"If I were tracking Alvaro, I'd go to the coast and ask if anybody borrowed a sailboat yesterday."

Though a philosophy minor should have taught me to avoid hasty conclusions, I had only imagined Alvaro in the mountains, because he started that direction, and because he was at home there. But we had lived both on the shore of Tahoe and thirty yards across the sand from San Diego's Mission Bay, where generous neighbors used to lend us their catamaran. Still, I suspected Pop had stooped to wishful thinking.

Across the bridge, we turned east and crawled the Eldorado over cavernous dips. In less than a mile, we stopped beside a footpath that led through a meadow to a stand of fir behind which stood a compound of three ancient travel trailers in horseshoe formation. An American flag drooped from a branch above one trailer. A pair of yellow cats perched like sentries atop a pile of composting garbage alongside a forest of corn stalks and dead sunflowers.

We were between the car and the compound when an army of *niños* burst out of the trailer and rushed us. Dark with round, flattish features. The oldest was twelve or so, the youngest no older than two. None of them wore shoes. Three little ones wore nothing. As they neared, they skidded to a stop, in a bunch behind the tallest, a boy in jeans and a Ricky Nelson T-shirt.

"You guys cops?"

"Want to see our badges?" Pop asked.

"Your guns."

"Locked in the car. My name's Tom, this is my son Clifford. You are?"

"Pedro Marti."

"Good name. These your brothers and sisters?"

"The baby's my big sister's."

"Any of you the kids who found the body day before yesterday?"

A boy a head shorter than Pedro jumped out of the bunch and raised his hand. Pedro said, "Yeah, Joey got there first. He screamed."

"Did not," Joey yipped.

The kids dispersed from behind Pedro to cluster around Pop and me. A tiny girl leaned against my knee. I patted her dusty hair.

When Pop asked, "Who saw the body?" all except the baby shouted "Me," or raised a hand.

"Did your mama or papa come look?"

Pedro nodded.

"Are they home?"

"Course not," Pedro said, as though Pop had asked if they owned a Ferarri. "They're picking cherries."

"Sure. Tell me, guys, what'd the body look like?"

"Dead."

"Bloody."

"Not bloody."

"Ugly."

"White."

"Big? All puffy?" Pop asked them.

"Just real white," Pedro said.

"Who called the police?"

Pedro jabbed a finger at his own chest. "We got no phone," he snapped, as though blaming us for the lack. "I had to run to the Crossroads, that payphone out front. Cost me a dime, and it didn't do no good. Somebody else called first. 'cause I heard the sirens even before I hung up."

Joey shouted, "We don't even got a TV."

At the car, Pop said, "I did it again. All the talking. Next time, kick me."

I climbed into the Caddy. He joined me and fired it up. "So who found the body before these kids did?"

"Maybe Pedro's mixed up," I said, "or while he was on the phone, the station radioed a cruiser that was already down this way for some reason."

We rattled east along the trail until I spotted a shack as hidden in the woods as the Martis' compound of trailers. It had a bowed roof out of which a stovepipe snaked. Pop speculated it was built by a miner prospecting Whiskey Creek a hundred years ago. A row of smallish redwood trees, equally spaced like a giant fence, blocked it from the road. The only sign that anybody lived there was a mastiff on the porch, lashed to a redwood post that supported what remained of a porch roof. Without a bark or growl, the giant ambled toward us, to the end of its leash, then sat on its haunches and lolled its tongue back and forth.

"Friendly?" Pop asked. "Or licking his chops, imagining how good we'd taste?"

"It looks stoned."

Pop hollered, "Anybody home?" After two attempts, he said, "How about I distract Bluto while you creep around and find a window to peek in?"

I backtracked a few steps, strolled toward the trees to our right, hid behind one, then tiptoed to the next and so on, until I had circled the shack. Crossing the clearing, I listened for the mastiff. What substituted for a window in the rear of the shack was a porthole-sized opening so high on the wall I needed to grab the ledge and execute a pull-up to see in. I saw or heard nobody inside, but the place looked as neat as though a maid dropped by every Friday. The old brass single bed was made, with a flouncy quilt and extra pillows. The only table had a tablecloth that looked ironed, and a bowl full of pine cones in the middle.

While we drove farther east, I told Pop we had found the lair of a female hermit. He asked how I drew that conclusion. "It's neat," I said.

Soon we came to the next house. It wasn't so hidden as the others. Between the road and the double A-frame cabin were a homemade swing set and jungle gym, and a primer-splotched '47 Dodge pickup with a wooden camper like a miniature house, with leaded glass windows and shellacked walls. A flock of white chickens pecked around the house, playground, and garden. As we neared, the three cupids darted out of the house and rushed the chickens. The flock scattered but the mid-sized cupid dove and tackled a hen. He stood, clutching the paralyzed fowl by its legs with both his hands. His brother and sister cheered. Their father stepped outside. "Othello," he called. "Go get the powder."

The tallest cupid ran to a shed beyond the garden while the father crossed the yard to meet us. By the time I remembered Pop didn't know this was Sara's family, the man had reached us.

"Lice," he said. "Are you here about Jimmy Marris?"

Pop gave him our names. The man nodded and said, "Yeah," as if he already knew them. "I'm Royal Van Dyke. Roy. You know, I promised my kids we'd leave pretty soon for the jamboree."

When I looked over at Pop, he was staring at me. I turned back to Roy. "Ten minutes?"

He motioned with a thumb toward the A-frame. We followed him in, to a storybook house. Aside from the kid-sized shirts and shorts, and the jump-ropes, rag-balls, wooden paddles, and such scattered around, the place was art. The walls and ceiling were cedar, oiled and rubbed. Mobiles of gnarled twigs, painted egg shells, and origami figures fluttered. Kitchen cabinets, a hutch, and bookshelves of oak and cedar appeared so flawlessly crafted that Pop, who had built our Tahoe cabin, sounded awed when he asked, "You do all this?"

"We did." He motioned toward a sofa-like bench made of oak slats, where we sat facing Roy, who slouched in a chair that matched the bench. The house was dim, most of the shutters closed. Roy used a Zippo to light a sand candle. He looked as noble as his name, graceful and slender. His hair was a million strawberry blond ringlets, just a shade lighter than Ava's. His beard was scraggly, perhaps a week old. I imagined he'd stopped shaving when his wife died. The hazel eyes that gazed back and forth between Pop and me flickered in the candlelight.

The top shelf of a bookcase at my elbow featured Aristotle, Brontë, Byron, Chaucer, Coleridge, Dante, Dickens, Dickenson, Dostoyevski and so on. Roy watched me read the titles. He said, "We were lit majors at Berkeley before Othello came. We moved up here to get our baby out of a culture we didn't care for." He looked too wretched to weep.

Pop nodded at me, so I asked, "Did you know Jimmy Marris?"

Roy shook his head.

"How about Alvaro?"

"Yes."

"Was he growing weed?"

Roy must not have expected so blunt a question. He stared, then blinked as though his eyes hurt. "No."

"Did you hear the shots?"

"No. When I sleep, I sleep hard."

"How about your wife and kids?" Pop asked. "Did they hear shots?"

Roy stared past Pop and me, toward the open door, as though he expected his wife to return. "Sara was already gone, and the kids sleep harder than I do."

I supposed Pop believed Roy's wife had ditched him. He sat nodding. I asked, "Who killed Jimmy?"

Roy closed his eyes and kept still as though waiting for the air to whisper an answer, until Othello ran in and announced, "Daddy, we loused Daffy and Petunia. Now can we go?"

"Mind your manners," Roy said. "Go pack shoes and T-shirts for Oedipus and Ophelia, and you guys be ready and waiting in the truck." He turned back to us. "I wish I could help, but…I can't, that's all."

I looked at Pop. When he stood, so did I.

Roy sat with his chin braced up by his hand, staring at the candle while we walked outside. The cupids were in the cab of the old Dodge pickup, little Ophelia tuning the radio knobs, Oedipus at the wheel.

I said, "Pop, his wife didn't leave him. She's the one I told you drove her VW into a ditch about two weeks ago. The one who swerved to avoid running down a drunk Cossack. She's dead."

"Jesus." Pop grimaced, then patted my shoulder and said, "Sorry," as if he mistook me for Mama, who preferred we didn't use her savior's name as an epithet.

"I'll bet you noticed Roy looked like he'd heard of us both. I mean, everybody in town's heard of me. But if he'd heard about you, doesn't that tell us he was better friends with Alvaro than he let on."

"I hear you," was all Pop said.

We continued east on the trail, about a mile and past a couple For Sale signs on vacant lots. One featured a well beside a trailer pad or foundation, with no structure.

A hundred yards before the trail ended at an arroyo, behind a small grove of pear trees was a shack that might have been cloned from the shack where the hermit lived with her mastiff. But this place looked like a clubhouse for teenagers rebelling against their fastidious mothers. The ground outside and floor inside were strewn with Cracker Jacks boxes, Frito bags, stomped beer and soda cans and shattered bottles, the shredded remains of quilts and a sleeping bag. I found a wine bottle filled with Coleman fuel and capped with a rag, the kind of firebomb people used to call a Molotov cocktail, and two large pieces from broken vials. I noted the smell of ammonia. "A meth lab," I said, and Pop didn't argue.

It could belong to the Cossacks, I thought. Or to somebody the Cossacks chased off. Not to Alvaro, I hoped to God. But the year before his shotgun wedding to the army, while playing guitar all night in Tijuana nightclubs, he'd gotten strung out on methamphetamine. And after Vietnam, he'd done it again.

Chapter Thirteen

The sputtering roar of Harleys intruded on our deliberations. "Across the river," I said.

We hustled to the car and Pop asked, "What do you think? Does their being where we were when the plane spotted us mean the pilot radioed Willis and he snitched our location to the Cossacks?"

"Or the pilot, who was probably Knudsen, snitched us directly to the Cossacks. Maybe he's not a Fed at all."

"Or," Pop said, "the Cossacks could have a police band radio."

"Whew." I caught my breath and leaned back into the seat. "I like that answer best."

"We can like it," he said, "but let's not count on it."

In Evergreen, we stopped at the Richfield station. While I pumped gas, Pop said, "Tell me why Alvaro ran?"

"He just got spooked? Like some holiday weekend, a couple months after Alvaro got out of the army, a bunch of us went to Mexico. San Felipe. He smoked a little grass, and when the fireworks started across the bay, I saw him twitch with every bang. And then, he started swilling tequila. Besides, the way those sheriffs came charging into the camp like a platoon of Viet Cong, I almost spooked and ran."

"You didn't, though. And he's been home more than a year now."

"Okay, but Alvaro knew the cops didn't like him. So, he'd heard the shots that night like I did, and when he saw the sheriffs…I don't know. Instinct or infantry training or something told him to run. And once they were chasing him, he didn't stop for fear they'd shoot him down."

Pop shook his head. "Some guys might've done like you tell it, but not your brother. He thinks fast. First, he knows we're not going to let him take a fall for something he didn't do. And he knows the odds of getting killed, or framed, rise like the moonshot as soon as he runs. His mind makes connections in a jiffy, it's how he survived on the streets and in war."

"You aren't saying if he ran he's guilty, are you?"

Pop reached for his pipe. "Or else he thinks a sheriff killed the Marris boy. Or he's covering for somebody. As long as the sheriffs are chasing him, whoever really shot the kid can make his getaway."

"Who, then?"

"You tell me."

I thought of Simon, Big Dan Mills, and Quig. Other faces I had seen around Evergreen crowded into my mind. I even thought of Ava. "I give up."

"Someday," Pop said, "when the killer's long gone, after the truth's out, your brother can turn up, and nothing's lost."

"Except he's busted for resisting arrest."

"Son, any rookie public defender could beat that charge, using the argument you gave about him being spooked."

"Okay, but why's he so sure the truth will come out, that he'll ever get cleared of the murder."

"Because he knows you. If the police fail him, enter Clifford Hickey."

"Make that Tom Hickey and I'll buy it."

"Tom Hickey and son, then."

As we drove through Evergreen I tried to convince myself that, like Pop believed or hoped, Alvaro might have run with a noble purpose. But Pop was sixty-six, this past year of caring for Mama had worn him down, and the fugitive was his son. Given all that, even Pop could sucker for wishful thinking. Especially if his brain had started to soften.

Still, he could be right, which made me return to wondering who might be so dear to Alvaro that he would risk his life and sabotage justice to help a killer go free. Alvaro didn't make tight friends easily, and he had only lived around Evergreen the past few months. On the phone or in his letters, he had mentioned no partners or sidekicks. Unless the fact that he'd quoted Phil Ochs was meant to send a message.

One of his Vietnam buddies might've shown up. I thought, Suppose a guy from his platoon came home and joined the Cossacks.

Jimmy might have cheated the bikers on a dope deal, or stolen one of their motorcycles. The snakes in my belly woke from their nap, to think my brother might be covering for a Cossack. Or, Alvaro could've fallen for a girl. Even the sister of a Cossack.

Traffic crept along River Road. Hippies in orange vests carried signs that advised people to park on the shoulder and walk to the jamboree. We followed their advice, joined a line and trudged like pilgrims toward the gate. Since Pop was old and wore a baggy cotton sport coat and a straw fedora even though his face had a sheen of sweat, people stared and smiled, no doubt thinking he must be a blues musician. They weren't far wrong. Until Claire's death broke Mama's spirit and Pop could rarely leave her, he had blown clarinet with a jazz group at Harry's North Shore Casino.

The few Harleys in the parking area were Sportsters and one full dress Power-glide. No choppers. I wondered if getting ejected yesterday meant I was banned from the party for good. But none of the gatekeepers was anyone who had chased me out. Our gate-keeper was a braless hippie in a loose-knit top. Pop handed her a twenty for two admissions and told her to keep the change. She grinned. He asked where we could find Big Dan Mills.

"You an old friend of his?"

"That could be," Pop said.

"Well then, Dan's going on in a half hour, right before Phil. Look for him around the main stage."

The crowd was so thick, I doubted we could reach the main stage in a half hour without lowering our shoulders and charging through like a blocker and running back.

Body heat and the sun made the jamboree air feel like tea-kettle steam. From the heat and the crowd, I got edgy, near claustrophobic. I felt like socking the next person who clipped me from the side. But Pop weaved through the maze, alert and adventurous, like a tourist who'd just stepped off the cruise ship. I wondered if he had temporarily forgotten his wife was borderline catatonic and one of his sons was running for his life while the other might get jumped and stabbed by a Cossack disguised as an ethno-musicologist. He paused for double-takes. Of a garden spigot hanging from a man's ear. A triple-braided beard. A T-shirt with holes in all the right places. A parrot riding the shoulder of a girl in a silk harem halter and bloused shorts. He killed a minute watching a dozen females from tots to grandmas dance around a black fellow with a Santa Claus beard who stomped a pedal that pounded rhythm on a bass drum while he blew screeches and moans out of a chromatic harmonica.

I led the way around the portable shed where they locked up sound gear to a roped-off area behind the main stage. One of the Security hippies patrolled the periphery. Pop approached him, opened his billfold and flashed it like a badge, then quickly folded and stuffed it into his coat pocket. The fellow cocked his head.

"We're here to see Dan Mills," Pop said.

The hippie squinted and must've seen from Pop's expression that questioning us would only waste his time and effort. He shrugged and walked over to Big Dan, who was beside the stage, facing away from us and leaning on a mike stand as if it were the cane in a soft-shoe routine. The hippie tapped his shoulder and spoke. Big Dan turned and gazed as though trying to place us. Then he waved us over.

As we climbed the rope, Pop said, "Mind if I handle this fellow, keep you from offending a guy who could help your career?"

"Please do."

Big Dan Mills, though hatless, stood taller than Pop, including his straw fedora. Big Dan's shoulders appeared too wide to fit through doorways. He was fifty-something, with bushy black hair and beard and leathery skin. His teeth looked capped. He shook Pop's hand first. Then mine. "Yeah?"

"Name's Tom Hickey." Pop laid a hand on my shoulder. "My son Clifford. He's on the bill. So was his brother Alvaro."

Big Dan frowned as though Alvaro had run off just to inconvenience him.

"You know Alvaro?" Pop asked.

"I met him. Ochs said give him a break. He auditioned, that's all. You're gonna tell me he didn't kill Jimmy Marris."

"And you're going to tell me he did?"

"Tom, I liked the kid, but you and me been around long enough to know—just because he's a likeable kid, or even a good kid, doesn't mean he didn't shoot the boy. Hey, you and me been around enough to know anybody's capable of anything. Charlie Manson's bunch, do you think all them were born murderers?"

"I hear Charlie doped and brainwashed them."

Big Dan grumbled, "Tom, it's awful simplistic to blame those murders on dope."

Pop had no patience with anybody who patronized him. The way he sucked at his teeth as though trying to dislodge a strand of tobacco meant he would've rather made sure Big Dan's repertoire would be strictly instrumental until his mouth healed. But he said, "Dan, let's get together sometime and discuss the human condition. For now, though, how about you tell us what all you know about Jimmy Marris."

"Never met the kid."

"Alvaro then. Who were his *amigos*? Why would the FBI keep tabs on him?"

He rolled his eyes and glanced my way. I said, "What kind of work does Alvaro do for Phil Ochs?"

Big Dan shifted toward the stage, as though looking for an excuse to ditch us. "Man, didn't I just say I hardly knew him?"

"Could be I don't believe you," Pop said.

Mills laughed, as if he appreciated a worthy adversary. "Partner," he said, "I'm on the road half the time. The best I can do for you is ask around. Right now, I got stuff needs doing."

"Sure. Ask around. We'll be back, or you can leave us a message at Quig's."

We had only climbed the rope when a pair of Security hippies climbed it going in. Before we reached the concessions, one of the pair caught up with us. Out of breath, he gasped, "Big Dan said to tell you the Cossacks did a run through Quig's."

When he scooted off, Pop said, "I guess Big Dan keeps an eye on every little thing. Let's go check on your mother."

He agreed to go for the car while I used a short cut, the trail along the river. I ran over the knoll where Ava and I had first talked, past the workshop where a woman was teaching autoharp and Alvaro would have taught slide guitar tomorrow had he not been otherwise occupied. I tripped down the bank to the river. Dozens of kids splashed and frolicked in the shallows. Near the line where the jamboree grounds met Big Dan's commune, the sloping bank steepened and the path narrowed to the width of a tightrope. A mountain goat would have tiptoed that stretch, but I kept running, powered by fear that the Cossacks had snatched Mama, and maybe Ava, on account of my waylaying Hound Dog.

I slipped, toppled, rolled, and splashed into the river at a place where the water was shallow and rocky. When I stood, my knee was loose at the socket, my bad hand stung even through the tingling numbness, and the gouges in my back felt bloody, though I didn't reach around to make sure.

Giving up the path, I waded, limping, near shore until the sharp bank gave way to a slope and the path widened again. I ran limping the last quarter mile to Quig's and entered the grounds by the trail west of the Chattagua hall. Outside the hall, the residents too broke or sick to attend the jamboree had gathered. I ran past a topless pregnant girl, the guy who had practiced yoga in the jail cell across from mine, an Asian fellow who talked with his hands, a freckled redheaded boy with a cast on his foot, and the boy's plump little sister. I kept running, over motorcycle skid marks, around the bathhouse and gazebo, to the A-frame Pop had rented. The door was open. I dashed in calling, "Mama!" One look told me she wasn't there.

As I ran out of the A-frame, a police car bounded into the compound. Also, hippies were arriving on foot, some along the path and others from River Road. Word had spread fast through the jamboree.

I reached the yurt and yanked up the flap so hard it ripped. When I saw them, I dropped to my knees, and yowled from the pain that shot through my wounded knee.

They were sitting side by side on the futon. Mama crawled toward me. "What's wrong, Clifford?"

She looked more alive than since before Claire died.

I led her outside and held her hand while we waited then watched the Eldorado skid into the compound and to a stop beside the A-frame. Pop jumped out and wheeled his gaze until he saw us. I let Mama go to him alone.

Back in the yurt, Ava was sprawled on the futon. "Worn out?" I asked.

"Uh huh." She sat up. "Did you guys learn anything?"

"Nothing that seems to matter. What did you do to make Mama so happy?"

"Well, I was reading her a Psalm she likes and the next thing she asked if we could pray together, for your brother." She flashed a stern look I couldn't interpret.

"What's wrong?"

"It was hard." She looked up above us, wearing a face that could mean a legion of spiders had appeared on the ceiling. "Maybe I'm not sure he didn't kill Jimmy."

"Yeah, okay. Did the bikers hurt anybody?"

"I guess not." She stood. "Let's go look around."

When we were outside, walking toward the sheriff's car around which people had gathered, she said, "They just rode through, with Vic in the lead. They made five or six circles and loopty-loops. I'll bet they were showing Quig what they can do if he doesn't turn you over to them."

If Willis noticed us, he didn't let on. Pop stood with an arm around Mama, listening to the stories of people who had witnessed the Cossack invasion. As we approached, he let Mama go and reached for Ava's hand. He kissed it as if he were a priest and she were the first woman Pope.

Then he took me aside. He said, "Marry that girl, will you? I think she reminds your Mama of Claire, great big heart and all."

"She's still not convinced that Alvaro didn't kill Jimmy Marris."

"Well, all the better. It means she's smart and honest. If you find a woman who won't tell you pretty lies, you've already got a better deal than most men."

I thought I heard a gunshot. The same or a similar report and about as far away as those the night of the murder. But nobody reacted. I was about to conclude stress was giving me auditory hallucinations, when the police radio crackled. We turned to watch the sheriff go for it. He listened, mumbled a few words and tossed his clipboard onto the cruiser's front seat. He ambled around the car and slid behind the wheel. As he started the motor, he told the crowd, "Somebody took a potshot at the communist."

A hippie with sores on his face and arms asked, "Which communist?" But Willis had already pulled away.

Chapter Fourteen

Ava agreed to stay with Mama, as long as we promised to come back with any news. Pop and I followed the cruiser. As we passed the gatekeeper, Pop asked me, "This communist would be Dan Mills?"

"Phil Ochs."

He rubbed the bridge of his nose and lifted his hat to wipe his brow. "Thank God," he said, and I thought the same, because we, not the sheriffs, had noticed and made off with Alvaro's magazines.

In the jamboree parking lot, while we waited for a rainbow colored Chevy van to leave its slot, we saw Phil Ochs. He was riding out of the lot in the shotgun seat of an equipment van driven by the Texan Security hippie. The van must have picked him up at the gate, because a rowdy mob of at least a thousand clustered around the entrance.

We parked and nudged our way into the middle of the crowd, where Willis stood listening. A long-necked deputy took notes. A middle-aged woman in pigtails and a shirtless, emaciated speed freak with the sniffles interrupted each other, both telling the story of a bullet that zinged over Ochs' head while he sang "Changes." Nobody saw the shooter's exact location, but it came from the across the river, most likely from the forested rise east of the Cossacks' hill. Security hippies were guessing the bullet had probably hit the ground somewhere in the old community garden. While the witnesses repeated their story and the deputy listened for significant details, a Cessna I felt sure was Knudsen's came buzzing out of the south.

We were standing behind Willis and I hadn't noticed him look our way when, as though he had rear-view eyes, he turned to Pop and said, "Your boy ain't so cagey after all."

"What?"

"The Mexican."

"You lost me, fella," Pop said.

Willis rolled his eyes.

"You're saying Alvaro tried to pick off Phil Ochs?"

"Yes, sir. Ochs is a traitor. He makes our boys in Vietnam out to be murdering scum. Now, you give me a vet like your Alvaro, a shell-shocked Mexican gone *loco* from smoking that *sinsemilla* the hippies grow, already killed one man, he knows he's a goner and figures he might as well take a big shot commie with him. Between you and me, if your boy had of picked him off, I mighta considered asking for leniency on both charges."

Pop rubbed his neck and spoke softly, though his face had reddened. "My son's a distinguished expert rifleman. Sheriff, Alvaro could clip a pea off the top of your head from a thousand yards. If he was shooting at Ochs, he could put a slug in one ear at the proper angle so it comes out the other."

I stood astonished that Pop, whose creed included the injunction not to give away any more than required, had told the sheriff something he might find a way to use against Alvaro. He must have a reason, I decided, and returned to thoughts the sheriff had sparked.

"A man goes crazy," Willis said, "could be he's gonna lose his aim. But thanks for the warning. I'll be sure and tell the hunters to shoot first before he gets his turn."

Pop said, "I told you how risky that would be. And if you think those heavies that came around were from Hollywood, you've been watching too much TV."

"You send 'em?"

"Nope, but I've got an idea who did, and he didn't make his fortune by inventing the hula hoop."

Willis snuffed and started to turn away. "Whoa, Sheriff," I said. "The crazy vet you're talking about isn't Alvaro. It's Hound Dog."

A crafty smile softened Willis' poker face. "You'd like to see us take Hound Dog out of commission, wouldn't you?"

While a man dressed like a salesman going to a luau told the same story as the others, Pop and I gazed over the spectators at the forested hill. At least eight men in uniforms climbed, ducking from tree to tree, each with a weapon held in position to drop and fire. On a hunch, I peered at the east slope of Sugar Hill, hoping to glimpse the shooter creep around. Then I reasoned that even Cossacks weren't so stupid as to shoot at somebody from their own neighborhood. But even before I completed the thought, the flaw in my reasoning appeared—I hadn't a clue how stupid Hound Dog or some other Cossacks might be. For all I knew, the greatest brain-challenge any of them had faced was learning how to shift a Harley.

I went to Willis and tapped his arm. "Have you sent anybody up to the Cossacks' camp, just in case Hound Dog or another one of them runs in from the east all sweaty and packing a rifle?"

The sheriff plucked a toothpick out of his pocket and held it in front of his chin. I wondered if he wanted to stab me in the eye. He stuck it into the corner of his mouth. "Suppose you go on up there and bring me a report."

"Why me? Because you're scared of them?"

The sheriff crammed his hands into his pockets as though to restrain them, then turned to Pop. "Get him the hell outta here."

"Yes, sir."

On the way to the Cadillac, I asked Pop, "Why else would a biker want to shoot Phil Ochs, unless he's the *loco* Vietnam vet Willis makes Alvaro out to be?"

"How about—so the sheriff will pin it on Alvaro. Which could mean one of them saw Alvaro's magazines, or talked to him, or overheard him talking about Ochs."

"Okay, let's suppose. What's that mean?"

"You tell me."

My brain felt like a Mixmaster. "A Cossack killed Jimmy Marris?"

"Killed him because…?"

I gave the only wild guess that came. "Say Brady Barker's in their pocket, and Jimmy Marris figured that out, say from a remark Lola made. And say Jimmy was trying to squeeze his uncle Brady into going straight."

"Why would Jimmy want to turn his uncle around?"

"Ava said Jimmy talked about ethics. Maybe he thought he could turn Brady into a good guy? Or maybe he hated the Cossacks and wanted them gone, so Ava's sister would get a fair chance to kick her speed habit."

"What's he care about Ava's sister?"

"For Ava's sake, maybe?"

"And how did the Cossacks learn about all this?"

"Say, Jimmy let on to Lola, and she snitched."

Pop grabbed the scruff of my neck and kneaded. "You wouldn't be hanging this whole mess on Barker because he pinched your hand? Still, just because you've got motives doesn't mean you haven't hit on the truth. Did you run any of this by Ava?"

"I just now dreamed it up."

"Could she be covering for her sister?"

"Huh?"

"The way you paint it," Pop said, "if Lola snitching on Jimmy resulted in his death, she might get nailed as a conspirator."

Although I would've preferred to deny that Ava had lied to me to save her sister from prison even though the stakes included my brother's life, I had to allow she might have. I mumbled, "Let's go ask her?"

Pop let go of my neck and walked around the car.

The shooting had chased half the crowd from the jamboree and most of the deserters were already gone, so the line of cars exiting the lot was only a few minutes long. While we waited, Pop asked, "Mind if I drop you at Quig's, let you talk to Ava while I run an errand?"

"What errand?"

"Nothing you need to worry about. If we split up for an hour or so, we cover twice the ground."

I knew by the set of his jaw and the way his fingers thrummed the steering wheel, he didn't intend to chat with Jimmy's school teachers.

"Nope," I said. "Where are we going?"

Pop cocked his head and watched me long enough to know he couldn't shake me. "The sheriff suggested we should talk to the Cossacks."

"Pop, they're not going to let us stop by, have a chat and leave."

"So I'll go alone. I'll be nice. Friendly."

"You go, I go."

"Clifford," he said, "I'm so damn old I might keel over any second without their help. Whereas, you've got fifty good years, anyway."

"Yeah, and what do you think I'm going to do if the Cossacks waste you?"

"I'd suggest, anytime you're thinking about revenge, meditate on Numbers thirty-five in that book your mama's always reading."

"Go left," I said as our turn to exit came.

He studied my eyes. I noticed him swell with pride and stiffen with worry or maybe a dash of fear. Then somebody honked and he swung onto River Road, and soon turned off onto a trail only fit for motorcycles or dunebuggies. The dirt was soft and the path narrow, but the Eldorado rolled along, threatening to crush the rickety bridge over the river, then knocking brush out of its way and scraping gouges in its previously immaculate sky blue paint. Pop asked, "You scared?"

"Yep."

"Good," he said. "I'll let you out and go alone."

"Forget it. Should I strap the gun on?"

"No." He stopped the car, shifted into neutral, and pulled the handbrake. He climbed out, went to the trunk, and opened it. After moving a folded blanket, he picked up a weapon I had never seen. A scattergun. A Remington shotgun with the barrel shortened to about eight inches.

For a moment I wondered if all these years Pop had fooled us into thinking he was an upholder of law, when in truth he had worked as an enforcer for Harry Poverman. He caught me gawking and said, "I borrowed it. In case we had to bust Alvaro out of jail. You ever use a shotgun?"

"A couple times."

"Left-handed?"

"No."

"Good. It's only a prop."

"But it's loaded, right?"

He reached into the trunk behind the spare tire for a canvas pouch stuffed with shells. He handed it to me. "Don't point this monster at anything higher than the dirt unless I tell you." He reached under the seat for his holster and .38. He threw the strap over his shoulder.

While we floated up the hill I readied the shotgun, loaded each chamber, locked the safety, aimed the barrel out the window and gave the trigger a half squeeze to get the feel. Then I unlocked the safety. On the middle stretch of hillside, I worried that I didn't have the nerves for this job, that when Hound Dog or somebody reached to scratch himself, I would spook and the gun would spring up and one squeeze would topple eight or ten Cossacks.

I told Pop that last year Alvaro and I camped atop Sugar Hill. He asked, "What's the layout up there? Any buildings?"

"An old barn with a room on top, full of bats and mice."

"What else?"

"Lots of stubby black pine. A dead apple grove. An old outhouse. A well with a concrete cistern."

He chopped the wheel left to maneuver a switchback. Something clunked underneath us. Pop said, "Our family's going to survive this trouble, but our vehicles might not."

As we crested the hill, at least twenty bikers and a half dozen tattooed girls appeared in a ragged line fifty yards away, shuffling and swaggering toward us from their camp, which was a circle of tents around the old barn. "Leave your door open," Pop said.

We climbed out. I followed Pop. We stopped and stood directly in front of the Eldorado. Already I wanted to aim the gun. But I managed to hold it pointing down like he'd told me to.

As they neared, Little Vic came through the pack and took the lead, walking a step ahead of Crutch, whose burgundy skin glistened with sweat, and on the other side a Cossack whose forehead from the middle down to his right cheekbone was marked by a scar shaped like a lightning bolt. I peered all around, looking for Hound Dog. If he was in camp, he was hiding or catching a nap.

I caught a glimpse of Lola, in the rear of the pack. Every few steps she rose onto her toes to peer over the others.

When Vic was ten yards off, Pop raised his hand, palm out. "One of you fellas go sniping?" he asked, as though it were a casual inquiry. "How about you, soldier?" He pointed to a wiry, shirtless man with a Huey helicopter tattooed on his hairless belly. "You look flushed, like you might've just run up the hill."

Before the man could answer, Little Vic threw a silencing look his way. Then Vic turned to Pop and bared his teeth. "Who shot who, Grandpa?"

"Come on," Pop said. "Let me in on it. Which one of you boys made the communist wet his pants, down at the jamboree, even though you missed by a mile?"

Vic barked a laugh. Most of the others joined him, but the guy with the lightning bolt scar only leered at me.

"You the new deputy, Grandpa?" Vic shook his head. "How many badges is Willy Willis going to give out? Hey—" he turned to his followers. "I'll bet he'll give us some stinking badges if we ask nice." The others chanted a chorus of affirmations.

"So, Grandpa," Vic said, "what makes us suspects?"

"Proximity. Possession of firearms. Motive."

"Motive?"

"Big Dan had you chased out of the jamboree yesterday. Right? Besides, this gig brings too many hippies to Evergreen. The more hippies, the tougher it is for you to rob them. Business sense dictates you shut it down."

Again Vic turned to his gang. "Hey, I like the old man. Sure he's a pain in the ass, but he's smart. What I don't get, how'd he fuck up so bad when it came to making sons? Must be the mothers' fault, huh? I mean, Alvaro is a ten *centavo chingadero* and the Pretty Boy here is a swish."

When Vic aimed a finger-pistol at me, and Crutch leaned forward, my shotgun sprang up to about forty-five degrees. Pop flashed me a look. I let the barrel fall.

"Little fella," Pop said, "on account of you're clearly upset about something, we're going to forgive you that crack, as soon as you settle up with us on the bill for restoring Clifford's '55. We shopped around. The best estimate's two grand. You want to give it to us now, that's okay, or you could drop it with the gatekeeper at Quig's."

Little Vic woofed a laugh. "Or how about this—you haul ass off our hill, Grandpa. The swish…" He hitched a thumb at me. "He gets to stay and party with us. Crutch and Boomer…" He hitched his thumb first toward Crutch then to the man with the lightning bolt. "…they're gonna follow you down, keep you company for an hour or so. Hound Dog, he's sticking around for the party."

No matter if you're a football fan, if you see a hail Mary pass that a receiver plucks out of the sky in the end zone, you'll thrill at the sight and treasure the memory. Watching Tom Hickey make his move felt the same.

With the shotgun on my left side, Pop didn't have to step, only reach, to grab it. He yanked it out of my hand so fast, I wasn't aware of letting it go.

And with the gun raised and sweeping across their ranks, he said, "Don't misinterpret, the weapon's not my ace in the hole. My ace is what I'm willing to do. Boys and girls, you're looking at a dead man. Cancer in the back of my mouth, working its way up to my brain, where by next Easter it'll kill me. Do I care about losing six months of misery? Naw. And you know what they say about misery loves company. I'd be delighted to take a bunch of you with me. Lola," he called out, "come up here, would you please?"

Her head poked up over a biker's broad shoulder. Vic raised his hand and waved her forward. The gang parted a walkway up the middle, and Lola shimmied through, prancing like stripper on a runway. She stopped beside Vic, but Pop used a finger to beckon her. "Get in the Cadillac, please."

Vic stood still. He tapped his lips. Then he gave Lola a nudge. When she failed to move he grabbed her elbow and shoved her toward the car.

Some of the gang murmured. Lola gave her hair a toss and shimmied our way. At the shotgun door of the Eldorado, she turned and raised a bony finger at Vic and others.

Vic said, "Give them a good time, baby."

She dove into the Cadillac. Pop asked me to keep her company, and when I was seated shotgun, with Lola in the middle, he announced to the gang, "Any more runs through Quig's, or even one of you stops by there for tea, we're going to use the tank here to mash every chopper we see." He patted the Eldorado. "And hear this—people are saying Alvaro's *loco*, and Clifford's getting the same reputation.

"Well, I'll promise you my sons are level-headed, easy going, mellow, compared to me."

Pop climbed in behind the wheel and held the scattergun aimed out the window while he sped the Cadillac backward and whipped it around as if it were a Grand Prix racer.

Chapter Fifteen

We crashed down the hill twice as fast as we had climbed it. Lola sat pressing her arms into her sides as if we had open sores she feared touching. Her chipped crimson fingernails dug into her knees. She craned around and looked up the hill. Then, hardly moving her lips, she demanded, "Where are we going? What'd she tell you about me?"

"Who?"

"Right, like you don't know my so-called sister. The one with the halo." She caught a clump of hair with her mouth and chewed it.

From the base of the hill all the way to Quig's, she cussed Vic. "Just you wait, Victor, you needle-dicked midget, I'm going to…"

We parked beside the yurt and climbed out. Pop asked Lola to go inside. To our surprise, she did. I hung back. When Pop came around the car, I said, "Promise you were lying about cancer."

"Sure. I promise."

"Pop, did you notice the layout up there? Their tents circling the barn like an old wagon train."

"What could that mean?"

"Could be they've got some treasure in the barn. Like a meth lab. Like they moved it from the shack across the river from Alvaro's camp, say after they killed Jimmy Marris down there."

Pop stared over the Chattagua hall at Sugar Hill, about a half mile of woods and meadow away. "And if they're so bold as to brew the stuff in their own kitchen, would that mean they've got the sheriffs in their pocket?"

Out of the yurt issued, "Bitch!" and other pet names.

Pop unstrapped his holster and shoved it under the driver's seat. He returned the shotgun to the trunk. We ducked into the yurt. Mama and Ava sat cross-legged on the futon. Lola stood with her fingers gouging her hipbones. Bent toward her sister, she yelled, "It's *my* life, Holy Joe. Daddy can't stop me, and you can't either, and neither can these geeks!" She waved at Pop and me.

"I didn't send them," Ava said.

"Yeah, right." Lola fished in one front pocket of her tight cut-offs for a hard pack of Marlboros and in the other front pocket for a lighter. I studied her features. Silver eyes, wide mouth and chin. She and Ava might be twins, I thought, one raised by angels, the other by a coven of witches. Lola was twenty pounds skinnier. Her breasts didn't fill the halter out of which a marijuana leaf tattoo grew. Her legs were dirty and nicked as if she had shaved with a hack saw. Her bleached hair, as long and thick as Ava's, hung straight and stringy. She had a raspy voice and skin that looked infested with tiny blisters. I saw no needle tracks.

Pop said, "Let's go sit somewhere."

When he touched Lola's arm to lead her out, she snapped, "Back off, pervert," and ducked outside on her own.

Mama rose and stood by me. "Did the motorcycle boys hurt her?"

"She hurt *herself*," Ava said, in a harsh voice that didn't seem to be hers. "Why's she here?"

I said, "Maybe she'll turn on them. Maybe she'll clean up and be your sister again."

"Yeah. We should expect miracles." Now she sounded like a cynic, an unbeliever.

I followed her outside. We saw Pop and Lola at a park bench beside the playground. Ava caught my elbow and tugged. We let Mama walk ahead.

"Just before you came into the yurt," Ava whispered, "not this time but last, before the shots at Phil Ochs, Wendy said, 'X is nearby.' Who is X? I asked her but she'd already spaced out."

"X is my brother, Alvaro Xavier." I spelled out his middle name.

Mama had stopped to wait for us. We caught up. In the playground sandbox, a little brown girl held a bucket of water and taught three younger ones to make drip castles. Pop motioned for us to sit in the lawn chairs beside the bench, as though he preferred having Lola to himself. But we overheard.

He asked why Vic had let her go without a fuss. She said, "'Cause he's got a hard-on for these two sluts Boomer dragged up from the Bay."

"Boomer's the scar-faced guy."

"He carved it himself."

"You like Vic?"

"Do you?"

"I hardly know him."

"He doesn't get any better. Hey, what's the deal here? Am I like a POW? You're gonna torture me with my pants down like you did with Hound Dog?"

Pop gave me a look that meant he'd be asking about the pants down part.

"You better torture me, Grandpa," Lola said, "or I'm clamming up. I don't feel like talking anymore."

"That'll be the day," Ava remarked.

Lola turned tome and pointed to her sister. "Thinking about Jesus makes her come."

"Stop it, Lo. Help us out."

"Why should I?"

"For Jimmy."

"Give it up, bitch."

Ava walked over, knelt in front of Lola and laid a hand on her sister's knee. "Okay, what'd I do to make you hate me?"

Lola only sneered, though her face clouded.

While Pop gave her a minute to answer, Mama and a scrawny child in the sandbox waved at each other. Then Pop asked, "You knew Jimmy Marris?"

Lola pinched her lips with her thumb and middle finger as though clamping them shut until the glue dried.

"Brady Barker, you know him?"

She began to hum, and Pop said, "My son figured out who killed Jimmy, and why. Care to hear?"

Lola reached for her Marlboros, lit one, and sucked on it while she stared at me.

I said, "Jimmy found out, maybe from you, that his uncle Brady was in the Cossacks' pocket. He hated them because they terrorized his town. He thought he could pressure his uncle into chasing them out. And what made him wild was, he thought you were special. The way he saw things, Vic and the speed he turned you on to were killing you off. With the Cossacks gone, you'd get clean and healthy and beautiful again. But he let on to the wrong person what he was up to. Word got back to Vic, who then sent one or two of his boys out hunting. They dropped Jimmy off the bridge into Whiskey River."

During my story, she had sucked a whole Marlboro, made hissing sounds, and wiped her dribbling nose. She tried to laugh. It didn't work. A silver spot glistened beneath her left eye. "Bullshit." She lit another Marlboro. "Hey, Grandpa. Some fool told me the Cossacks from Russia got famous for eating their buggers. That true?"

Pop smiled. "We've got appointments. Stick around, would you please, Lola?"

"You gonna make me?"

"Nope." He stood and came to Ava and squeezed her hand. Then he then kissed Mama and turned toward his car. I said goodbye to the women and followed him.

In the car, Pop said, "Poor kid." If Pop had a tragic flaw, it was compassion for women in trouble. "I could use a sedative. Know any bars close by?"

I pointed up River Road. "Ava told me that a few minutes before the shot at Ochs, Mama said Alvaro was nearby."

"God tell her?"

"Maybe. She didn't say."

When we parked outside Louella's Lounge, on Manhattan Avenue halfway between the jail and the Safeway mall, I told Pop about the proprietor having been enjoined by Barker and Knudsen to report to them if I showed up there. Inside, Pop found the place most congenial for its jukebox that featured Benny Goodman, the Ink Spots, and Billie Holiday, and because it was dark and smoky like he thought a bar ought to be, or else you might as well drink at home.

I ordered a Moosehead, Pop called for his usual double shot of Dewar's on the rocks. I spotted the owner who looked like my English profs. When he glanced our way, I waved him over and asked him to please call Barker and Knudsen like they asked him to, because we wanted to talk to them.

The man nodded and left but didn't go near a phone.

"What now?" Pop asked.

"Go back to the crime scene?"

Our drinks came. Pop asked the bartender if we could use the phone. The bartender said no. Pop still tipped him. We drank fast, then traded the dim blue light of Louella's for a blast from the sun as it approached the western horizon. "We've got a little better than an hour of daylight," Pop said on our way to a pay phone outside the Safeway.

He called the Riverside Lodge. The desk clerk rang Knudsen for him. The Fed picked up. "My son told me you're a good man," Pop said, and asked for an hour of his time.

When they hung up, I asked, "Did I say he was a good man?"

"If not, you're learning what a godawful liar I am, which is a lousy fact for a guy to know about his old man."

"I'll need therapy."

"Send me the tab. Should we tell Knudsen we figure he's FBI?"

We found Agent Knudsen outside his cottage across Moonshine Road from the lodge office, pacing the riverbank and peering into the water, his aviator sunglasses in his hand. As he walked toward our car, he hitched the glasses on. We had climbed out of the car. Pop stepped forward to shake his hand. I didn't.

"Tom Hickey. I believe you know my boy here."

"We've talked."

"I've heard," Pop said, "that you're not what you say but a G-man who's taking notes on my other boy. Tell me it isn't so, would you?"

Knudsen's little smile flashed into a big one. "Proud to know you, Tom."

"Want to show some ID?"

"Either that, or we could try to cooperate." Knudsen motioned toward the Caddy. "Shall we?"

He rode shotgun. "Nice wheels."

I sat in back watching for motorcycles or other enemies, hoping they would descend upon us while our team included a federal agent. Unless, I thought, Knudsen was corrupt and on the payroll of killers.

For all I knew, he might have conspired with Brady Barker and the Cossacks to rip off a thousand-kilo *sinsemilla* harvest from Quig, Simon, or whomever. Jimmy could have learned from Barker and tried to cash in by blackmailing the Fed, giving Knudsen no other option but to waste Jimmy, since cops knew better than to pay extortion.

Though I reasoned the odds against that scenario might run as high as several billion to one, the past three days had driven me to a place beyond reason. I'd arrived in Evergreen dreaming of the big break, of a kiss from Mimi Fariña and some carefree days with my brother. But I'd gotten jailed and maimed, had my car mutilated, kidnapped a guy, seen my brother get chased into the mountains, gone with Pop into the lion's den to snatch Ava's sister, and met and found myself in danger of falling for Ava, all in four hours short of three days.

Up front, Knudsen questioned Pop. Having read Alvaro's military and criminal records, he knew my brother was adopted, that he had graduated from high school, spent two years at community college, gotten busted at the border with amphetamine pills, and joined the army in preference to serving a year in road camp. Knudsen knew Alvaro had earned three bronze stars and two purple hearts, one for the M-16 shell that nearly sliced his Achilles tendon and one for the shrapnel that chipped the bone above his left eye. Knudsen knew details, but not my brother's mind or heart. After mentioning some of those facts and alluding to others, he asked, "Alvaro came to the redwoods hoping to strike it rich panning for gold?"

"Naw," Pop said. "Whoever told you that is mistaken."

"It's the line he used on the locals."

"He was putting them on then," Pop said. "Alvaro doesn't give a fig about rich. He just loves the woods. So, how do you figure this shooting? Any specifics on the location, the distance, how many shots were fired, how many hit Jimmy?"

The Fed glanced back at me. "I guess Alvaro's at home in the out of doors. A hunter."

"Except in Vietnam and a few trout," Pop said, "he never killed a living thing bigger than a mosquito, as far as I know. I wouldn't be surprised if over there, he shot to miss. He's a delicate boy."

Knudsen made a wry face. "An innocent."

"That's the word. Now, since you and Mister Hoover are fascinated by Alvaro, do you suppose I'm one of those parents who's always the last to know?"

After a long time scratching behind his ear, Knudsen said, "I can tell you he bought a dredge, suitable for nothing I know except sluicing gold out of creeks and rivers. From McNees Emporium two weeks ago. Thursday morning, the dredge wasn't in Alvaro's camp, even though we picked up a sieve and a gold pan there, and the lab found a clean set of Marris' fingerprints on the pan."

Pop stared up the road, probably groping for an explanation, like I was. He shook his head. "Clifford, you have questions for the man, don't you?"

"For starters," I said, "if Pop wants to be your friend, that's peachy. But I don't, and I want to see your ID, and hear why an FBI agent would masquerade as another kind of Fed."

Knudsen chuckled.

I considered asking what he knew or thought about the Alvaro and Phil Ochs connection. But that might clue him to something he didn't yet know.

We drove past Alvaro's camp and a mile or so farther east to a riverbank site where Knudsen pointed out foot tracks, several of them colored gray from the casts investigators had made.

"Army boots," Knudsen said. "No doubt Alvaro kept his. Probably his most comfortable footwear, broken in." He swept his hand as though scattering grass seed, to point out the course of the tracks leading down and into the water. "Deep tracks for a guy Alvaro's size. What's he weigh?"

"About one-fifty," I said.

"One-fifty. Then he must've been carrying either Marris or one of these redwoods, to make tracks that deep. Now, tell me if I'm right—Alvaro wears size eight."

I said, "And you'll tell us how many Cossacks wear size eight army surplus boots, right?"

He pursed his lips. "I may do that."

He led us, backtracking the route he claimed Alvaro took carrying Jimmy. It looped to the west of Alvaro's camp, over mosses and ferns, through vines and into and out of tracts of composting needles and bark, soft as quicksand. By the time we had followed the boot-prints to a creek, the sky's complexion had gone bone gray.

The boot tracks started at the edge of the creek near a wooden frame. Knudsen pointed. "Alvaro's dredge fit into this thing. Look, let's say Jimmy happens to see Alvaro buying the dredge. He thinks a few nuggets could pay his college tuition. Why not give it a go. He's got a beef against Alvaro for hitting on his girl. So he and a partner come out here to snatch the dredge.

"In the right vehicle, you can get from Moonshine to here. They call this one Wild Turkey Creek. It runs between the south and middle forks of Whiskey River. Late night, Jimmy and a partner are loading the dredge when somebody starts shooting."

"Who's the partner?" Pop asked.

Knudsen gave us a cryptic smile.

"Who says he had a partner?"

"A couple reasons. One, Jimmy didn't have a vehicle."

"Two?"

"I've got my ideas. But you're going to have to come up with your own, Mister Hickey." He looked over at me. "And son."

We tromped through the woods toward the Caddy, each of us absorbed in his own thoughts. Mine regarded the partner. If somebody had accompanied Jimmy into the woods, the shortest route to the truth was to find the partner.

A picture of Simon flashed in my brain. Then came one of Ava.

Knudsen saved the rest of his story until we were back in the car and rattling along Highball Trail. "Look, say Jimmy and his partner are a little tipsy and pumped with adrenaline, and they're laughing, loud enough to wake somebody like Alvaro who learned to sleep light, when he was in Vietnam and out on patrol. He jumps out of the tent, picks up his rifle, runs up the trail to his dredge, and catches them stealing the thing. Look, these aren't your Boy Scout type woods. They're one of those places where criminals come to score big or die trying.

"Who knows, maybe Jimmy or the partner take a shot at him. However it played, the partner gets away, Jimmy doesn't."

"Who's this partner?" I demanded.

Knudsen turned to me and spoke softly, like someone trained to act patient even when he didn't feel that way. "We're going to find more footprints and casings from Alvaro's gun and whatever else is out there. We'll find the rest of the pieces of the puzzle after we free up some men, after they bring in Alvaro. It's a done deal."

"Crap," I said. "More likely a Cossack in size eight army boots swiped Alvaro's dredge and carried it on his back through the forest, making all those tracks."

Pop glanced over his shoulder and flashed me a look he had used when I was a mouthy kid. Which made me want to yell, What, do you expect me to think and ask questions, or don't you?

◇◇◇

After Pop turned onto the highway, he asked, "If you're so sure Alvaro's the killer, why are you handing us your theory? Makes me suspect you're telling us to find a crafty lawyer who can shred your evidence."

"Actually, I'm hoping you'll recognize the truth and back off. Mister Hickey, you might love this boy, but he's not your blood. In the nature versus nurture controversy, you might find the answer's a little of each. Even if you raised the kid to be a model citizen, he might've grown out of a bad seed."

Bad seed, my brain echoed. Just yesterday, when I met Little Vic in the jail, I had thought of a movie with that name. God just might've fed Knudsen those words, I imagined, to assure me Vic was the killer.

Knudsen said, "I'm hoping you and Clifford will look at the facts and quit stirring up what's already a volatile brew. Before it explodes all over you and other people, like Marris' girlfriend.

"Look, the bottom line is, you two can either leave Evergreen with a son going to prison where he ought to go and serve his debt, or find yourselves invited to a whole string of funerals. Which will be on your conscience, provided you're decent men."

Pop filled and lit his briar. "You're okay, Mister Knudsen."

"What's that mean?"

Pop shook his head and blew a chain of smoke rings.

I wracked my brain for ideas about Jimmy's partner. Nobody talked until we pulled up at the Riverside Lodge and Pop said, "We're not disregarding your advice, Agent Knudsen of the FBI. We're going to sleep on it, and take a new look at things in the morning."

Knudsen saluted. "You might want to add this to the brew. Phil Ochs is a revolutionary. And your boy is closer to Phil Ochs than you may know. Whether he came to the woods to forage or to get rich, he spent the bulk of his time snooping around. Just like you two. Good night." He turned and marched off toward his cottage.

I climbed into the front. As Pop swung a U-turn and back-tracked to Cognac Lane, the Fed's accusations stabbed me like a poisoned dart between the eyes. For the first time I allowed the possibility that Alvaro might be the killer. All my reasoning had begun with presuppositions. Everything I knew about Alvaro was tainted with love. And similar thoughts plagued Pop, I suspected, when he pulled up at the curb outside Frosty's Liquor.

He handed me a twenty. "Dewar's for me," he said.

As I came out of the store with quart of Scotch and a six pack of Oly, I saw Pop closing a pill box and dropping it into his breast pocket.

"Headache?" I asked.

"Heartburn," he said, and sat still for a minute with his eyes closed before he started the car.

Chapter Sixteen

On the way to the commune, Pop asked, "How about we chat with Quig this evening?"

We found Mama and Ava on the deck behind the Chattagua hall. They were on a bench, feet hanging over the edge of the deck, watching the moonlit river. Mama loved rough water. In Tahoe, every few days she and Claire used to hike up Mount Rose and sit beside one of the mightier streams, the way other women met for coffee or tea. When we lived in our shack on San Diego Bay, Mama often tagged along when Alvaro and I toted our boards a mile each way up the sidewalk of Pacific Beach Drive, going to surf beside Crystal Pier. She would sit on the damp sand, her feet in the tide, looking enchanted.

She gave me a happy smile. "Ava will take us to church tomorrow."

"You got here just in time," Ava said. "Another five minutes, the leftover food gets composted. We'd better hurry."

"Where's your sister?" Pop asked.

"In the yurt, crashed out."

Ava led us into the Chattagua hall, where diners sat cross-legged on rugs that looked woven out of rags, or on the plank floor, or lounged in bean bag chairs, plates on their laps. Simon and a girl who could've passed for a grown-up Raggedy Ann sat facing each other on a mat in front of an out-of-service fireplace. People saw us and backed away as if we all had mumps.

The only tables were three long fold-outs near the door to the kitchen. They were set with wooden and glass bowls of white rice, brown rice, millet, Swiss chard, yellow squash, zucchini, lemon Jello, chocolate tapioca pudding. Ava noticed Pop hovering over the bowls, scrutinizing each dish. "Nothing you like?"

"I'm looking for the pot roast." He winked.

Ava laughed, low and sweet as a cello. "Try the millet with your eyes closed and think 'pot roast.'"

"Which one of these characters is Quig?"

She nodded toward a circle on the floor, five women and three men, all young, all staring at us, and a plump older fellow with a bald crown and a ponytail the color of sunflower seeds. The plump man and Ava waved to each other.

We carried our plates and Kool-Aid to the deck and all squeezed onto a single bench. Mama nibbled, like always. I believe she only ate for nourishment. Pop grimaced while chewing his brown rice and squash, but he gobbled the wheat bread with butter that Ava informed him was churned from milk freshly out of Dolly, Quig's one cow. When he had eaten all he cared to, Pop asked who wanted a drink of something more medicinal than spring water. He set his plate on the deck and walked around the hall to the Eldorado and his cooler, and returned with a Dewar's on the rocks and an Oly for me. He sat between Mama and Ava. After Ava had quit eating and put her plate on the deck, he said, "Introduce me to Quig?"

"I'll go get him." She collected dishes and carried them inside.

Pop reached for Mama's hand. "I'd like to be here when the salmon run."

"Alvaro loves salmon," Mama said.

"We're taking care of Alvaro, babe."

"Guaranteed?" she asked, smiling because Pop issued guarantees most every day.

"You bet."

I said, "Pop, should we ask Quig what all he can tell us about the Cossacks? You said the kingpin usually knows everything."

"Good call. And he's also usually shrewd enough to get to know his enemy."

Soon Ava returned, leading Quig by the hand. He was the shorter, with sawed-off legs and tiny feet. A few more pounds and twenty years, he could play Santa Claus. With his head cocked and hairy chin uplifted, he reached a miniature hand out toward Pop. "You're a private investigator, I understand?"

"Used to be. Now I'm a guy with family problems."

"So I hear." Quig pulled a bench closer to ours and sat. "Mind if I smoke?"

"It's your place."

"Really it belongs to the people. I only pay the bills."

"Why's that?"

Quig reached into his shirt for a joint as fat as a cigar and torched it with a stick match. "Why do I pay the bills?" He sucked a drag, pressed it deep, and offered the joint around. We all declined. "I predict the stock market. I send out a newsletter. People who make money off my advice pay me. I use my earnings to feed my family. In return my family gives me love."

"Some family," Pop said.

"I did the nuclear thing, and it was a bust. My blood kids want to have me committed."

Pop managed a sympathetic frown. "Jimmy Marris, you think he was a snitch?"

"I got bad vibes."

"You grow that stuff you're smoking?"

"I'm getting bad vibes again."

"To sell?"

Quig let the accusation pass. "Jimmy wanted money. He proved it by the questions he asked, the girlfriend he picked." He glanced at Ava. "And by the conversations he tuned in to. My guess, he was a poacher. This forest…" He waved in a broad circle. "In dollars and cents, there's more ganja than lumber."

"Who'd he poach from?"

"My best guess? Alvaro."

"How about your next best guess?"

He shrugged. "Excuse me, Visalia needs me to hold her hand. She's been freaking." He made a little bow and rose. Pop glanced at me.

I tapped Quig's arm. "Aren't you going to kick me out like you promised Little Vic?"

"You'll be gone by morning, right?"

"No."

He laughed and turned toward the door that led inside. I jumped up and around him and blocked it. "If you helped us out, maybe we could get rid of the Cossacks for you."

He looked both ways as if for assistance. None came. "Help how?"

"Tell us what you know about them, that's all."

He crooked his mouth and folded his arms. "I did look into their backgrounds, and found nothing remarkable, for bikers. Except, considering today's assassination attempt, you might be intrigued to know that Ronald Moore, the one they call Hound Dog, was a Marine sniper. If I think of other tidbits, I'll pass them along. Now, please stand aside." I did. He strolled into the hall.

Ava was still fuming over Quig's reference to her and money. "Talk about bad vibes," I said, "that guy's nothing but." Her chin quaked like a baby's before it bawls. I touched her shoulder and tried to sound merely curious. "You've got money?"

"Quig probably thinks I could give him a fortune if I wanted to. But I don't and I can't get any and I don't want to and even if I did, I wouldn't give it to him."

"Where does Quig think you'd get money?"

She glared with defiance. "My real dad's Paul McNees."

The sudden knowledge that Ava's dad owned at least a lumber company and a builders' and outdoor sports emporium felt to me like when the swell of a Tahoe excursion boat flipped our dingy. But Pop didn't even look surprised.

He said, "I'd make book Mister Quig takes more loot out of this place than he brings in, besides the fringe benefits." He watched Quig and the girl stroll toward the river. "Like holding Visalia's hand."

Mama yawned. Pop walked her to the A-frame. Ava and I ducked into the yurt where her sister rolled and tossed, gasping as though from nightmares and squirming as if bugs had infested the futon. Ava tucked a Mexican blanket around her and patted her cheek. After Lola jammed her head under a pillow and lay still a few minutes, Ava and I left her alone and walked to the park bench beside the playground.

Ava wasn't talking, so I said, "If I ever write an instruction book for detectives, rule number one is to ask everybody's last name. Right, Miss McNees?"

"Lots of people change their names," she said. "Maybe I should."

"Why's that?"

"Around here, McNees is like Rockefeller. People hear it, they get ideas."

"Like me, when I ask if you can get a list of buyers of 30.06 rifles, or ammunition for them, from your dad's emporium?"

"Yeah, like that," she said.

I wanted answers, to hear from Ava everything she knew about her sister and Vic. I wanted her to swear to God she wasn't in the forest with Jimmy Wednesday night. But first I needed her to drop her guard. So I gave her Knudsen's theory, that Jimmy had tried to steal from Alvaro, and my brother overreacted.

All through the story she kept shaking her head. "Jimmy used to shoplift, but we were in junior high then. Clifford, how's your hand?"

"I can wiggle my index finger," I said, and wondered why she had changed the subject.

"Can I see it?"

I reached out my bandaged hand, she cupped it in both hers and kissed two fingers before she noticed Pop coming, holding a tumbler of Scotch. He sat beside me, across from Ava.

"Mama sleeping?" I asked.

"She fell asleep praying for these hippies. She's worried about them."

"Because of the Cossacks?" Ava asked.

"Because of the devil." Pop filled his pipe, lit up, and sipped his Scotch.

Ava asked, "What do you think about the hippies?"

"Looks to me, no doubt you've got some idealists, some true believers among them. But plenty of the rest are stalling, trying to put off growing up."

"How do you know when somebody's grown up?"

"When they take care of other people instead of letting other people take care of them."

The way Ava hung on Pop's words, she might have advertised for a dad and granted him an audition. "What about Quig?" she asked. "Is he just using the kids?"

"He's a rat, the same as most of us are. The good folks, the people of constant good will, like Wendy... Well, look how the world has clobbered her."

"You're not a rat," she said.

"I am. Don't make me have to prove it."

She peered all around and whispered, "If Quig's getting rich off the harvest, do you think he might've shot Jimmy?"

"Whew." Pop glanced at me and hitched a thumb toward Ava. "This young lady's got an aptitude."

I thought of asking how Ava could live with the "family" of her boyfriend's murderer without catching a clue, but I recalled that my friend Nancy had lived with the Manson family all through their murders, and she hadn't suspected until after the arrests began.

"I'd best turn in before I break down and pour another." Pop drank the last sip from his glass. "Where are you sleeping, son?"

"In the Chevy."

"I'll be there at dawn sharp to rouse you." He checked his watch. "That's about six hours."

As Pop ambled away, Ava stood up. I walked her back to the yurt. We stood a minute outside. I stared at her eyes and imagined a kiss, before Lola's groans called her sister inside.

When I peeked in and asked to borrow a Bible, Ava was already kneeling and petting Lola's hair. She crawled to a pile of books and fetched me a King James.

After a trip to the bathhouse, I slid into the back of the Chevy and into my sleeping bag, flipped on the overhead light, and browsed every article about Phil Ochs in Alvaro's magazines. Not a word about his politics.

I opened the Bible to the verse Pop had referred me to before we climbed Sugar Hill.

The words he wanted me to read stood out as though in bold lettering—"If **anyone** kills another out of **hatred**…or **anger**…he is a **murderer**."

About one, having only dozed fitfully, I bolted up, startled by the distant noise of sharp pops. Like my first night in the forest. Only the shots sounded different. A pickup was skidding through McNees Park, terrorizing the campers, I decided. I slipped out of my bag and crept to Pop's car, hoping it was unlocked. I wanted a gun beside me before I tried again to sleep. But the Eldorado was locked.

In the Chevy, I covered my head with the sleeping bag and imagined Hound Dog creeping down Sugar Hill and then paddling across the river, one handed because his other hand held a gun aloft to keep it dry. My head was still covered when the first rap sounded and the rear window rattled. I gulped hard, choked, and thought, as soon as my head poked out of the bag, he'd pull the trigger. The bag was unzipped. I imagined I could sneak my foot out, find the latch handle to the rear door, which opened upward. Gripping the handle with my toes, I could turn it, then kick with my other foot, and lunge for the door. My foot was still groping for the door when Pop called, "Snooze you lose, Clifford."

The world remained bleary all the way into downtown Evergreen. Then Pop pulled to the curb in front of Babe's and I asked, "What about Quig?"

"You mean is he the killer?"

"Maybe not the shooter but the guy who ordered it done."

"Give me a motive."

"Jimmy was sneaking out at night and harvesting Quig's plants."

"From what you told me, the Cossacks go out harvesting everybody's plants. Why hasn't Quig killed any of them?"

"He caught Jimmy in the act. He's scared of them, but not of Jimmy."

Pop said, "Or Quig might have his eye on Ava?"

"No way," I grumbled, miffed by just the thought. "She's thirty years younger than him."

"So's Visalia," he said. "And Ava could be heir to a fortune."

We bought coffee and bear claws to go. On the sidewalk, Pop said, "Seems to me the law's kept busy exploring the north side of the river, because they're so damned sure Alvaro did the shooting, and his camp's on that side. But you said the shots might've come from the south side, right?"

"Yeah, and they were about as loud as the ones I heard last night." I told him about the shots and my guess that they came from McNees Park.

"How far is McNees Park from Quig's?"

"Say a mile and a half."

"What's that tell you?"

"Okay, where I slept Wednesday night was about four miles by the odometer off the highway. So we follow the river, on the south side. Anywhere we look, say two to six miles from the 101, we might hit the jackpot."

The first gray daylight appeared as we passed the compound of old trailers where the Mexican family lived. A small man had paused from ripping up dead corn stalks to watch us pass. Two of his *niños* played in the dirt beside him. At the next shack, the mastiff rose on its giraffe legs and uttered a sleepy bark. I watched closely, hoping for a glimpse of the dog's hermit mistress. She didn't appear. Likewise, I didn't catch any sign of life around the Van Dyke A-frame. A hundred yards past the deserted flop house we parked at the end of the road.

"Lock your door," Pop said.

"Shouldn't we take the guns along?"

"Not unless you're scared of bears. If any people turn up and object to our trespassing, we're bird watchers. And since I'm the old guy, I'll take the first trail we come across, if we come across any. You take the next one."

We crossed a shallow arroyo and tromped over spongy ground for a few minutes before we discovered a path along which mulch had gotten packed and scuffed away. Pop followed it, straight east. I tromped another minute and discovered a similar trail into the woods. I turned southeast onto the path. A spotted doe watched until I almost could've touched her, then she bolted. Dozens of birds joined in a chorus that sounded like a choir of Pentecostals singing in tongues.

Pop had played baseball as well as football. His favorite position was first base, so he'd taught himself to cheer the pitcher with a loud, two-finger whistle. Though I had heard it a thousand times, this morning I mistook it for one of the birds, maybe telling the others to shut up. But no bird I knew could shout, "Clifford."

Jogging toward the voice, hoping my sense of direction was reliable, I cut left and right between the trees, second growth redwoods with trunks of about the same girth as a sumo wrestler. As I rounded one of them, I would've crashed into Pop if he hadn't sidestepped.

"Check this out." He pointed to an ankle-high stalk.

I knelt and looked. The top was sliced clean, straight across as though done with a sharp machete, and fresh enough so lines of resin still glistened. I leaned closer and sniffed. "Weed."

"How do you know?"

"Never mind."

He turned a mock scowl on me then motioned with his hand, pointing and sweeping. "They're all over, dozens of them, tucked between every tree in this grove. Let's not cover the same ground. You take the right flank, I'll get the left."

We started ten yards west of the first plants and swept eastward, angling in until we reached each other's territory, then going out ten yards beyond the northernmost stalks, still close enough to the river so we could hear it rush and tumble. I spotted birds' eggs, a long green snake, the feathery carcass of a chicken hawk, and a chaos of human footprints.

Pop spotted the 30.06 casing. It lay in plain sight like an Easter egg a mother had put on display to make certain her kid wouldn't pass it by. It was leaning with the business end up on the base of a redwood stump, thirty yards beyond the last stalk.

I found distinct tracks. They commenced only three paces from the casing and headed west. One set was large and deep like the boot prints Agent Knudsen had showed us. The person in boots had taken long strides. The other set looked like a bare foot without toes. They were man-sized even though the strides measured half as long as those of the fellow in boots, and they only continued for a dozen steps before they turned into skid marks. At that same place, the boot prints turned, so now they were those of a man walking backward.

We followed the tracks into and out of poison ivy, stumbled into culverts hidden by mulch and over fallen branches. The tracks detoured around stumps and trees but otherwise headed straight to the river. A man in boots walking backward, dragging behind him the barefoot person without toes.

The tracks led straight to the riverbank. A nest of branches and fallen logs had collected in a small cove, as if they had come to find shelter from the rapid current. Pop stared at the river. "Suppose the killer dragged Jimmy over here and put him on a log, lashed him to it with a vine or something, and pushed him into midstream. You think he could've floated down to where he beached in, say, four hours?"

I stumbled down the slippery bank, waded knee deep alongside the nest, and used a branch to pry loose the big log nearest me. It was long and round enough to make a small canoe. I walked it out of the cove and shoved it into the midstream current. It whipped sideways, then straightened out and flashed away downriver.

Turning to the bank where Pop waited, I called out, "Less than four hours."

As a reward, we sat on the bank and rested. But my glee dissipated as I recognized that even if the clues we had found could rout Knudsen's "evidence" against Alvaro in court, coming from the prime suspect's father and brother, they wouldn't convince Willis to call in his bloodhounds. And if they managed to hunt my brother down, the odds of him standing trial were puny.

"Now what?" I asked.

"You tell me."

"Cut it out," I yelped, which shocked me. Pop didn't allow disrespect, and we didn't give it. I closed my eyes and breathed deep. "See, I can't handle you trying to make me be something I'm not. And every minute you waste on it could be the one where my brother gets killed."

He reached into a pocket for his pipe and tobacco, stuffed the pipe, and lit it with matches from Louella's Lounge. "Son," he said, "You're a man now. You're smart. But let's don't presume you're wiser than I am."

I hung my head.

"How about this," he said. "Should we pick up the casings or leave them and bring the sheriff out here? Either way, he's going to accuse us of planting them."

I said, "We could dream up a lie to get the sheriffs out here on their own. We could call in an anonymous report about the marijuana stalks."

"And they'd get around to investigating first thing after Halloween."

We decided to leave the casings where they had fallen and report them to Knudsen, who Pop said was the lawman with the fewest loyalties in Evergreen.

We walked to the Cadillac and drove to the Van Dyke home. Othello, the oldest cupid, was throwing his pocket knife, trying to stick a log. Pop reached across me to the glove box, opened it and pulled out his Instamatic. Then he leaned out the window and asked for Roy.

"My dad went shopping," Othello said.

Pop climbed out of the car. He squatted beside the boy and handed him the camera. "You know how to work one of these?"

"Sure. We got one."

"Anybody comes by, going that way…" He pointed east. "Snap a couple pictures. Don't let him see you doing it, though."

The boy aimed the camera at his brother.

Pop gave the boy a dollar and said, "Save the camera for what I asked, all right?"

Back in the car, Pop said, "Tell you what. I'm going to find Deputy Barker, have a talk. You go to church, ask your mama to pray we make the right move."

"Church?"

"Your mama needs an escort, besides Ava."

"No, if you don't want me there with you and Barker, I'll get busy questioning everybody I see, at Quig's and the jamboree, till I know who was out in the woods with Jimmy."

"Do that. After church, if I'm not back to Quig's yet. Your mama wants to go to church, and I'm not letting her out of that compound without one of us along."

"Why?"

"It's a rule of mine. Clifford, anytime I'm making dangerous enemies, I settle my family out of the way. How many times growing up did you and your brother and your mama stay over at Claire and Harry's when you didn't know why?"

"Five or six, I guess."

"Now you know why."

"Nobody's after Mama," I said. "If you're worried about the Cossacks, what good would kidnapping Mama do them?"

"I couldn't tell you."

"Pop, she hasn't gotten kidnapped in twenty-two years."

"Strange. That's exactly how long I've been going by this rule." He used a look he rarely gave, because it could sear flesh and made plants wither. "It'll please your mother."

Just because Pop was my hero, I thought, didn't give him the right to make believe I was the brains and then, at his convenience, treat me like a dull-witted kid. So I sulked until we reached the highway and he said, "Look alive, Clifford. For your brother's sake. Tell me this. Since the casings fall where the rifle's shot, why did we find them so close to the place where the murderer started dragging the body? According to the newspaper, Jimmy's murderer shot from at least fifty yards away."

Chapter Seventeen

When Pop let me off at Quig's main gate, I plodded into the compound thinking church was the last place on earth I wanted or needed to be, especially now that we had some clues about the murder.

I found Mama and Ava sitting on the steps to her cabin, dressed for church. I sat beside Mama and told them about our walk through the woods. When I explained what the tracks meant, Ava covered her eyes. "Moccasins," she said. "Not bare feet. Except for sports, Jimmy wore moccasins everywhere."

I see the booths in Babe's Cafe all occupied when Pop enters at 8:50 Sunday morning. From the way they stare at him, the patrons look like a potential lynch mob of loggers, retired loggers, and the children and wives of loggers.

Placing his hat on a stool at the end of the counter, Pop sits on the stool next to it. Then he orders coffee and eavesdrops. From the nearest booths he hears talk about the bullet meant for Phil Ochs. Two groups lament that the Mexican had missed and threaten to run the commie Big Dan Mills out of town for inviting such a traitor as Ochs to Evergreen.

Pop hasn't seen Brady Barker or asked me for a description, but the deputy isn't hard to recognize. He's the man who walks in wearing a badge and gazing around with burning eyes. Neither does Barker have difficulty recognizing Pop, who stands and offers a handshake. But either the deputy doesn't want to touch a Hickey or he suspects that even at sixty-six, Pop can grip hard enough to break fingers.

When Pop moves his hat to the counter, Barker comes over, sits on the end stool and yips at the waitress, "Coffee, Midge." He leans on the counter as though he has worked graveyard and the swing shift before it. "I've got a minute is all."

Pop drains his coffee. "Let's get to business then. You ever been sued?"

Barker only sighs.

"I can't imagine my boy is the first suspect you've brutalized," Pop says.

The deputy rises off the counter, stiffens his posture, and rotates the stool so he faces Pop squarely. Keeping his eyes on Pop, he drinks a swallow of black coffee, slaps a dollar on the counter, and stands. "See you around."

"Whoa. One other thing."

"Make it quick. I've got to round up a Mexican."

"No need. Clifford and I did a little snooping and came up with a pair of 30.06 casings as well as a trail of footprints that beat the devil out of the ones your team found."

"Where?" Barker demands. And the shift in his eyes and the hitch in his voice tell Pop that if the deputy isn't in on the murder, he knows somebody who is.

"My boy and I will keep that information to ourselves for now, until we talk to FBI Agent Knudsen. We've got an appointment." He checks his Bulova. "In an hour."

"Knudsen's flying."

"Right. I got patched through to his radio. We're meeting at the airport. Here, I'll tell you this much. What I'm going to give the Feds makes a strong case that you're gunning for Alvaro for reasons of your own."

Barker's crossed arms fall free. One hand makes a fist. His lower jaw pushes out, but he doesn't speak.

Pop stands, grabs his hat and pipe from the counter, and tosses down two dollar bills. "If I'm you, I'm rushing to tell the hunters nobody better shoot Alvaro. If they do, you're conspiring to murder. And Clifford and I, we'll invest our hearts and souls to see the charge gets made and to make it stick."

As we neared the church, I wondered how God viewed the fact that I had gone surfing on Sunday mornings and had ditched chapel all through my five years of college, disillusioned by preachers charged with embezzlement or worse or whose every third phrase expressed or implied a plea for money. I couldn't abide another admonition about serving God with tithes and offerings from a snappy dresser with razor-styled hair. And in the midst of the Vietnam war, the blind patriotism of too many Christians had made me think of most churchgoers as Pharisees.

Ava had recovered. She was holding Mama's hand. I asked, "What's your pastor like?"

"He got saved out of the drug scene in Haight Ashbury, only about six years ago. He planted our church on his own, in the back room of Burgers and Brew. He raised enough to buy this lot at the river bend, and he built the church himself, with some volunteer help. He lives all alone in the attic."

The shoulder of River Road served as the church parking lot. I pulled in at the end of a lineup of vehicles. My ball-peened Chevy looked in its element with flowered buses and old pickups with body and fenders all different colors. People here might call my many-dented wagon a work of art.

We followed a trail through a meadow and a maze of berry vines behind a girl probably younger than I was who looked about a minute from delivering her fifth child. The other four climbed on or clung to her or the hairy bear of a man at her side.

Music lilted out of the church, a redwood structure with a peaked roof I suspected didn't leave much standing room in the pastor's upstairs living quarters. Stained glass in simple patterns of crosses, Holy Spirit doves, and fish embellished the front and side walls in random locations.

Pastor Bob stood at the door. From twenty yards, I saw him peering at me. He was wiry, about thirty, had dark brown wavy hair and a clipped mustache and goatee. He wore *huaraches* of the Tijuana street vendor variety, cotton slacks, and a collarless, three-button muslin shirt. Even while he kissed and shook hands with the family of six and a half and ushered them through the double doorway, he kept one eye on me. He gave Ava a chaste hug, mostly shoulder. She introduced Mama and me. His hasty nod told me he already knew about us.

He only said hello and welcome, but in the press of his hand I read compassion, a peculiar reaction from a resident of Evergreen. During the past three days I had learned that people hold the brother, father, and mother of a killer to blame. Pastor Bob, I thought, either doubted the charges or considered us victims like Jimmy's mother and Ava. Or he was a master con man.

The church appeared to seat about a hundred. Half the spaces were occupied. Ava chose a row near the back. She slid in. Mama followed her. I sat on the aisle. Above the padded altar at which a few people knelt, four musicians performed. A gray-bearded man played guitar. Three young women, on dulcimer, autoharp, and tambourine, all wore gypsy dresses of gay colors, but their music was melancholy.

I noticed the benches were joined with pegs rather than screws. Even those upon which kids squirmed didn't creak. On the walls, the base boards and window moldings were perfectly mitered, and the flooring was laid in star-shaped designs. The windows that from outside had appeared randomly set, from this angle created an abstract design I interpreted as believers ascending a road to heaven. I gazed around, looking for curly blond hair, but saw none. I asked Ava, "Did Roy Van Dyke help build this place?"

She nodded. "How did you know?"

"We were at his house yesterday. You don't find many real craftsmen like him."

"Roy's an angel," she said. "So was Sara."

I watched Mama patting her knee in time with the music and silently mouthing the words.

"What can wash away my sins,
nothing but the blood of Jesus…"

My first clue that Pastor Bob wasn't just going to preach out of McClaren's Sermon outlines was the songs.
They sang:

"There is a fountain filled with blood…"

And they followed that with:

"There is power, power, wonder working power
in the blood of the Lamb…"

Next came:

"Grace that can pardon all my sins…"

Five songs, each about sin and redemption, before the pastor left his post at the door. Because the musicians faded one number into the next, I knew the topic and sequence were scripted.

Which could mean the pastor believed that all, some, or at least one of his flock needed lifting out of a place deep, dark, and foul. Like the guilt of doing murder, I imagined. Either Jimmy's killer was in this church or Bob had expected him to attend. I would've bet my Gibson Hummingbird.

A few minutes after the musicians completed their set and carried on with an instrumental medley of the songs they had already played, Pastor Bob left his post at the door and walked at bride-speed up the aisle. He stepped to the pulpit, excused the musicians, and sent off the children, who ran toward the doorway where two grinning women stood with picnic baskets.

The pastor stared at the doorway at least a minute before he opened his Bible to Kings 11 and read about King David catching an eyeful of Bathsheba and arranging for her husband's death. Which led him to a story from the Haight.

In a crash pad where he had stayed, a hippie who lusted after a certain girl implied to a drug dealer that the girl's lover was a snitch. Soon the lover disappeared. The lonely girl turned to heroin, and she gave the hippie what he wanted until she knocked herself cold with an overdose. Now the hippie, haunted by guilt, landed on the streets. Hunger and pneumonia drove him to repent.

The pastor directed us to Luke 15, about the prodigal son who asks his father for his inheritance, squanders it on riotous living, and after hitting bottom returns and asks for a place among his father's servants. After he read, he closed his Bible and stared another minute at the doorway before he asked, "Did the father ask if he'd been out gambling?"

"No."

"Had he robbed anybody?"

Ava said, "Now comes Isabel's part."

Isabel was balding, stoop shouldered, and corrugated with wrinkles. All along, even through the music, she hadn't let a minute pass without hollering amen or a synonym. "Maybe he did!" she yelped.

"Well then, had he raped anybody?"

Isabel flung her hands in the air. "He just mighta done that too!"

The pastor shook his head. "But at least he didn't kill anybody."

Isabel sounded outraged. "Who says he didn't?"

"You caught me there, Sister. Could be, out there in the hard world, he could've got so lowdown he did murder. We don't know. It's not recorded, is it? Strange. I mean, Jesus was telling this story. Maybe storytelling wasn't his gig. Maybe he was in a hurry to get to the moral. How about that, Isabel?"

"Go on, you."

He laughed, then gazed over our heads toward the open doorway, as though waiting for the entrance of an actor dressed as the prodigal son. "The father looks at his son and he sees through his eyes to his heart, and that's all he needs. The son's heart is broken. The father opens his arms. The end.

"Could be the son was a robber, a rapist, a murderer. But he is none of those things anymore. Now he's wearing party clothes, drinking new wine, carving the roast beef. He's born again."

"Yes he is!"

Next he concluded the story he had left behind, about the hippie whose actions had turned a sweet girl into a corpse. "Now that sinner, who was as sorry an excuse for a man as you'll ever meet, has got a darling wife, a healthy son, and a radio ministry.

"Brothers and sisters, even Judas Iscariot could have asked God to forgive, and God would've forgiven. Does anybody think Judas lost his portion of the Kingdom by turning the Lord over to his enemies? Because if you do, you've got it all wrong. He only lost his salvation when he failed to believe that the father loved him enough to redeem him. And so he hardened his heart."

Pastor Bob reinforced his point with a few more verses and a closing prayer. He didn't take a collection, didn't even mention the basket on the table by the door. The musicians returned.

On the way out, I dropped my last five dollars into the basket, the least I could give to repay Pastor Bob for what he had given me—a conviction that he believed one of his flock was a murderer.

I only had to cajole or squeeze him into telling me which one.

Outside, Ava introduced us to a dozen hippies, a rancher couple, and a spastic man who walked with a cane. I tried to etch their faces in my mind and caption the faces with names. After all but a few had left, while Ava introduced Mama and Isabel, I caught Pastor Bob alone.

"Powerful message," I said. "So is sin and redemption your favorite topic? I mean, you're so passionate about all that."

His eyes narrowed and his lips crimped sideways. "I think of the prodigal son's story as a capsule version of the whole Bible."

What would Pop do, I asked myself. I doubted he would drag the guy out back of the church and thrash him, or offer a bribe, or go to Simon and pry out of him whatever made him distrust Bob, then come back threatening to expose the dark deed. Pop had a catalog of methods to draw people's secrets out of them, I suspected. All I could think to do was fix my gaze on his eyes and lower my voice a half octave. "Something tells me you were talking to one of us in particular."

He stood rigid and still, waiting for me to go on. When I didn't, he said, "Excuse me, I'm going to the jamboree."

While we drove back to Quig's, I told Ava that one of the flock had killed Jimmy. And I told her who I thought it could be.

Her face darkened, as if her opinion of me had plunged. She said, "You missed the whole point of Bob's message, that we all are the prodigal son." But Mama, a veteran churchgoer and expert on sermons and pastors, touched my arm and nodded.

Chapter Eighteen

Evergreen's airport is a mile south of the Crossroads, directly across the 101 from a migrant camp that lies beyond a craggy burnt hill. The airstrip runs parallel to and in view of the highway. The building that serves as office and control tower looks like a three-story fruit stand. The only airplanes, three of them huddled close, are ancient crop dusters.

Pop pulls up beside Knudsen's government Fairlane. I see him smoking his pipe, glaring at the sky. He leans out of the car and knocks the bowl clean. He starts the motor and turns the car around to face the highway, for a faster getaway.

The Cessna sputters in from the east, circles once for position, drops out of the sky, and bumps and skids a landing. Agent Knudsen jumps down, goes to his car for a steno pad, and climbs into the Eldorado. Pop has the motor running. Before Knudsen gets buckled in, the car has sped out of the lot and up the highway.

"What's the rush?"

"I'm expecting a visitor."

"Mister Hickey, it occurs to me that you might be in contact with Alvaro, and for some strategic reason, are trying to get me out of the air. If that's the case, if you're running any kind of scam here, it'll come back to haunt you."

"No scam."

On Highball Trail and across the bridge he reminds Knudsen about my campout beside the river, my hearing gunshots and my estimate of their proximity. He says, "Clifford suggested we snoop the other side of the river. Because, at least as far as we know, nobody else has gone there."

"Why didn't your boy tell me about hearing the shots?"

"I'll bet you didn't ask nice."

Across the bridge and up the trail, Pop points out the residences and summarizes what we found in each. And as they near the Van Dyke home, at first he looks for Othello. Then he watches for any sign of the boys or their father. But nothing appears. And Roy's old pickup is gone.

He drives to the end of the road and parks. Instead of using the circular route by the river, he leads Knudsen along the path we had walked coming back to the car, a few paces over fifteen hundred, not far short of a mile, to the first marijuana stalks. He points to them and says, "The motive."

He leads on through the forest of stalks and stumps to the redwood under which we left the bullet casings. Ten yards away, he slows and shades his eyes to better peer into the forest beyond the crooked tree.

The big chunks of bark with which we had covered the casings lie far from the spot. Pop strides to the tree, leans the palm of his outstretched hand against it and stares at the ground, while Knudsen asks, "What are we doing here, playing charades?"

"Brady Barker's been here and gone. I told him we found the place, almost an hour ago. And a boy who lives up the trail, unless he got distracted playing mumblypeg, may have some proof for you. It was Barker," Pop assures him, although he knows somebody could've tailed us or been hiding in the forest watching. "We told nobody else."

Knudsen yawns. "Why'd you tell him?"

"As a test. He flunked." Pop marches off, looking for the boot and moccasin tracks to the river. Traces remains but the continuity of them is gone, replaced by scrapes and scuff marks, which he points out to Knudsen. Then he squats in shade, and reaches into his shirt pocket for a pill box.

A few minutes later, Knudsen sits in the Cadillac parked beside the Van Dyke home while Pop goes to the door. He sees a small paper sack with the top rolled down. He picks it up. "Hickey" is printed with block letters in red crayon.

He knocks, then unrolls the sack and looks inside. Nothing but a camera. The counter reads "4."

He takes the camera to Knudsen. "Get this developed."

The agent says, "If Brady Barker's on here, you've got me interested enough so I'll have a talk with him. But look, if it appears you're playing me, stalling for time so your Alvaro can dash across some open field while I'm on the ground, I'll find out if you've ever done any acting, even been the rear end of a horse in second grade, or if you've ever run for politics. Look, what I'm saying, if I suspect you're a liar, I'll bust you. Clear?"

At Quig's, while Mama and Ava went to change from dresses to shorts, I walked across the compound to Simon's trailer. His microbus was gone. I knocked and was still waiting when the gatekeeper Ava called Blackie stumbled out of a neighboring army tent. "Simon split," he said.

"When?"

"Yesterday noontime."

"Where to?"

"Hey, do I ask you where you're going?" He careened away toward the bathhouse.

By the time I returned to Ava's yurt, Pop was there. He looked like an old fighter in the tenth round, worn out but dogged. His face was flushed almost to purple.

He told us about his talk with Brady Barker and the trip with Knudsen to the crime scene. I gave him my theory that Pastor Bob could hand us the killer if we could find a real detective to squeeze the secret out of him. He looked at the women, for their opinion. Ava shook her head, but Mama said, "Pastor Bob can help Alvaro."

The women headed for the bathhouse. When they'd gone far enough to give us privacy, I told him who I believed shot Jimmy Marris.

Pop's look implied I was betting a long shot. "You want me to talk to this pastor. Do you think he'd still be at the church?"

"At the jamboree."

"Get your Hummingbird. Put it in the trunk. We might not come back here before you're due backstage."

I said, "Huh? I'm supposed to stop trying to rescue my brother just to play a couple songs?"

"You're on the bill." He plucked a folded schedule from his pocket, opened it, and pointed to my name. "Three-thirty."

"Yeah, with three other acts for a half hour set. They'll cover for me." I had started to raise my bum hand and to argue that I couldn't even hold a flat pick and sure couldn't manage the open tuning finger-pick style Alvaro had taught me, which was my best. But Pop's face told me he was appalled to hear his son making excuses.

With my Hummingbird in the trunk, all four of us rode in the Eldorado. Pop's spirits had lifted. "Sure," he said, "if Knudsen would've showed up on time, we might've caught Brady Barker out there. Sure, that's what I hoped, but look at what plan B gives us. Barker's on the run. He's going to slip and fall. Meantime, Agent Knudsen's at least thinking twice. I've been watching." He pointed straight up. "I haven't seen him up there. When I left him at the airport, he was standing beside his car. He could be in a darkroom already."

Ava leaned forward. "Do you think Alvaro's really nearby, like Wendy said?"

Pop liked most people, admired many, loved several, trusted the intentions of a very few, confided in his family, but knew better than to count on anybody. Ava had charmed him, but she wasn't family. So he wouldn't give her anything she could use to endanger his son. He reached for Mama, eased her closer, and kissed her cheek. "Alvaro could be anywhere."

An hour after the jamboree gates opened at ten, the attendance was half of yesterday's, before the gunshot. If Hound Dog or whoever shot at Phil Ochs meant to bankrupt Big Dan's jamboree, he'd succeeded as well as a rainmaker could have. Before, hoards of children had roamed around on their own. Today, the only small kids I noticed were junior hippies from one of the communes whose folks didn't have the option of an early retreat from Evergreen.

The schedule board announced that Hoyt Axton would appear on the main stage at noon. I had jammed with Hoyt after hours at the Candy Company, my favorite San Diego coffee house. Now, Malvina Reynolds, a favorite of mine for her wise and witty lyrics, was onstage singing:

> "And the children go to summer camp
> and then to the university
> where they all get put in boxes
> and they all come out the same.
> Little boxes on the hillside,
> Little boxes made of ticky-tacky…"

We passed moping vendors in the concession aisle. As we started up a knoll, a girl came running to Ava. She was squat and freckled and had blue eyes as brilliant as Pop's. "Gawd, Ava, I haven't seen you all summer, since biology. Jeff's waiting for me, gotta hurry. But listen. That Mexican that killed Jimmy. A few weeks ago, he came into the bank. He looked kinda weird, like he was going to rob me or something. He came right to my window and cashed this check on some Beverly Hills bank, from some record company. Hog Farm Records or something like that. I was gonna tell the cops, but I saw you here first and, you know…" She glanced down the hill and must've thought her boyfriend looked miffed. "Call me." She turned and ran to him.

I told Pop, "Alvaro would've called us about any record deal he'd made. Or even any studio work he'd done. I think."

Now I felt sure. Ochs had arranged for a record company to pay my brother for something. Maybe to recruit militant farmworkers into the anti-war movement. I was about to tell Pop when Ava spotted Pastor Bob.

He was talking to a shirtless, vanilla white kid with a guitar strapped on his back. As we approached, the pastor said, "It might feel like the Holy Spirit to you, but is it really? I mean, how're you going to know what the Holy Sprit's like unless you meet him at least once when you're not stoned?"

The kid used our presence to cover his escape. The pastor laid a hand on Ava's shoulder and asked if we had come to pass out tracts, but his shifty eyes proved he knew better. Ava held his arm and introduced Pop while we all climbed a knoll. Pop motioned to a patch of thick grass as close to private as any available. We sat. Pop glanced at me. I shook my head.

Pop didn't sit well on the ground. His seasons playing fullback and sixty-six years of living had wracked his knees. He shifted his legs and wiped his brow with the bandana handkerchief he carried, while the pastor watched and waited, rubbing the spine of the Bible on his lap as though working air bubbles out of the glue.

"So…" Pop gazed around and all at once attacked the man with a stare. "Why are you protecting the killer?"

Ava covered her mouth with pretty fingers.

Pastor Bob squinted as though to look at the sun, though it was straight overhead. He stood, nodded to Mama, and started down the hill, but he didn't make three steps before Pop caught up and led him toward the river.

We watched Pop speak briefly and the pastor give one-word answers. A few such exchanges passed before the pastor handed over his Bible. Pop leafed through it, spent a minute reading, shook his head, and looked up another passage. The fourth try he found the right one.

Pastor Bob appeared to read the passage before he slammed his Bible shut. He stared at Pop long and hard. Then he wheeled and marched to the river at the sandy beach beside the shallows, where today only a few hippie kids splashed. Gripping the Bible under his arm, he squatted at the water's edge and picked up a stone. Like a catcher, he sprang up and threw the rock, into the woods across the river.

He strode back to Pop and spoke a few words, then tromped off toward the gate and parking lot. When Pop returned to us, Ava's hands were clasped together beneath her chin, with thumbs dug into her throat. "He told you who killed Jimmy?"

"Told us meet him at the church in an hour is all."

"What verse did you show him?"

"Way up front. Leviticus, um, five."

"What's it say?" I asked. Pop winked at me.

From the way Ava stared at him, I suspected that whereas she had previously only considered Pop a remarkable guy, now she was in danger of confusing him with God.

The instant we climbed into the Eldorado, she grabbed her big purse and fished out her Bible. She found the passage and read it aloud. "If a person sins because he does not speak up when he hears a public charge to testify regarding something he has seen or learned about, he will be held responsible."

◇◇◇

On his way back to Quig's from the meeting with Knudsen, Pop had gone to the jail and asked to see the sheriff, meaning to report that Brady Barker had swept away tracks and stolen evidence. But the sheriff was gone, and without his radio, the desk officer claimed.

With me, Mama, and Ava along, Pop made a second visit to the jail. He went in alone. When he came out, the purplish tint of his face had darkened. "Willis is still out of touch," he said. He crooked a finger at me. I climbed out and followed him a few steps up the block. "And now," he said, "they're adding attempted murder to Alvaro's alleged crimes. The man says they found the shell that missed Ochs. Looks like it could've come from a 30.06."

I didn't tell him what I'd deduced about Alvaro and Ochs. First, I wanted at least a guess about how that theory connected to the death of Jimmy Marris.

We crossed the street to Foster's and picked up a sack full of burgers, which we ate on the way back to Quig's. Between bites,

I said, "We should find Knudsen. Maybe he's got the pictures developed."

"If he has," Pop said, "and it's got a snapshot of Barker, he'll tell Willis. But is that going to make the sheriff pull his dogs off Alvaro?"

Ava said, "Not if they say Alvaro shot at Phil Ochs."

I wadded the remaining half of my hamburger, stuffed it into the sack it came in, and smashed it between my knee and my good hand.

At Quig's, outside the yurt, Ava and Pop had their first spat. A rule he lived by held that you didn't take women into rowdy bars, battlefronts, or anyplace where guys shoot each other.

Ava's chest heaved, an inspiring sight. "For three days I've helped you guys and now I'm too frail to go with you?"

Pop shook his head and lit his pipe. "Too valuable."

"He's *my* pastor," she argued, but Pop only blew a kiss at Mama and walked toward the Cadillac.

"I'm the only one of us who even *knew* Jimmy," she yelped.

"Let's go, Son." Pop climbed into the car.

Ava threw her hands in the air and turned to Mama.

"Wendy, this isn't fair."

For her sons, Mama had fought dogs, neighbors, teachers, and devils. But never had she taken sides against Pop. "I don't want to go," she said. "Please stay with me, Ava."

Like Pop, I had played first base in high school and college. In championships, and when games depended on my bat or glove, I had learned how adrenaline works. So for other frightful or challenging times, I was prepared. But never, not even when I had gone to waylay Hound Dog, had adrenaline pumped so hard as on the drive to meet Pastor Bob. Thinking about Simon's opinion of the man, I feared we were on our way to an ambush. My eyes burned. Sweat streamed off my scalp and circled my ears. When a slow caravan of campers and trailers turning west out of McNees Park stalled us, I would've yelled and blasted the horn, had I been driving.

When we arrived at the church, Pastor Bob was already waiting, perched on the hood of a dusty '64 Falcon Ranchero. He jumped down and approached Pop's window. His eyes were slits, his jaw looked swollen. His voice sounded muffled. "Follow me."

We tailed him at a distance because his Falcon spewed green fumes. Through Evergreen and down the highway, the pickup chugged so slowly and with such a smell, Pop asked if I thought the pastor had converted it to run on chicken manure. I said, "Maybe so, but don't you think he's also stalling, that he snuck a call to the killer and promised him time?"

"If he was going to do that," Pop said, "why not just lie to us?"

My eyelids began to twitch, and instead of seeing the road, I imagined bullets zinging past our heads. "I'm feeling weird, though," I said. "Like I'm having a premonition, and this guy's leading us into a trap. I haven't seen a Cossack all morning."

Outside the Crossroads, a logger was replacing his pickup's slashed tires. When the Falcon turned onto Highball Trail, Pop said, "Looks like you might've solved the mystery, which would make you the detective in the family." And the little crooked smile he gave me told a big story. He wasn't joking or trying to boost my confidence. He was proud of me.

"But suppose I'm wrong and Bob's the murderer. I mean, pastors go bad. Maybe not as often as lawyers do. But Simon told me Bob's just a con, fleecing the sheep. Say Jimmy Marris found out Bob was the last escapee from Alcatraz. He laid low in the Haight, where Simon knew him, but his past won't leave him be. So now and then he's got to bump off somebody."

Pop chucked my arm. "By Jove, Holmes, I think you're on to something."

When I was a boy and reading Sherlock Holmes, Pop used to joke with me, like he'd just done, except back then he called me Watson.

Because I felt more at ease while imagining, I dreamed up scenarios. "The murderer could be the owner of the mastiff, or the cousins of a myopic cherry picker who can't afford glasses and lives in a camp like Alvaro's, and he was out poaching and thought he was shooting at a buck, but it turned out to be Jimmy Marris. Or the killer might be some logger out to rid the world of communists." When the Falcon made the turn to cross the bridge that led to South Highball Trail, I reached under the seat for the holstered gun.

Across the bridge, the Falcon turned left. The Mexican kids were on their porch, gobbling tortillas and drinking out of paper cups. Two of them waved to the pastor. He didn't wave back.

A mile east, the mastiff trotted on shaky legs from its porch to the roadside and barked so feebly I feared it was in the last hours of starvation.

The Falcon stopped beside a post, which I guessed marked the Van Dyke property line. A minute passed. Then the pastor drove on. He parked near the chicken coop. I grabbed the handle of the gun on the seat beside me. As we pulled in beside the Falcon, I lifted the holster to strap it on.

Pop touched my leg and shook his head. I didn't argue. He would win. He might ask how I'd feel if a gunfight started and among the casualties was Othello, Oedipus, or Ophelia.

Roy's Dodge pickup wasn't in sight. Nobody was outside where I expected to find anyone except the infirm or hung over on that fragrant, silver-blue day. Although, since we left the jamboree, the heat had risen to wicked. Sweat dripped off my brows and burned my eyes. Still I felt as if my teeth were about to chatter.

Pop reached under his seat. As we climbed out of the Cadillac, he crammed his .38 under the waistband of his trousers.

Without looking our way, Pastor Bob walked to the house. He knocked. Othello flung open the screen door, then vanished. The pastor's head leaned into the dark house before the rest of him followed. I was only inches behind Pop. As he stepped inside, I saw his right arm bend into position to grab for the gun.

Chapter Nineteen

The only light entered through the door. The stained glass windows, the picture window facing the forest, and the skylight were shuttered or shaded. Othello and his brother and sister were in the loft, leaning over the edge and looking ready to pounce on us.

Before I saw the face of the man in the craftsman chair facing us, I spotted the revolver on his lap. His hand was in ready position. He seemed to be staring at the gun, his head bent and covered by an old Brooklyn Dodgers cap, his golden curls tied back in a ponytail.

"Sit," he said.

Pop took the rough-hewn chair by the woodstove, leaving Bob and me the sofa bench. I sat on the outside, so the pastor was between us. Pop hitched his thumbs under his belt, his right hand an inch from his pistol. "My son's out there running from guys who think he's a *desperado*. Let's don't waste time on polite. You just tell your story."

"Yeah." Roy kept his right hand on the gun and used his left to move his cap back. Then we could see his whole face. It looked so gray and mystified, I wondered if he had taken poison. He spoke like a dreamer. "I was camped out, keeping watch, because Othello was fishing the river last...Monday, three days after Sara, and he saw five Cossacks."

"Six," the boy yipped.

"Okay, six of them. He tagged behind and watched. They parked their hogs on one of the trails that end at Old Crow Creek, and they crossed it on a log bridge, and went straight to my plants, like they knew exactly where to look.

"Those plants were…You see, we had our eye on a sea-view lot on a hill across Highway One, north of Shelter Cove. We wanted to build a spec house. Passive solar. With the income, I could build another house. And so on. It wasn't like I meant to grow weed for a career." He snatched off his cap and squeezed it like an exercise ball. "No way was I going to let the Cossacks rob us. They already killed Sara.

"Wednesday night, Pedro from down the road, he watched my kids and I went out to guard my plants. But Alvaro must've got lonely and hiked over to visit. He got to playing my violin, and told Pedro he could go home if he wanted, and he'd stay over.

"I was fast asleep in my bag when something woke me. I heard a man's voice, way out there past my plants. I yelled something like 'Get out of my life!'

"I stood still and listened, until I heard a shot and saw a little flash, and a bullet came whizzing by me. On instinct, I fired at the flash. Or maybe I wanted to kill somebody, I don't know. A second later, boom, and this time not just a warning. It might've got me except I had jumped behind a tree. But I saw the second flash too. I lifted my rifle. Boom. Then not a sound.

"I waited and listened. You know, for feet slapping while they ran away. But nothing. They were waiting me out, thinking I'd come look around, I guess. So I didn't. Not until daybreak. By then…I didn't see bodies or even any blood. And my plants were okay. I thought everything was okay. So I went home. And Alvaro was there. I told him what happened, and I crashed. That's all."

"And Alvaro took your gun," I said.

"It was his gun. He'd loaned it to me. I didn't own a rifle. Just this." He patted the barrel of the gun on his lap. "When I heard about Jimmy, and Alvaro running, I knew. But…" He raised the revolver and slipped his finger into the trigger housing. "No way I give myself up and go to prison and leave my kids to grow up in Yorba Linda with Sara's folks or in Brentwood with mine. No way do I let my kids go back to the American sell-out nightmare. No way." He stared at the ground.

I wondered, and still do, what all he'd lived with that sent him on a quest to find or make a different world for his kids. Maybe horrors. Or maybe he was raised a spoiled brat and couldn't abide growing up.

His hand fell limp. The gun pointed down. A minute passed before he broke from his trance and glared at us, all the handsome gone, his face contorted as if we had just brought the news about Sara's crash. He shuddered so hard it looked like a seizure. "Are you going to try and stop us?"

Pop lifted the pipe and tobacco from his shirt pocket, careful not to spook Roy into thinking he would pull a gun. He filled and lit the pipe. "Clifford, should we go to the law?"

"Law," Roy growled. "Since we moved up here, a year ago April, just in this county five guys are dead, either shot poaching or shot by poachers. Three go down as hunting accidents, the others go unsolved." With ratcheting gasps, he filled his lungs. "Two weeks ago tomorrow, a drunk they call Hound Dog killed our Sara."

Oedipus wailed. His sister scolded, "No, Daddy said no."

Roy declared, "The law's a fiction, man." He fixed his gaze on the pastor.

Pop shifted his pipe into his left hand, and used his right to point at Pastor Bob and Roy in turn. "Good thing you believe in God, probably got saved or whatever they call it. I mean, so your salvation's secure, even if you kill a boy."

The pastor had shifted and leaned toward Pop as though anticipating a wise pronouncement.

"What I'm wondering," Pop said, "the boy you kill, suppose he never made any magic profession of faith. What do you think, is Jimmy Marris in heaven?"

While Pop stared at him, Roy's mouth crimped into a jagged line. Pop turned his stare on the pastor, who gazed upward as though awaiting the answer to a question he couldn't field on his own.

◇◇◇

When Pop stood, so did I. He shifted one eye to the loft and said, "Othello, did you get the pictures I asked you for?"

"Our dad took them," the boy said.

Pop waved me around and ahead of him. I sidestepped to the door, watching Roy's gun. Once I was outside, Pop followed me, walking backward. Then he turned and we hustled to the car, glancing over our shoulders.

"I'll hold the shotgun," I said.

"What for?"

"Aren't we going to take him in?"

"Or we can go talk it over. What do you say?"

I was thinking, Roy Van Dyke would sacrifice my brother to keep his kids from spending a few years with their grandparents. For that, I couldn't even start to forgive him. But I wasn't ready to consider myself wiser than Pop, even if he was getting senile. I climbed into the Cadillac. Pop drove, stiff and mute and scowling.

Sunday lunch at the Crossroads was barbecue on the deck that overlooked the river. The parking lot was crammed with pickups, cars, and a semi-tractor. No Harleys. I guessed the Cossacks were off striking fear into another town or home mending their socks since today, at the Crossroads, the loggers would have them severely outnumbered.

Every third man in the bar wore a McNees T-shirt with the chain-sawing beaver. The patrons chomped ribs, chugged brew, swapped jokes and sports predictions, played checkers or rummy or stuffed quarters into the jukebox. We stood at the bar.

While we waited for Cherry, and while Elvis crooned "All Shook Up," I asked, "Are we going to phone Willis?"

"In a while."

"Pop, they're not going to call off the bloodhounds until they catch Roy and he confesses."

"Suppose Willis goes there and Roy says, 'Those Hickeys are liars.' Then what?"

"That pastor will set them straight. Unless Roy already killed the pastor."

Cherry stood over us. "Somebody killed a pastor?"

Pop shook his head. "Dewar's on the rocks and…"

"Same," I said. "Make it a triple."

She flashed us her toothy smile. Pop watched her drift down the bar. "Nice gal."

"She did me a big favor."

He studied me a moment. "I hope you didn't make her help you torture Hound Dog."

"I didn't torture anybody."

"Anyway, she's a doll. No so much compared to Ava but—"

"Pop, we're here talking about girls when some deputized redneck might be shooting Alvaro dead, right now."

"You think your brother is still around Evergreen? Why's that?"

"Because," I said, "as soon as he got out of immediate danger, he would've got us a message somehow."

He reached for an ash tray, tapped his pipe clean and refilled it, then laid it on the bar as he assumed the expression that prefaced every lecture he had given me. "Clifford, a fellow ought to look out for his own. But his own's not the only people he ought to look out for. The world's full of people, and your mama would say that if we saw them through God's eyes, they'd all look just about as precious."

"You mean Othello and Oedipus and Ophelia."

"And Roy." He lit up, fed his lungs, then motioned a finger at the barmaid. When she came, he asked, "Who owns this place?"

"Frank Hoppe."

"He around?"

She frowned as though Pop had delivered bad news. "Did I do something?"

"Nope. Would you bring Mister Hoppe here, please?"

She nodded and shot glances back at us while she filled a couple orders and shimmied her way between tables.

We finished our drinks. Pop smoked. The neon waterfall on the Hamms sign popped and sizzled. I thought, What good's it to solve a murder if you've got no evidence and you let the murderer get away?

Hoppe had a black beard. He wore an apron and a cook's tall hat. He walked with a limp that made his shoulder bob. He removed his sunglasses and wrinkled his nose. "Need somethin'?"

Pop stared at him. The man reached for a tap lever and held it as though for balance. "Come on, partner, I got ribs burning."

"A week or two ago, Hound Dog walked out of here drunk and climbed on his motorcycle and killed a fine little lady."

Hoppe leaned back and gave us a look that meant, Not this again. "No, partner. What he did was get in the way of a hippie gal who was driving stoned."

Pop shrugged. "Tell me, who was tending bar that day?"

The man leaned so close he could've kissed Pop on the nose. "Who are you?"

"Think of me as Sara's ghost. Who was tending bar?"

"Me, partner. I was. I served the Dog, but I'm not serving you, 'cause you're outta here."

Pop raised a finger. "My advice is, cut your losses and close the place down, sell your license before you lose it."

"Fella, you're too damn old to be with the Alcohol Bureau."

"That's a fact, but the guys that'll stop by here every other night aren't, and they're pals of mine, and the first minor gets a sip, the first logger stumbles on the way to his pickup, these young guys will rip your license into confetti." Pop tapped out his pipe, in foxtrot rhythm. "Go baste your ribs."

By now, Hoppe had leaned back away from Pop and lifted his hands off the bar. He sneered, made a poof sound, and limped away. Pop caught Cherry's eye and waved her over. She kept her distance, her head cocked with suspicion.

Pop asked, "Think you might like to work at Harry's Casino, South Lake Tahoe?"

She made her hands into spiders, tapped her fingers together and moved her stare back and forth between Pop and me. "You guys aren't pimps or something are you?"

Pop grinned. "We're on the level. So if you find yourself unemployed or ready for a change, think about it." He reached for his wallet. Along with a ten dollar bill, he handed her a business card.

◇◇◇

When Pop drove past the jail, I said, "Whoa!"

"What?" he said.

"We're not going to Willis?"

"You tell me to, we sure can."

All the way to Quig's I tried to decipher reasons for Pop's behavior, allowing the sheriffs to keep hunting Alvaro when we had at least a chance to stop them. The only reasons I could imagine implied Pop was truly getting soft in the head or heart.

We found Mama and Ava in shorts, sunning their legs, sitting on a blanket on the riverbank. Pop squatted beside Mama. "We found the killer."

Mama lunged and hugged him. He lost his balance and plopped onto the sandy dirt.

"Now we'll find Alvaro," Mama said.

I sat in the dirt beside Ava, who had pulled up her downy legs and was crushing them to her breast and wincing as if she feared the revelation. "Who did it?"

"Roy Van Dyke."

Ava closed her eyes. I began the story, but the instant I paused to breathe, Pop took over. He gave the details just as I remembered until the part where we left and drove to the Crossroads. Instead of the truth, he implied that we came straight from Roy's to Quig's, and that we would've brought Roy in except he was holding a pistol and to challenge him would be too risky, since a gunfight might've left us with dead kids and a dead preacher.

"Why did he tell you everything?" Ava asked. "I mean if he wasn't going to give up."

I offered, "The pastor might've told him confessing to us would buy him points with God."

Pop knew the reason Roy gave us his story. But he wasn't yet ready to let us in. He said, "And we didn't go straight to Willis because he's sure to think we're lying to run interference for Alvaro. But…" He fixed his gaze on Ava. "…if you went along and told him the story, made out you were with us at Roy's place, Willis has got to believe Jimmy's girl. Not a chance you're going to side with the murderer."

I expected her to spend a while with her conscience, maybe go for a walk beside the river. But she nodded and stood. We hustled to the car. We had opened our doors when Pop asked her, "How about we stop by Jimmy's mother's place, ask her to join us at the jail?"

"I'm supposed to lie to her too?"

"If you can see fit."

"The sheriff's out," a weary desk officer told us.

"Bring him in," Pop said. "We found the murderer."

"Yeah, right," the officer said, but his arrowhead nose wrinkled, and he moved to his right and pushed buttons on a radio on a shelf under the counter.

Accompanied by crackles, Willis grumbled, "Come on."

"Those Hickeys are here, and so's Jimmy's girlfriend. They want you to come in so they can hand you the murderer."

Even the crackling radio fell silent. Then Willis said, "I'll bite. Don't offer them coffee."

Delene Marris arrived, in shorts and a white blouse her red bra showed through, carrying an odor of cigarettes and misery and greeting me with a venomous look. Ava introduced her to Pop and Mama. She turned the same look on them.

A cruiser pulled up in front of the police station door. Willis climbed out, stretched, and walked in slowly with Barker at his heels. He tossed a glance over his shoulder as though warning the deputy to keep his distance from us. Without formality, he shooed us ahead of him and into the interrogation room.

Four of us sat. Barker and I stood at opposite ends of the room. I managed not to snarl. He popped his knuckles.

Ava told the story just like Pop had, implying that she was at the scene without saying so. While she spoke, Barker mumbled and cussed under his breath until his sister yelped, "Shut your mouth, Brady."

Ava said, "But Jimmy wasn't out there poaching. I don't know why he was there, but he wasn't stealing Roy Van Dyke's plants."

Barker aimed a finger at her. "Jimmy's not hardly even cold and you already jumped the fence." He threw his arms up like a basketball defender and held them up while his white-hot eyes swept from Pop to Ava, from her to Willis and Delene. "All they're doing is blowing a smokescreen, thinking we'll call in the hunters, so the Mex can escape."

The sheriff gave a diffident nod. "I wanta see this Roy."

◇◇◇

All the way to the Crossroads, I waited for Pop to pull over at a gift shop and ask the women to get out and wait. But he didn't. Once again, I wondered if his mind was slipping away.

So I asked, "We aren't taking the women, are we?"

Ava said, "Hush, Clifford."

"They'll be all right," Pop said, and Mama gave me a look as if she knew something I didn't.

When we turned onto Highball Trail, Agent Knudsen's Fairlane pulled out of the Crossroads parking lot and fell in behind us. Willis and Barker were in the lead. Behind it came another sheriff's cruiser that had joined us at the junction of Manhattan and 101. We came next, in the Eldorado. I rode shotgun. Jimmy's mother sat in back between Mama and Ava. Mama looked at peace, somewhat dreamy. Ava, all the way from the jail to the Crossroads, had rested her head on Delene's shoulder as though sending a message: If you still want to be a mom, you can be mine. Along the bumpy road and across the bridge, they held hands.

I sat hoping that the moment we pulled up at the Van Dyke place, Agent Knudsen would leap from his car, weapon drawn, and command Brady Barker to drop and surrender.

From a half mile away, I saw that Roy and Pastor Bob's pickups were gone. Even so, the snakes in my belly started chomping.

Our cars skidded in and formed a blockade line in front of the A-frame. Before anybody else had touched the ground, Barker was halfway to the door. I imagined him rushing the place, bursting in to silence Roy with bullets.

The sheriff marched over to us, grabbed hold of the car door while Ava was halfway out. "You ladies stay the hell in the car."

Willis and Agent Knudsen walked together toward the A-frame. By now, Barker was at the door, his gun drawn and up beside his ear. He yelled, "Sheriffs," and checked the knob with his free hand. Locked. He peered through the front window and turned with a sneer for Pop and me. "Doesn't look vacated."

Knudsen scratched his neck and peered over his nose at the deputy. His expression looked more like a psychologist's than a cop's. I felt sure he'd gotten the photos developed.

"Van Dyke must be at the jamboree with the rest of the hippies," Barker said, "'cause he didn't shoot Jimmy, and he never talked to these liars."

"Are we going in there?" Knudsen asked, pointing at the door.

Willis didn't answer, only scratched his lip with his teeth. He walked off the porch and back to his cruiser, where he picked up the radio handset. "Horst, call everybody, tell 'em to stop any forty-something Dodge pickups. Suspect is Roy Van Dyke. Late twenties. Blond. Slender. Could be three kids with him. He's armed. Might've shot Jimmy Marris….Yeah."

Pop tapped Knudsen's shoulder. "Did you develop the snapshots?"

"I did," Knudsen said. "A picture of each of three kids and one of a wall."

After Willis replaced the radio handset, he gazed at Barker, who stood kicking dirt. The sheriff scratched his lip again, as though trying to decide something urgent, before he turned and walked back to us. "Hickey, I don't suppose you coulda helped out, grabbed Van Dyke and brought him in. I expect you forgot how to do that part of police work."

Pop looked up and down the road. "We didn't think you'd approve, Sheriff. When you were deputizing everybody else in town, you passed us by."

"Yeah, well things woulda gone better for your Mexican boy, 'cause at least till we talk face to face with Van Dyke, Alvaro's our man."

As Willis turned toward his car, Pop said, "Find the pastor. He'll give you the same story we gave you."

"Hickey," the sheriff said, "we got a whole town to protect, and a few thousand tourists. You want me to talk to this pastor, you bring him to me."

Barker shuffled to the rear door of the Cadillac. "Get out, Delene," he yipped. "You're coming with us." But his sister stayed put between Ava and Mama. After scuffing his feet like a bull, Barker stomped to the cruiser and climbed in beside the sheriff.

Knudsen led the caravan back to the highway. He turned south, toward the airport. Willis switched his siren on and zoomed toward Evergreen. We lagged behind. On Manhattan Avenue, we saw Willis going into his office while his cruiser whipped a U-turn and sped east toward River Road.

We fell behind again but kept the cruiser in sight. As it passed the jamboree, Pop pulled to the side of the road by the entrance. "He's going to the church. My son and I will keep him company, if you gals would kindly go in here and tell whoever needs to know that Clifford will return in time for his set. And keep an eye out for Pastor Bob."

"What if Barker's going to kill Pastor Bob?" I said.

"You know Barker better than I do. Maybe he thinks Roy's going to hole up in the church, claim asylum, or wait until dark to make his getaway."

We sped past Quig's and McNees Park, which looked deserted, and skidded onto the dirt shoulder about fifty yards from the church. Barker was already out of his cruiser and half way across the meadow.

The musicians who had performed that morning stood outside the locked sanctuary. We kept our distance, about twenty yards, close enough to hear the woman holding the tambourine call out to Barker, "Is Pastor okay?"

Barker didn't speak until he reached the musicians. "Why do you ask?"

"He's supposed to be here, and he's not. When we saw you, we got worried."

"Nobody seen him?"

They all shook their heads or said no.

"Where's he live?"

The tambourine player pointed to the sanctuary. The guitarist said, "Upstairs."

"He shows up, tell him to call me." Barker handed each of the musicians a business card. Then he wheeled and strode past us wearing a look I hadn't seen on him before. It was almost serene, which spooked me more than his blazing eyes ever had.

Chapter Twenty

At the jamboree, the concessions were closing. Six or seven hundred people lounged on grass or blankets in front of the main stage. All that remained of the thousands who had trekked to Evergreen.

Ava, Mama, Delene Marris, and Steph the waitress were together on a Mexican blanket at the outer edge of the crowd. Mama saw us first. She waved and nudged Ava, who then convinced some hippies around her to get chummier and make a place for us. Pop stayed back where he wouldn't have to sit on the ground and where he could stand without blocking anyone's view and smoke his pipe without fouling as many people's air.

While I taped my hand, Ava finished telling Steph the true story of Jimmy's death, all except for the last piece of the mystery. She didn't know that piece.

I didn't tell her my guess about who had turned honest Jimmy into a marijuana poacher, accompanied him to the woods, and maybe shot at Roy Van Dyke. Pop always said guesses were dangerous, too easily confused with fact. Besides, I was occupied with pre-show jitters.

Ava told Steph, "We don't know if the person who took Jimmy into the woods and the one who dragged him to the river were the same or two different people."

"Cossacks," Steph declared.

This was Sunday, Woody Guthrie day. The gospel singers called Faith, Hope, Charity, and Mavis clapped, stomped, and sang:

"This Land is Your Land,
this land is my land,
from California
to the New York island
from the redwood forest…"

I asked for and got good luck kisses from both Ava and Mama. Pop gave me a thumbs-up. I picked up my guitar case and walked around the crowd to backstage.

The stage manager had decided to send us out in the order we showed up, which placed me last. He and the other musicians stared at my hand but didn't ask or commiserate. They might've supposed I was some nut who thought he could play better with his index finger and thumb taped together and a flat pick wedged between them.

In the twenty or so minutes before I went on, I didn't worry about Alvaro. Instead, I imagined forgetting every word of my songs or my bandage unraveling and getting stuck between the strings.

The stage manager pointed at me. I froze. He came over and pinched my arm. "You're on, Hickey."

I considered bolting out of there but decided I would rather die than run. On my way out front, I managed not to trip over cords.

The crowd looked three times the size it had when I was part of it. But as soon as I found and focused on Mama's loving eyes, I saw no reason to fear anything.

I teared up while I told the crowd it was my brother who wrote and had lived my first song, a ballad about the day his platoon's rotation would've put him on point except the previous day shrapnel wounded him. His best *amigo* took his place and got shredded by machine gun fire.

I sang:

We called him Chattanooga,
we called him Elmer Fudd,
but his real name was Ernie Dupree…"

No doubt most of the crowd had heard about Alvaro killing Jimmy Marris and shooting at Phil Ochs. At the end, when they clapped loud and hooted, I didn't know if it was for my performance or out of pity.

My next and last number was a favorite of Mama's, which my brother and I used to bellow around campfires mariachi style.

"De la Sierra Morena
Cielito lindo vienen bajando.
Un par de los ojitos negros
Cielito lindo de contrabando
ay yi yi yi
canta y no llores…"

While I sang, I felt Alvaro watching me.

I was backstage packing my Hummingbird when Big Dan Mills lifted his guitar overhead like a weapon and roared, "Everybody have a good time?" The crowd whooped and whistled. "Coming back next year?" The cheers multiplied.

"All right!" Dan shouted. Then, while I ripped the tape off my fingers and walked around the crowd to my folks, he sang:

"California is a Garden of Eden,
a paradise to live in or see,
but believe it or not, you won't find it so hot
if you ain't got the Do-Re-Mi."

When I reached my folks, Mama clung to my good hand. All the last performers but me, and a dozen more who'd played earlier, had gathered on stage alongside Big Dan. One of them gazed into the sky. Others joined her. Soon all of us stared at

Agent Knudsen's Cessna, which came from southwest as though tracing the route of Whiskey River. Passing over the sun, it circled the jamboree twice before it climbed toward the mountains.

We took Delene Marris home and went back to Quig's. Mama and Ava were freshening up, Pop and I were sitting beside the river waiting for them, when he told me they would leave Evergreen tomorrow morning.

"What about Alvaro?" I demanded.

"Kids grow up. Decide their own lives. If your brother chose to throw in his lot with a killer, all we can do is trust him, hope, and count on your mama's prayers."

"Whoa," I said. "Alvaro threw in with a killer?"

"I guess you didn't see the X and the date on the wall above the sofa bench in Roy's A-frame."

"So Alvaro helped him do something and Roy let him scratch his nickname on the wall to commemorate. So what?"

"The date was August twenty-six, nineteen and seventy two." He let the number sink in before he said, "Yeah. Yesterday."

"So…it was a message to us? Meaning he was going to help the Van Dykes escape."

Pop only nodded.

"And that's why Van Dyke snapped a picture of the wall."

"You bet it is."

"And it's why, when we went back with the sheriffs, you let the women ride along. You knew they'd be gone already. Why didn't you tell me?"

"I should've."

"Yeah, you should have trusted me like you've been pretending to." Ashamed, worried, and bitter, I stood and walked alone upstream.

Chapter Twenty-one

The sun is dropping below the trees and the forest beginning to darken when Agent Knudsen in his Ford meets Willis and Barker at the Van Dyke place. The sheriff has brought a search warrant. He knocks. I see Barker kicking the door near the knob. It flies, smacks the wall, and knocks down a watercolor of Ophelia in a peasant dress with a dozen tiny bows in her curly hair.

Searching mostly for weapons, ammunition, drugs, paraphernalia, notes or anything written, they empty the kitchen drawers, pull them out and stick their heads into the cabinet framing. Knudsen gets so impressed by the carpentry, he'll tell me later, "If we catch up with this guy, I may go his bail and have him build me a house."

From the walls they remove dozens of Sara Van Dyke's sketches and watercolor portraits. They roll aside the hand-loomed rugs and the futons in the bedroom and loft so they can check beneath for anything stashed there or for secret compartments. All they find that might incriminate Roy is on the porch in a box of garden supplies—a sack labeled Crook Neck Squash half full of marijuana seeds.

Willis finds a letter written to somebody named Bob. In it, Roy admits that if he didn't have his kids to look out for, he would go gunning for Hound Dog. On top of a heap of other evidence, the letter could certify that Roy's frame of mind was murderous enough to make him shoot at poachers, thinking they were Cossacks. But alone it means zero.

Knudsen remarks, "Van Dyke could've gone to hide out with this guy." He waves the letter. "You men know anybody named Bob? Yeah, okay, everybody knows a Bob or two, but the one I'm talking about might be what—a hippie, or what?"

"How about a pastor?" Willis says.

Though at first the place hadn't looked deserted, even Barker finally agrees the occupants have fled. In the bathroom they find no tooth brushes or paste, razor, aspirins, or ointments. Hardly any bedding remains. The only men's or children's clothes in the closet, the dresser, or the trunk on the loft are dressy. The Van Dykes have left no jeans, sneakers, jackets, or T-shirts behind.

Nobody takes note of the X and the date on the wall behind the sofa bench, except Knudsen, who had developed a photo of that wall and who knew my brother's middle name.

Mama and Pop disappeared into the A-frame early that night. The light that stayed on clued me they were reading. Pop's current book was a history of ancient Rome. Mama was sifting through the Bible, in case she missed something the first hundred times.

Ava and I went to sit by the river on a grassy bank a hundred yards beyond the west boundary of Quig's, so we could hear the music from the party at Big Dan's and pick out the voices or guitar licks of performers we recognized who had stayed over.

The moon looked like a gash in the sky. The stars appeared as bright clusters, and every minute or so, a meteor flashed from east to west.

Ava was barefoot, with a beaded leather thong around her ankle, a long black skirt, and a loose top. Now and then I glimpsed a bra strap. Among hippies, the bra indicated a Christian as clearly as a fish or cross did. Her hair shivered in the ocean breeze that followed the course of the river. In the starlight, her eyes were pure silver. "I've never met people like Wendy and Tom," she said.

I shook my head, meaning I hadn't either.

"If you're a cross between those two, strong like him and gentle as her, and wise as either of them, I ought to sell everything I own, give it to the poor, and follow you."

"How much can you get for everything you own?"

"Including my car, maybe two hundred."

"That's not much for a rich kid. Tell me about your folks?"

"My real dad, Paul McNees, he's got more money than the rest of Evergreen put together. Still, even after six divorces. He just built a resort on Trinity River.

"And he's pretty cool. He knows every joke ever told, and he's always telling them. I guess that's one reason he got so rich. Makes people laugh while he's sticking it to them. But he remembers my birthday, buys me Christmas presents. Every couple weeks, I meet him for lunch. Which is a lot, if you think about it, for a guy who has nine kids, at last count.

"My mom's a travel agent sometimes. She's sweet, but she can flip out when things go wrong. This year she turned forty and landed in the hospital after a drinking binge. But when I saw her last time, she looked okay."

"You've got a step dad?"

She grimaced. "He's the reason I live in a yurt. He likes me more than he likes my mom."

Even among star clusters, meteors, the starlit river flashing past and hills spiked with redwood and pine against a background of silver sky, of all the sights, Ava was the masterpiece.

If she was as bright, loyal, deep, and loving as I thought, I'd have to be *loco* to just move on and leave her here. But unless one of the folks who applauded for me yesterday showed up soon and asked to become my agent or offered a record contract, I was on my way to law school. Odds were high that with me in L.A. and her elsewhere, even if she chose to love me, I would lose her. I imagined marrying her and moving home, renting a shack in King's Beach, working security or dealing baccarat at Harry's Casino, giving my folks a grandkid or two. But Pop had always wanted me to succeed at the college he'd had to leave after two years on account of money, when a trick knee sidelined his football and the scholarship it gave him. At USC, he imagined I could become somebody with the power and courage to back the humble and whip the bullies and big shots in their own ballpark. Even if I chose to follow my own dream, to write songs and make music, it would mean a vagabond existence that didn't seem to fit Ava. I couldn't imagine her following any man around. But here I sat, becoming ever more enchanted. I said, "Now that we know who really killed Jimmy, and why, do you feel any better?"

She grabbed a clump of grass and tossed it to the breeze. "Clifford, mostly all day I've been trying to believe Roy's story."

"And…?"

"I don't. See, Jimmy obeyed the law, mostly. He wouldn't risk hurting Delene like it would if he'd got busted for dealing weed. There's no way he was out there poaching."

"Maybe he was there for something else."

"What?"

"Hunting?"

She sighed, pulled her hair back off her shoulders, and stood. "Jimmy didn't hunt."

While we walked toward the yurt holding hands, I told myself Ava must hold some wrong ideas about Jimmy Marris.

And I coached myself to trust Pop's assumption that Alvaro had proved he could evade the hunters, that he would deliver the Van Dykes to some sanctuary without anybody but us knowing he'd helped them escape. Pop had proven his judgment so often, Alvaro, Mama, and I used to consider him infallible.

Now I wasn't sure.

Before 7:00 a.m., Pop rapped on the tailgate window of my Chevy. In the bathhouse I used the sink and urinal while a girl about sixteen showered, dried off, and beamed at me. I told Pop about her. "Wake up to a sight like that," I said, "who needs coffee?"

He nodded. "I got an eyeful in the bathhouse yesterday. Since then, I've been going off to pee in the woods. Cut my odds of keeling over from a heart attack."

Something in his tone of voice kept me from laughing at his remark.

We stopped at the jail and got told the sheriff was at Babe's. We found him there, in a booth across from two loggers. When he saw us, the loggers turned to view the object of his interest, then straightened their caps and tossed greenbacks onto the table. They ambled toward the door and scorched us with looks they might use on a visiting ball team who had skunked the locals.

Pop led the way to Willis' booth and pointed at the vacated bench. "You mind?"

Willis shook his head and sipped coffee. Pop and I sat. The sheriff had already eaten. He shoved his plate aside. "Found the preacher's truck."

"No preacher?"

"Somebody ditched the junk-heap at the Sacramento Airport."

"How about Van Dyke?"

He scowled. "You holding something over Knudsen?"

"Never met the man till yesterday. Why?"

"It's him you can thank."

Pop raised his hands, palms up. "Elaborate, would you?"

"Time being, till we apprehend Van Dyke, we called off the search for your Mexican boy." With a final contemptuous glance at us, he slipped out of the booth and left the cafe.

I moved to the seat across from Pop. "If they find Van Dyke," I whispered, "they find Alvaro too, and bust him for harboring a fugitive or something."

Pop said, "They won't be looking in the woods anymore. Who sets out hiking through wilderness with three little guys?"

"Maybe X."

"Don't tell the sheriffs."

We celebrated the good news with coffee, orange juice, and chili omelets. "I'm thinking your mama and I need a day of rest," Pop said, "before we drive four hundred miles. I'm going to check out that Riverside Lodge, where we can get a real bed and I can fish myself to sleep. Whatever loose ends need tying up here in Evergreen, I'll take care of them."

"We can do it together."

"What I'm saying, Clifford, is you should get out of town. Put some miles between you and your enemies. Your mama agrees. Invite Ava up to the lake. She could use a vacation, I'll bet."

I grumbled, "So you think we can count on Willis to figure out who was in the woods with Jimmy Marris?"

"Does it matter?"

"Yep."

"To Ava, you mean." Pop watched me eat and shook his head. "Tell me something. What good will it do your mom and me to find out one of our boys is in the clear if the other gets knocked off by motorcycle thugs?"

I smeared berry jam on my toast. "They'll back off."

Pop fished for his pipe. "Maybe. And maybe Little Vic will give up the wild life and go to librarian school. Maybe Ava's sister will join up with Mother Teresa. Maybe…"

I believed I couldn't rest until I had the whole truth about the death of Jimmy Marris, though I didn't understand why finding the truth obsessed me. I might need to prove to myself, beyond any doubt, that my brother was as innocent as Roy claimed. Or maybe I hoped to win points with Ava. Or, I was in love and just wanted to help Ava feel better.

The rest of that Monday, I hung around Quig's, mostly talking to residents about Jimmy Marris, Quig, the Cossacks, and sheriffs, and listening for clues. Hippies asked to hear the story of our solving Jimmy's murder. Ava told me she wanted to visit her mother and Delene Marris. After she left, I tried to distract and untangle my mind by reading a biography of Clarence Darrow Pop had given me.

Simon's microbus sputtered into the compound. I caught him before he went into his trailer. On his rusty lawn chairs, he smoked while I told him about Roy Van Dyke shooting Jimmy. He flicked the roach in a fire pit. "Good story."

Then he appeared to get lost in space, probably contending with some profound issue.

I tried to catch him off guard, using my friendliest voice. "How come Ava says you and Jimmy Marris were tight when you told me you hardly knew him?"

He cocked his head and stared. "Define tight."

"Yeah, I misunderstood on account of semantics. Anyway, I'll bet you could give me some names, kids he hung with who might've gone with him to the woods." If he gave me names, I thought, he might be trying to deflect suspicion from himself. If he stonewalled me, either he was innocent or plenty shrewd.

"No good with names," he said.

I stared at him. He floated into space again.

"So you buy Roy's story?"

"It's a good one," he said. "But try this. The plantation belongs to Alvaro. Jimmy knows about it. Alvaro tries to pick up Jimmy's girl at Foster's. Jimmy figures an eye for an eye. A man goes to take from him, he's going take from the man, so him and a homeboy of his go out poaching, and what happens is like Roy told you, only it's Alvaro that shoots the kid. And Roy—see, there's somebody I was tight with, till he caught the faith and shied away from my pagan self.

"S'pose Roy figures he can take the heat off his *amigo* Alvaro by sneaking off before the cops show up to question him and staying gone long enough for Alvaro to get himself on down the road. See, what Roy said to you and your ol' man and the preacher, he's way smart enough to know that's no legal confession. All he's got to do is deny, man."

"Right," I said. "So when you were out there in the woods with Jimmy, you saw my brother?"

His laugh was high and giddy. "Poachers have got pockets full of cash, my man." He turned his front pockets inside out, then waved toward his rusty trailer and pointed at the '57 microbus with blotches of rust on the doors and fenders. "You think I'm sending my share of the loot to a Swiss bank?" He stood and wandered off toward the bathhouse.

Again, I tried to read about Darrow, but Simon's version of Roy's story had poisoned me with dread that Willis would hear or conjure the same version, that Roy was covering for Alvaro.

I needed to corner Jimmy's partner and get the truth. I took a walk along the river past Big Dan's, where the residents tossed horseshoes and played volleyball and school was in session, with two groups of a dozen children each sitting on grassy knolls by the river drawing or writing on tablets.

From the sandy beach at the west bend of the river, near the jamboree ground where one crew stabbed trash and another loaded portable stages onto a flatbed truck, I spied on Sugar Hill. I sat trying to convince myself that Roy was a heroic fellow who would stick by his conscience and confess to the law if they caught him. I watched Harley Davidsons with black skull flags waving from their sissy bars coast down the hill and chug up it, one every few minutes, none in a pack or pair, which alarmed me. Before, I hadn't noticed any of them riding alone. I imagined Vic had sent them out as scouts, trying to catch me away from Quig's.

And I realized something that should've come clear over breakfast. What was keeping Pop in town wasn't fishing. At home in Incline, our cabin was on the lake. We had a dock and two canoes. All that kept Pop in Evergreen was an idea that Little Vic might be waiting for the crazy old gunslinger to leave before he dedicated his gang's efforts to wasting me.

I found Quig on the deck behind the Chattagua hall. A middle-aged woman with pigtails and sun-blistered skin was reading his fortune with Tarot cards. I leaned on the deck rail nearby and eavesdropped. She saw water and air in his future.

When she concluded and left, he called me over and motioned to the flimsy wicker chair that matched his. "Roy Van Dyke, huh?"

"And you got it right," I added. "Jimmy was a poacher."

"Makes it double tough on a bright-eyed kid like Ava who thought he walked the straight and narrow."

"It'd be easier on her if she knew who was out there with Jimmy. Then she could blame Jimmy's death on somebody. It's tough to blame Roy, with all the stuff he had on his heart and mind. Who do you think was with him?"

He shook his head. "When you find out, if they don't bust him, I'll see he gets chased out of town."

"Powerful, are you?"

He winked. "I've got some power, like Big Dan does, and Paul McNees, and Vic. Like Woody sang, it's all about the Do-Re-Mi."

When Ava returned, the sight of her cheered me. Besides, I thought, if we sat by the river and reviewed everything we knew, maybe answers would arise.

But she had troubles of her own. She had caught her mom drinking vodka earlier in the day than usual. Her mom had encountered Lola and Vic in an aisle in the Safeway. Lola turned a caustic look on her and strutted past, holding Vic's arm. "And," the mom told Ava, "your sister looked half-dead."

Ava had found Delene Marris chain smoking and biting her nails, only able to talk in peeps. Ava finally gleaned that Delene feared a meltdown at Jimmy's funeral tomorrow morning. "It'll kill me," she peeped, over and over until Ava worried Delene would make the fear come true. If not physically, then in some spiritual way.

We were sitting on the bench by the playground when a guy Ava called Whit, my age with a chipmunk face and bangs, brought a message from the Bend in the River Chapel. Midweek Bible studies and the Wednesday evening service had been cancelled, and next Sunday, a Baptist from Eureka would preach. Because Bob got called to minister to an old friend in Toronto.

"Did somebody talk to Bob?" Ava asked.

"Ginger got a telegram."

Ava rushed off. She drove to Ginger's house. I walked back and forth along the riverbank from where I could watch Sugar Hill and the road that led down to Moonshine Trail. Ava wasn't gone more than twenty minutes. When I heard her car, I hustled back to the yurt.

She looked bewildered. "The telegram came unsigned from New York City. It only asked Ginger to arrange for a substitute preacher and didn't explain anything, except that Bob's supposed to be ministering in Toronto." In those days, draft evaders and drug fugitives saw Canada as home free.

"Does that mean Roy and his kids went to Canada with him?" Ava asked.

"Could be," I said, though I believed otherwise. I thought Bob and the Van Dykes had gone separate ways and Pop was right about Alvaro helping Roy and the cupids flee. But I wasn't ready to tell Ava my brother was aiding Jimmy's killer, though I knew she would learn soon enough, unless I ran off and tried to forget her.

As soon as dark made it harder for the Cossacks to spot Ava's car from their lookout on the hill, she drove us to the Riverside Lodge. Pop already had steaks on the grill, on the river view deck of their cabin. He wrapped ice cubes with a towel, which he smacked against the deck until the cubes were shards. He fixed Ava her first Scotch Mist ever. "Even if you're underage," he said, "you've got more sense than any of us."

Mama sat close beside Ava on a bench and stared across the river, as though any second Alvaro would dash out of the forest.

Pop said, "I made some calls. Guy at the *San Francisco Chronicle*. A news syndicate. A cop or two who'll send word around that the charges against Alvaro got dropped and the search is off. So X might read it and know."

He looked old, fatigued. Beneath a yellow bug light, his face was lavender. I said, "You guys need to go home in the morning. Get Evergreen off your minds. Think about stuff besides Alvaro. I mean, he came home from Vietnam in one piece. And I'll join you in a day or two."

While Pop finished his drink and sucked the ice, he stared at me. At Mama. Back at me. "We'll sleep on it," he said.

He refilled his drink, turned the steaks, and walked to the edge of the deck. I guess he hoped we wouldn't see him take out his pillbox. After he shook a pill into his hand, swallowed it and chased it with Dewar's, he came back and sat beside Mama.

In Ava's car, when she asked me how long Pop had been taking nitro-glycerin, I said, "What nitro-glycerin?"

She told me about her grandpa, who suffered from angina until he died last year. Right then I knew she was right. And I saw what I should've seen all along—Pop had been trying to impart to me all he could before he died.

The idea laid siege to my heart. Now I wanted to go home and spend every minute I had left before law school with Pop. Memorize his every word. Pry every secret out of him. Make him feel deeply loved.

But I still wasn't ready to leave Evergreen. Whether I needed to vindicate Alvaro or score points with Ava and help her through grief hadn't come clear. Neither of those answers felt like the whole story. Maybe something in my DNA made me need to grasp the truth, for no other reason than because it was true. And Pop knew me so well, he believed I would always be pursuing answers, about crimes or mysteries of the heart or spirit. Maybe that was why he tried to make a detective out of me.

Tuesday morning, when Ava and I stopped at the lodge on our way to Jimmy's funeral, Pop and Mama were sitting beside their packed luggage on the riverbank, waiting for us.

Mama rushed to meet me. Her eyes looked glazed, like when she felt prophetic. "Clifford, go home. The motorcycle boys are mean."

I looked at Pop and raised my eyebrows. He said, "Only a moron would ignore your mama."

From the way Mama kissed me and Pop shook my hand, I discerned that things had changed between me and them. They believed their boy was a man, whose judgment they trusted as much as their own. Or more.

Pop hugged Ava, then Mama did the same but held onto her for several minutes, as if she were Claire Poverman returned from the dead. Pop took me aside. "We're not going right home," he said. "Maybe tomorrow we will. Today we're going to the coast, eat a fancy meal, walk on the beach. Your mama misses the big waves.

"And," he said, "I'm taking the Chevy. You're going to keep the Eldorado."

I started to object but he held up his hand. "Fred Swank, used to work at the casino, he's got a body shop in South Lake now. I called him. He owes me a couple favors. Before you go to USC, that Chevy will look showroom new. What color do you want?"

"Sky blue," I said, because I didn't care and that was Mama's favorite color.

Though I suspected his desire to get the body work done was real, I knew he had another motive. He was putting me in a vehicle a half dozen Harleys might play kamikaze with and not make a dent.

Along with the car keys, Pop slipped me a hundred dollar bill. "The Eldorado's a gas hog," he said. "And, I left a pistol and the shotgun in the trunk. Leave them there."

Chapter Twenty-two

The funeral service was at the Congregational Church on Sherry Lane, a block north of Manhattan Avenue. I felt unworthy to attend, since all along I had cared more about clearing Alvaro than exposing the killer. Besides, I had allowed the Van Dykes to escape. But I hoped Jimmy's partner in the woods would show up at the funeral and somehow give himself away. And Ava wanted me to accompany her.

I had borrowed a suit from a giveaway closet in Quig's Chattagua hall. It was tight all over. Ava wore a simple cotton dress and a touch of makeup. I couldn't keep my eyes off her mournful face.

The church, one of the oldest buildings in Evergreen, had oak pews, but the altar and ceiling planks and beams were redwood. All the windows were opaque stained glass. The place was darker than Louella's Lounge.

Delene and Brady sat up front, close as lovers and bowed forward as though life had knocked them out. In the next row, four deputy sheriffs and Willis fidgeted. The rows behind them were occupied by locals about Jimmy and Ava's age. Short-haired fellows in suits as tight as mine, probably because after June graduation they became loggers and bulked up. Girls who, at eighteen, already looked like housewives, hair stylists, or second grade teachers. Behind the locals were empty pews and a few hippies. Simon in a flowered shirt. Quig, who showed up late, accompanied by the Tarot reader. They both wore muslin and sandals. No bikers came.

From the eulogy I guessed that if the preacher had known the deceased, it was during Jimmy's childhood. His remarks made Jimmy into a decorated Boy Scout. Not a word about his brains, dreams, or troubles.

From the line at the casket, I didn't see Jimmy's face until after I saw the rest of him. His legs were extra long. They had dressed him in a dark blue suit and a paisley tie. Ava clutched my arm and pulled me closer. Then I saw Jimmy's face, with its high forehead, the skin lightened by powder, the jaw with a deep cleft. Ava squeezed my arm as if she wanted to break it. No doubt she was seeing, like I was, that Jimmy could be my brother.

Steph hitched a ride to the cemetery with us. I was driving the Eldorado. The procession crept down River Road past the jamboree site, Big Dan's and Quig's communes, to the forest glen just across the bridge from the river bend and surrounded by young redwoods and blackberry vines.

Six young loggers carried Jimmy and set him on the rack that would lower him into the ground. The preacher read from Corinthians. "When the perishable has been clothed with the imperishable, and the mortal with immortality, then the saying that is written will come true. 'Death has been swallowed up in victory…Where, O death is your victory? Where, O grave is your sting?'"

I gazed at Ava and thought, Here, preacher. Here's the sting. Right beside me.

Since nobody at the funeral had clued me that he might've gone to the woods with Jimmy, I would test the one I suspected. If the test failed to convince me, I would need to go after the Cossacks again. Provided I could muster sufficient guts.

When I told Ava I was going to Eureka to hire a lawyer, she insisted on riding along. I didn't argue. On our way past Sugar Hill and through Evergreen, we didn't see any bikers.

Eureka felt like a metropolis. College students were registering, searching for apartments, applying for jobs, buying books.

Lots of them wore a T-shirt that demanded equal scholarships for women athletes.

We sat in a patio cafe and studied the yellow pages. From a phone booth, I interviewed three lawyers. The first two attempted to sound genteel and fair. The third, Kevin Dalrymple, pretended to be nothing but a shark. We drove to his office, in a strip mall, next to a Speedy-Mart. His receptionist was a baby-doll redhead in a mini-skirt and a sleeveless top that was supposed to button down the front but mostly didn't.

Dalrymple, young, pudgy, and sickly pale, leered at Ava even while he listened to me. But he licked his lips at the chance to sue a cop. I opened my wallet and pulled out the hundred dollar bill Pop had slipped me.

As soon as we climbed back into the Eldorado, Ava said, "Yuch." She repeated her assessment of the lawyer every few minutes while we drove. But she agreed Dalrymple was our man.

Alongside the 101 near the coast loop turnoff, a pair of sheriff's deputies had two Cossacks leaning palms-down on the trunk of a cruiser. Neither of them looked up as we passed.

I planned to stop at the jail and leave a message for Brady Barker, but we saw him on a bench outside Foster's Freeze, eating fries and drinking a soda. I pulled to the curb. Ava stayed in the car.

As I approached, Barker shook his head. "I used to think that girl had class."

I held up my bandaged right hand. "It's still dead." With my left, I handed him a Dalrymple business card. "I already filled out papers. We'd better talk, maybe cut a deal. Louella's in an hour."

◇◇◇

Ava wanted to go along. I argued that all her presence would accomplish was to further inflame Barker and besides, she was underage. At Quig's, when I started to leave her, she snapped, "Why'd you tell Brady to meet you at a bar. So you wouldn't have to take me, or is it a macho thing?"

"Macho thing," I said.

On my way into Evergreen, I saw Willis and a partner rousting a trio of Cossacks on the shoulder of River Road.

Louella's seemed darker than usual. The juke box was quiet. The owner only glanced at me, then looked away.

Barker sat at the table closest to the entrance. I went to the bar and bought two Dewar's on the rocks. I sat across from Barker and pushed a drink toward him. "You probably don't drink on duty. But this time you ought to."

"You think you're going to sue me, do you?"

"Did you guys decide to take on the bikers?" I asked.

Barker stared as though hunting for a speck in my eyes. "Sheriff thinks a Cossack dragged Jimmy into the woods."

"Why's that?"

"They're the poachers. He knew the forest better than them."

I played along. "How do you suppose they talked Jimmy into going along? Money?"

"Hell no. Not Jimmy. They must've scared him."

I drank half my Dewar's. "I don't buy that."

Barker's clenched fists rapped the table. "What do you know about Jimmy?"

"Not much. But if it was Cossacks," I said, "how come it was you that brushed away the tracks from the place where Jimmy got dragged to the river?"

Barker was halfway out of his seat, his face jutting forward. "So here's the deal," I said, amazed I didn't stammer. "You give me the truth. That's all I'm asking. Convince me. I'll call lawyer Dalrymple and tell him to go fish.

"And, as long as nobody's hunting my brother, what goes on in Evergreen is your business. You give me the truth, I don't snitch."

Barker kicked his chair away. It toppled. Without a word, without picking up the chair, he marched around me and out the door. I swallowed the rest of my Dewar's, then reached for his, which he hadn't touched. I gulped it down.

In the car, I realized never before had I drunk two double shots of liquor with hardly a buzz. "Adrenaline," I mumbled.

All the way back to Quig's, I imagined the next second a bullet would whiz out of the woods, smash through a window, and put an end to my meddling.

When Barker pulled into Quig's, the residents gathered around as though he were a popsicle vendor. He ignored their queries and walked straight to where I sat beside Ava on a stump outside her yurt. He motioned with his head. "Just you."

I followed him to the riverbank on the west boundary of the property, at least fifty yards from the closest ear besides ours.

He pointed to the ground. I sat. He squatted beside me and frisked me with his eyes. "That a tape recorder in your pocket?"

"Wallet." I showed it to him.

"Empty your pockets."

I complied. He stared at the river. "You're gonna tell Ava. She'll get it out of you. I know what women can do. But nobody passes it on to Delene, understand?"

"Deal. If Ava won't promise, I don't tell her."

"You're going to make her swear on her stack of Bibles, hope to die. Word gets around, gets to my sis, I got no reason on earth not to hunt you down. You can tell that to Ava."

His face had narrowed, his eyes gone to flame. He kicked a rock the size of a football. It rolled, picked up speed, and tumbled toward the river. "Jimmy was panning for gold along the creek. He heard somebody laughing and snuck up close enough to see who it was, three or four Cossacks. He caught them talking about coming back that night. So he came into town and told me."

"Why?"

"I had a deal with Quig. He was gonna pay Jimmy's first year tuition to Stanford if I'd chase the Cossacks out of town. They'd been costing him plenty, and the big harvest was still to come. Give Jimmy one year at any damned college, he promised he'd keep his nose in the books and win him a scholarship for the rest. So him and me went out that night. Me to call in the bust. Jimmy for an eye witness. He wanted to do something to earn his money. He was like that. Wouldn't take something for nothing. The idea was, as soon as they start harvesting, I radio in. By the time they finish and drive the trail up to the highway, Walt and Omar are waiting."

"Who're they?"

"Deputies. Graveyard shift. That's all there was to it." He jumped up and put his hand out flat, meaning if I stood, it would be at my peril. "Like I said, word gets out, not even your smartass ol' man or the gangster he's chummy with can save you."

"One question?"

"What?"

"Who fired the shot that made Van Dyke shoot back?"

"None of your damned business."

While he marched off, a kind of warmth rushed through me. I muttered, "Good for you, Brady." He was still covering for his dead nephew. Because Jimmy must've fired the shot, since Roy took aim at the gun's flash.

As my grudge against Barker passed away, I felt a shock-like jolt in my right ring finger, the first sensation in that hand since Thursday.

Barker's cruiser left a cloud of dust behind. I sat a minute and rehearsed a speech I could give to Quig—"Here's the deal, big shot. If you want me to keep to myself the news that you tried to lay a bribe on a sheriff's deputy, you'd be wise to get out of Evergreen and take your damned money with you."

But I had promised Barker silence, except to Ava. And long ago Pop had convinced me that unless people hold promises sacred, the world caves in.

◇◇◇

Before I could tell Barker's story to Ava, a pack of Harleys came roaring our way. Vic and a half dozen Cossacks skidded up to Quig's gate. The gatekeeper sent a boy running to us. "Um, are you Hickey?" he said.

"One of them."

"These…out here…the little devil says you better come talk to him."

Ava wanted to go alone, as my emissary. I declined her offer. She marched beside me anyway. "Let's go get Quig and bring him along," she said. "Quig needs to be here. Or at least we should take a bunch more people."

I walked faster, too anxious to stop and explain that in macho confrontations like sports and war, every time you exhibit fear or even concern, the enemy scores.

The bikers still perched on their Harleys. As we neared them, Ava grasped my arm. Vic was grinning, holding an envelope. He raised it above his head and waved it slowly back and forth like a hypnotist's prop before he tossed it to me, on the right side. I had to lunge and catch it backhand. He laughed.

"Pocket change," he said. "Fix your car with it. Call it a reward for snooping out the guy that shot Jimmy."

While the Cossacks behind him nodded and murmured approval, Vic kick-started his chopper. They rode out of sight before I looked inside the envelope.

Hundred dollar bills. I counted twenty.

"Thank God!" Ava said. "I mean, not for the money. But Vic is calling a truce."

She kissed my cheek and beamed. Probably until now she had feared every minute that her new friend would soon be as dead as the old one.

We sat on the futon in the yurt while I explained why I didn't feel safe or relieved. I told her about my friend Toby who liked partying and motorcycles. He joined the Iron Horsemen. One night at an open party at the Hell's Angels clubhouse, everybody had to check their weapons, put them on a table. Toby was standing by the table when a Hell's Angel cussed a partner of his. Toby's partner cussed back. The Hell's Angel picked up a knife and slashed at him. Toby grabbed a gun and killed a Hell's Angel. By some miracle, he escaped.

A few days later, he landed in jail, but when the case came to trial, his lawyer got him off for self-defense, since juries aren't partial to Hell's Angels. Months passed. Then, after a concert at the stadium, Toby got found in the home team dugout, sliced to ribbons. He lived, but the surgery lasted two days and cost his mom's insurance a quarter million. Another year passed, then the Highway Patrol stopped him for reckless driving. When they searched his car, they found a dead Hell's Angel in his trunk. "Outlaw bikers don't forgive and forget," I said. "It's against their principles."

"Then you can't stay in Evergreen."

"I could leave," I said, "now that I've gotten the truth."

She cocked her head. I reached for her hand and held it while I told her how Brady Barker and Jimmy had gone to the woods to set up the Cossacks. I told her Quig had offered Jimmy a year's Stanford tuition for his and the deputy's cooperation.

Ava dropped my hand, clutched her belly and doubled over. She rolled onto her side and drew her knees up close. I thought she was going to suck her thumb.

"You okay?"

She said, "Money. Guns and money."

"Yep. I was thinking, we could go to visit my folks, and we could hike to Marlette Lake. Way up high, nobody goes there. We could play Adam and Eve. They didn't have guns or money."

"Or clothes."

"I guess we *could* take swimsuits."

She rolled off the futon and stood. Wiping her face, she walked out. She went to the bathhouse and returned after five minutes with her hair and face shiny wet and her eyes bright as new.

◇◇◇

We stayed at Quig's until after dinner, then finished packing. All of my gear including the Hummingbird and everything Ava thought she needed for a week in the mountains only required half of the Eldorado's cavernous trunk.

When Quig lumbered toward us, wearing a look so dismayed, I wondered where his smugness had gone.

He didn't even glance at Ava. To me, he said, "You're needed at the hospital."

Chapter Twenty-three

If my folks had done like Pop told me they would, spent Tuesday night in Ferndale, found a sea-view restaurant with good Scotch and T-bone steaks, our family and Ava might've spent Thanksgiving counting our blessings. But Pop and Mama worried about me.

So Pop drove my ball-peened '55 Chevy wagon back to the 101 and turned north, toward Evergreen. And the devil prompted Vic and a pack of his Cossacks to walk out of the Crossroads minutes before my Chevy approached from the south.

Little Vic was like politicians Phil Ochs wrote songs about who don't hesitate to endanger others. He gave the order, or the dare. The one they called Crutch, the guy with burgundy skin, jumped onto his chopper. He kicked the starter, revved the motor, popped the clutch, and roared out of the Crossroads parking lot in front of the Chevy he thought I was driving.

Pop always swerved to miss deer, dogs and cats, even possum. For a tough guy, he had a wide soft streak. He swerved to miss the biker.

The Eldorado took us twenty miles in ten minutes. Ava didn't flinch or lift her arm from around my shoulders even when logging trucks blasted their air horns as I passed three and four vehicles at once on the two-lane highway.

The hospital was on the southern outskirts of Eureka. I sped through the parking lot and skidded a turn to stop at the main entrance. We dove out and ran through the doorway and to the information desk. "Hickey, Tom and Wendy," I shouted at an old lady in a green frock. Her face crimped and her eyes clouded, probably from fright, maybe from sorrow. She couldn't speak, only shake her head.

A tall, Indian nurse appeared beside her. "You are?"

"Clifford Hickey," I yelped.

She nodded. "The lady is gone. To the morgue."

I didn't hear the rest. A few beaches get waves that peak but don't roll. They break like sheer cliffs. If you're crazy enough to ride one, your legs will fly up while your head goes down and you'll tumble right and left, spin and flip and splatter on the sand. A wave like that had caught me.

Ava pulled me out of it. "Tom is alive," she said. "He's the one that needs you now."

She led me down a hall and into a waiting room and lowered me to a couch where I sat and imagined Pop would implode like Mama had when Claire died. His spirit would perish. He would stay mute forever. Ava sat close and rubbed my neck and shoulders and wept. I didn't weep, though I longed to.

When they let us see Pop, he was sitting up. His only visible wounds were covered by a bandage around the top of his head. The only change to his face was in his eyes. They used to be sky blue gems. Now they were granite.

He let us hug and kiss him, and motioned us toward the chairs. "I sure hope there's a heaven," he said, his voice parched and scratchy.

After a few silent minutes, he told us about the wreck. How Vic waved and the dark-skinned biker fishtailed onto the highway. About the soft shoulder that sent them into a spin and a roll before they landed in the ditch. The way Mama's head crashed through the windshield and her neck twisted half around.

"What are you thinking?" he asked me.

I wanted to shout, Why the hell didn't you run the biker down? But I wasn't going to stoke the fire of Pop's misery.

"You're already making plans, I'll bet," he said.

"I've got to do something."

"Well, you know what your mama would want you to do. Right?"

"What?" I snapped. "Forgive them?"

Pop made a stiff nod. "She would remind you her savior preached it takes no character to forgive your friends or people who do right by you."

"Okay, but—"

"And she'd say how you deal with your enemies proves whether you're the kind of man she wanted you to be."

"Come on, Pop," I said, "remember Danny Katoulis."

His eyes hooded like most always when he had to think about the years during the world war, just before he met Mama.

"In the story I heard, you didn't have a lot of mercy on that slime."

He stared without blinking at me, then at Ava. When he spoke, he accented most every word. "Then what it comes down to is, are you going to be like me, or like your mama and Jesus?"

I felt Ava staring at me. "Hey," I said, "Jesus could turn the other cheek and walk away and sentence the guy who socked him to hell."

"Even so," Pop said, and raised his voice to command tone. "When it comes to following examples, you'd better look at Jesus. Or at Wendy. Not at me."

I sat a while, pounding my bandaged hand against my knee, glad for the pain that shot up my arm, through my shoulders and all the way to my skull. "A couple days ago you said we don't get to choose who we're going to be, on account of life has ways of making us become who we are."

His granite eyes locked on mine and stayed there until they closed and the Indian nurse informed us she had slipped him a heavy sedative, just before she let us in.

◇◇◇

Pop was wise. I believed in him. But he was wrong if he imagined I could act like anything like Jesus. If I resembled God in any way, I thought, it was the one you can find in the Old Testament, who created hell so he could send his enemies there.

For the first time since I had come to Evergreen, I felt no doubt or compunction about what to do. Pop had spoken for Mama, not for himself. One of us would kill Vic. And if anything stopped Pop and me, as soon as Alvaro found out, he'd run across the mountains or through machine gun fire to avenge our mama. If Alvaro failed, Harry Poverman would pawn his casino before he would let Vic keep living. Vic was a dead man.

Outside, I marched straight to the trunk of the Eldorado. I dug through my gear and Ava's bags and grabbed the holster and gun Pop had left me.

When I pulled it out, Ava yipped, "What's that thing? How'd it get there?"

I slammed the trunk lid and walked around the Cadillac to the driver's door strapping on the holster. Ava grabbed my arm. "Take that gun off," she shouted. "I hate guns."

"Shhh."

"No," she screamed. "Don't you get it? If there hadn't been a gun with Jimmy in the woods that night, Roy wouldn't have shot him. And if Roy hadn't shot him, Alvaro wouldn't have needed to run. And then your folks would still be in Tahoe, alive and well."

"Roy isn't Little Vic," I said.

"What's that supposed to mean?"

"It means you can blame what Roy did on his having a gun, if you want. But Vic doesn't need weapons. He's like a germ. A plague."

She reached for the holster belt and unhitched it so fast, I didn't move quick enough to stop her. "I'll keep the gun."

While I tried to think of ways to get it back without hurting her, she said, "Because men can't be trusted with guns, that's why."

I didn't argue. I knew better. All the lawyers in D.C. couldn't win that argument. Besides, I would be more lethal with the sawed off shotgun.

"You know how to use a gun?" I asked her.

"Come on," she said. "Didn't I grow up in Evergreen?" She stomped around the car to her door, climbed in, and crammed the gun into her purse.

As I pulled out of the lot and turned south on the highway, she asked, "Who's Danny Katoulis?"

"Way back during World War II, before my dad got drafted, before he met Mama, he chased a hit man all the way to Denver. Pop knew the guy from when he was a cop in L.A., and he knew the slime had gotten away with plenty. Now Katoulis had a contract to knock off a certain swami who was on the road raising funds for his cult. Pop's friend Cynthia Jones had hired Katoulis. She was a jazz singer, kind of crazy. She claimed the swami raped her. Pop didn't want to see her become a murderer. So he found Katoulis in Denver and killed him."

"Self defense, I bet."

"Nope. He played God."

She turned her head and stared at the moonlit forest. After a minute, she turned back and touched my arm. "Well, I bet he wouldn't do it now."

I shrugged. "Maybe thirty years with Mama made him more like her than like his old self."

Or, I thought, he was just telling me to lay off Vic because he worried Vic would kill me. Or he hoped to recover soon and do the job himself.

I drove behind the slowest vehicles, wondering how to get rid of Ava. She asked where we were going. "Back to Quig's," I said. She laid her arm around me and her head on my shoulder. I turned into Evergreen on Manhattan Avenue. "Hungry?" I asked.

"Not really."

"I am." I pulled up to the curb in front of Foster's Freeze, parallel with no cars in front of me. "Would you mind getting me a burger and a malt?" I asked.

Most people would've flashed a look that meant, Go get you-rown stupid burger. Some, being of suspicious natures, would've guessed my motive. Ava kissed my cheek, slid over, grabbed her purse off the floorboard, and climbed out. Before she closed the door, she said. "Double burger and chocolate malt?"

I nodded and felt an honest smile rise at the thought of what a pure, trusting soul she had. When she reached the counter and started to order, I floored the Cadillac and raced away. In the rear view mirror, I watched her jump and wave her arms, then shake her fist at me.

Chapter Twenty-four

That night, I wasn't human. I couldn't reason, or feel pity, or think beyond what I needed to do. I didn't notice anything alongside the road. My mind didn't toss around ideas or reflections. I had no hunger, thirst, aches, or discomfort. I had become a soulless demon programmed to seek, destroy, and self-destruct.

I didn't harbor much anger toward any Cossack except little Vic. Hound Dog was crazy. The others might be as cruel as Vic, but all I knew for certain was that they answered to him, like Manson's bunch answered to Charley. My friend Nancy knew all the Manson family murderers but wouldn't even guess which of them were monsters and which were only caught in a drama that made them act like monsters.

If I needed to kill other Cossacks, I would. They just didn't matter. Only Vic did. I thought about driving straight to their camp, making a suicide run. But up there, even if I performed a massacre, I might die without touching Vic.

So I parked behind a shed, hidden from River Road and Sugar Hill, in the field that had been the jamboree parking lot. I went to the trunk and dug out Pop's Remington shotgun.

While I sat behind the wheel watching the road down the slope of Sugar Hill, regret for what I was about to do began to distract me, and it prompted a deeper regret about forsaking Ava. I fished in the glove box, found a flashlight, a pen, and a notepad. I wrote a note, though I had no plan for getting it to her. I apologized and promised that I admired her more than

I had any business admiring anybody I had only known a few days. And I tried to explain that I turned into a killer because every vicious act Vic did or instigated from now on would be mine to account for, unless I killed him. In a sense, I wrote, Vic was part of me. The most evil part, I hoped. And a part that needed to die.

I thought of explaining that a worse sin than killing Vic would be leaving the crime to Pop or Alvaro when it was me who turned Vic loose on my family. But then Ava might believe I was groping for excuses.

I folded the letter and wrote Ava's name on the outside. I thought of going to Quig's and placing it in the mailbox. But Vic might come roaring down the hill while I was gone. He might race off somewhere before I could run back to the Cadillac and give chase.

A minute after I set the letter on the dashboard, I saw Ava. She had just passed my hiding place, striding toward Quig's, on the other side of River Road. For a second I wanted to leap out of the Cadillac, shout her name and run to her. Maybe I could hand her my note and say goodbye, at least.

But I closed my eyes and covered them with my good hand. I counted to one hundred, long enough for Ava to go beyond the range of my vision in the moonlight. Then I opened my eyes, blinked a few times, and measured the length and depth of my breaths. A few minutes later, I heard the rev of one Harley, then another. The noise came from atop Sugar Hill.

From the revs, I imagined the whole gang would come roaring down, but only four appeared, moonlight glittering off their chromed machines. I started the Cadillac's motor and let it idle. The Harleys crept down the trail sputtering in first gear. All I could tell about the riders from that distance, at least two hundred yards, was that they'd brought none of their women along and that the lead rider was little Vic. He looked no bigger than my old teddy bear.

At the base of the hill they stopped and pulled two abreast, as if to confer. Then Vic fishtailed off and the others tagged along. Where the trail met River Road, they turned right and gunned their motors.

I mumbled, "Yes. Yes." They might be heading into the woods to scout or rob a plantation. Or to the Bend in the River Church looking for the pastor so they could beat him into giving up the whereabouts of Roy Van Dyke. Or to the waterfall to skinny-dip and flagellate each other. Whatever they were up to, I had caught them going away from civilization.

The first few miles or so, I hung back. They passed the church and clattered across the covered bridge and over the river, and past Jimmy's grave. On the grade, when the road widened through a foothill village of orchards and lighted farm houses, I sped up to seventy-five and began to close on them. Now they rode four abreast.

The road narrowed as the last house fell behind us. I floored the pedal. Light from the sliver of moon dimmed out as the forest thickened and the trees got taller. Redwoods grew higher than the night allowed me to see. Their fragrance, like fumes from a magic potion, made everything appear otherworldly.

When the asphalt gave way to a dirt logging trail, one rider dropped back, then another. The one on my left was Hound Dog, whom I hadn't seen since I left him tied to a tree. The other was taller.

I didn't intend to run those two over. I only meant to nudge them off the road. But as I neared, they peeled off. When their tires hit the mulchy roadsides, they went crashing into the forest. I heard their squeals.

Little Vic had gone ahead of the other, who I guessed was Boomer, with his lightning bolt scar. He zigzagged. He backed his speed down as though trying to help his leader put some distance between him and me. For an instant I admired the biker's loyalty and courage. Then once again I changed from human to pitiless.

I punched the gas again, caught him in a zig and slammed my right fender into his front wheel. His Harley reeled into a spin. His arms lashed around and over his head as if he hoped to grab a branch. He flew off and tumbled like a spastic high diver, into the black woods.

Years must've passed since a logging truck drove this road. The Eldorado barely fit between the roadside brush, manzanita, and small trees. Branches whip-cracked the fenders and roof. For too many moments, I concentrated on driving. Vic pulled farther ahead. I thought I heard other motors roaring up from behind, and airplanes above, and banshees screaming all around. But those noises were whispers compared to Vic's machine racing flat-out through woods so high and lush, the road became an echoing tunnel.

I would've caught Vic and crushed him in another half mile, except motorcycles can do things Cadillacs can't. Besides, he knew the forest road. I didn't. He skidded around a bend. In the couple seconds it took me to make the turn, he disappeared. But I heard his motor sputtering and saw the totem.

Though I had only been to the swimming hole once, I remembered the directions. When you see the hippie totem pole, a psychedelic phallus carved into a redwood log, on the right side of the road, look for a path on the left side. I stomped my brake pedal and skidded to a stop just past the totem. I threw the gearshift into park, grabbed the shotgun, flung open the door, and jumped out.

As I started down the path, I heard the Cadillac motor purring. I had failed to shut it off, only shifted to park. The key was still in the ignition. For all I knew, Vic was on foot now, circling around and hoping to steal the Cadillac. I lost a minute or two running back to turn it off, grab the keys, and lock the doors.

The path was steep, slippery, and narrow. Stumble one step to either side, I remembered, and you could sink waist-deep in mulch. I gripped the shotgun, crooked my finger into the trigger guard, and started down. I dug my heels into the powdery dirt. In my memory, the pool was fifty yards from the road. Now the whoosh and splash of the waterfall made it sound closer, but it felt like history's longest fifty yards.

Between the squawks of birds or banshees, I heard a squeal that sounded human. After a few careful, silent steps, I heard it again. A light blinked through the brush. I ducked, to make a smaller target.

The path cut right. Vic had barely made the turn. Then his front wheel had lodged in a bush. The rest of his chrome and black-lacquered Harley was leaning on a stump. It looked like a scrap pile.

I squatted and peered all around. Vic could be hiding in the brush, leveling a gun at me. Yet I didn't flinch or feel the slightest fear. I was a creature without feelings that stepped, stopped, peered into the dark, listened for another squeal through the waterfall's swoosh and rumble.

The last twenty yards to the pool, the path was straight and even steeper than before. On this slope the trees had been thinned by erosion. As many lay fallen as stood, which allowed for shafts of pale moonlight to reach the ground. In one of them I saw Vic. A few yards beyond the pool, he was hobbling. A mangled leg dragged behind him. I lifted the shotgun, shoved the butt against my left shoulder. From twenty some yards, I suspected the scattergun might not kill him. But at least it would hurt and make killing him easier.

Someone yelled, "Hold on, wait." It wasn't Vic. I thought it came from in front of me, down the slope. But then I thought echoes might've tricked me, and it could be Hound Dog or Boomer. I had spun and was staring and aiming the shotgun into the dark up the hill when I heard a girl yowl.

She had tripped over a fallen branch. She and her boyfriend had come dashing out from behind one of the manzanitas that made a hedge between me and the waterfall. She was dressed only in panties. He was in boxer shorts. Their hair dripped, their hands and arms clutched sleeping bags and rucksacks.

The boy grabbed the girl's arm and towed her behind him, climbing toward me. "We don't want to see anything, man," he yelled. "We didn't see anything, swear to God we didn't."

I lowered the shotgun, let them run past me, and watched them disappear into the dark. Then I crept on down the hill.

The swimming hole, about ten yards in diameter, was in a rocky, sandy clearing. The waterfall, on the far side of the clearing, was more like rapids plunging down over jagged rocks. On sand beside the pool sat a flickering lantern beside a fire ring with hot coals and a pan that hung from a stick. I smelled pork and beans.

The clearing was a wide ledge in the hillside. The path ended at the pool. The only trail Vic could've followed without sinking into mulch or getting blocked by thick manzanita was along the streambed. In late summer it was dry.

He had hobbled beyond my field of vision, but I heard him scuffing sand and stones. I walked at a zombie pace and paid no mind to the crunching gravel. The shotgun stayed in position beside my waist.

When I saw him, just a few yards ahead, he was on one knee, the other leg still dragging. His hands were stretched out in front, grasping toward something, maybe a rock he imagined he could sling at me. He crooked his head around, stared straight at me. He tried to shout but only managed a high, breathy whisper. "Hey, old man, it was Crutch that ran your kid off the road, not me. Anyway, he was just dueling, playing chicken."

Though his eyes bugged, he couldn't see me. Maybe the crash blinded him. Maybe his eyes were dripping blood. Anyway, he thought I was Pop.

I had no reason to give him the truth. I tensed my finger and might've shot him right then except a volley of banshee cries made my head jerk to glance into the forest. And Mama spoke to me. I don't know whether she came from heaven, from the past, or from out of my heart. She said, "Love your enemy, Clifford."

But all she accomplished was to make me feel like hell. Vic was crawling now. I stalked a couple arm's lengths behind him. Again, he crooked his head around and tried to shout. "Hey, I paid off your kid to get lost, just like you wanted. So why the fuck was he coming back north? Have you thought about that, old man?"

He crawled again, his right hand in the water, his neck craned around over his shoulder while he rasped, "Hey, your kid tortured Hound Dog, so Crutch, being the Dog's brother, took the kid on, put him to the test. Your kid lost, that's all."

I stopped still. The shotgun nearly dropped from my hand. I thought Vic might not need to die, now that I saw who was even more to blame for Mama's death. I had gone after Hound Dog instead of calling on Pop that first day. If not for my stooping to defend wounded pride, Mama would be alive.

Vic crashed head first into a fallen log. After he snaked over it, he gasped a few times and croaked, "Hey, you win. Look at me. You're the man. Let's call it even."

A weird thought came. What if, instead of Alvaro, my folks would've adopted Vic? What if he'd gotten raised by a mother like mine?

He'd have become a better man than me, I thought. Like Alvaro, who was risking his life to help Roy Van Dyke and his cupids.

I quit thinking and watched him crawl, his head crooked almost straight backward to stare bug-eyed in my direction, until his front hand reached over a rocky ledge. "Hey," he yelled, as he tumbled out of sight.

He only fell about eight feet, down what must've been a waterfall in spring, but he landed on a jagged hunk of granite. It made a diamond shaped gouge in his forehead. He didn't even scream.

◇◇◇

Vic didn't go gentle. He was still breathing. I carried him like a bag of cement, over my shoulder. He couldn't have weighed much over seventy pounds. That night, I could've carried a ton. When I reached the road and the Eldorado, he was still breathing in little gulps. I laid him on the ground, opened the trunk, and made a pallet bed out of my sleeping bag. He fit crossways with room left over. I used a piece of tent cord to tie the trunk lid open just enough to give him air. I lashed the rest of the cord around him and my duffel bag and guitar to keep him from flying up and smashing into the trunk lid when I drove over ruts and fallen limbs.

I drove fast, until I neared the place where the other bikers had crashed. Then I slowed and looked for them. Even their Harleys were gone.

Around midnight, I stopped in front of Quig's and opened the trunk. Vic lay on his back, staring up. The trunk light made his moist eyes sparkle. His lip curled. He didn't say anything, but I recognized the look. I had seen it on a boy when I worked for a group home, and in a snapshot of Manson my friend Nancy showed me, and on my own face, in the mirror while I chased Vic into the forest. A cannibal.

I don't remember picking up the tire iron. But I remember seeing Vic's smashed and bloody head and finding the tire iron in my hand. I dropped it, then slammed the trunk closed, fell onto the car, and pounded with my fists until the gatekeeper Ava called Whitey came out of the dark with his finger to his lips. "Hush, man. No screaming after midnight."

So I sat on the ground, picked up dirt and sifted it with my fingers, while I stared at the sliver of moon but saw Vic's face like it appeared at the jamboree when he said, "See you in hell, Pretty Boy."

Chapter Twenty-five

Ava was awake. The flap that served as the door of her yurt was clipped open. Maybe she didn't care if anybody came in and raped or killed her. I found her sitting cross-legged in the dark on her futon, in her T-shirt with the silk-screened beaver and its chainsaw. Her eyes were wide but registered no alarm or surprise. Her voice came out flat and sounded raw, as if she'd caught strep throat during the last few hours.

I brought in her duffel, her rucksack, and the Mexican shopping bag into which she had packed her climbing boots and spare sandals. She said, "Did you kill them?"

"Little Vic anyway."

Her eyes, cheeks, and even the crown of her head appeared to deflate. I dropped her bags and remained standing, staring at her and feeling like someone who can see heaven from hell across the river and knows he can gaze upon its delights for eternity but never touch or taste them or hear the songs.

"I'm going to the police station," I said. "Only, maybe I don't have the guts to walk in there alone. Maybe on the way I'll spook and run."

After she sat still so long I thought it meant No, leave me alone, she pushed herself up. She walked past me, barefoot, out the doorway and straight to the shotgun door of the Cadillac.

All the way into Evergreen, she stared at me as though I were a fugitive madman. Still I hoped that suddenly her eyes would moisten, her lips part, and the softness in her voice would absolve me. Like Mama's voice would have. Mama could forgive anybody, for anything. But the closest Ava came was to ask, "Do you feel better now that it's done?"

I pondered, but soon realized the words to explain how I felt didn't exist. Not in the English or Spanish I knew. "I can't even remember who I was before. I mean, not just today. Yesterday, last week. I'm not who I thought I was."

"Who are you then?"

"Something evil, I guess. Like Vic used to be."

I parked at the curb in front of the jail. After one last gulp of Evergreen's crystalline air, I climbed out. I took the car keys with me. On the sidewalk, under a streetlamp, I glanced at Ava, saw the horror in her face better than I had in the dark yurt or car and knew if I tried to even touch her hand she would scream and jump away.

But she was brave. She followed me inside. The lanky deputy with a birthmark where a sideburn might be glanced up from a magazine he preferred we didn't see. He closed it and slipped it under the counter.

To keep from collapsing, I leaned on the counter with the weight on my good hand. "You know Little Vic?"

"Everybody knows Little Vic."

"I killed him."

The deputy leaned backward and gaped. "Come again."

A sob came from behind me, from Ava. The deputy made a half-turn and called to the jailer, who was at a desk scraping corrosion off a flashlight. "Spence, come here on the double."

Spence hustled our way. "Where did you leave him?" the deputy asked.

I handed him Pop's car keys. "The green one opens the trunk."

Spence led me down the hall toward the cages. Though I heard Ava sob again, I didn't turn or look over my shoulder. I wanted to see her crying no more than I wanted her to see the despair that was squeezing the life out of me.

I said to the jailer, "The car belongs to Tom Hickey. Please keep it somewhere safe for him."

Chapter Twenty-six

Alvaro had dodged a brush fire, bloodhounds, and airplanes but never traveled more than ten or so miles from Evergreen until, after two days up and down the foothills and into the Trinity Wilderness, before dawn Saturday morning he had returned to the outskirts of Evergreen to finish the job one of Phil Ochs' *amigos* had paid him for. Keeping Phil alive.

Ochs had told this *amigo* he was spooked of the jamboree, outdoors in firearm and redneck country. When the *amigo* heard a decorated soldier who was Phil's friend would be there, he and my brother made a deal.

In July, Alvaro went to a party, danced and drank with a girl who ran with the Cossacks. She didn't know details, only that a Cossack had gotten paid by somebody to whack the commie songwriter.

So Alvaro studied the terrain, learned from Big Dan where the stage would be set up, and calculated where a Cossack sniper's best position would be. And when the sniper I believe was Hound Dog lowered the sights on his rifle, Alvaro sighted his 30.06 and fired into the dirt at Hound Dog's feet.

As the biker wheeled and ran, so did Alvaro. Through the woods close to the river, he crossed the creeks called Jim Beam and Old Crow, to Roy Van Dyke's A-frame.

Sunday afternoon, while Roy confessed to us, Alvaro was hiding out at the migrant camp across the highway and over a hill from the airport. After we left, Pastor Bob followed the

Van Dykes' neighbor, Pedro Marti Sr., who drove Roy's Dodge to the migrant camp. He gave the truck to a mechanic with instructions to strip it and use the parts. And he delivered a note to my brother.

The note asked X to meet Roy and his cupids that night after dark five hundred paces along Grizzly Creek north of Highway 36.

Alvaro guided them over a pass through the Trinity Wilderness, where Ophelia turned her ankle. The men took turns carrying her. In a village called Wildwood, they arranged with a farm worker to drive them in the camper bed of his pickup across the Sacramento Valley. He dropped them near Mill Creek. They climbed into the Sierra Nevada and reached the Pacific Crest Trail, along which serious adventurers hike from Canada to Mexico and some *campesinos* trek a thousand miles to make a few dollars an hour.

Through September, my brother and his troop lived like bears, on fish and berries. Roy got bit by a rattler while deflecting its attention from his kids. Oedipus came down with a rash like hives.

South of Mount Whitney, where the mountains were dry and the lakes cesspools compared to those they left behind, Roy traded *sinsemilla* to campers for dried fruit and nuts and powdered eggs that sustained them until they crossed the Mexican border.

◇◇◇

Pop had a broken collarbone and internal bleeding. He would stay in the hospital at least three weeks. A lawyer named Ramos gave me the diagnosis when he came to introduce himself and say Paul McNees had hired him to represent me.

"Why should McNees pay for me?" I asked.

"I guess that's his business, not ours," Ramos said. "He sure didn't tell me."

I hoped Ava had put him up to it. More likely, I thought, McNees was paying off the killer of his daughter Lola's rotten boyfriend.

I told Ramos everything. He suggested I might go free if I bent the truth, claimed Vic had ordered me at gunpoint to follow him into the forest with my Cadillac, since the trunk was big enough to carry a mountain of poached marijuana. If that were the case, Ramos mused out loud, "It could be that Vic meant to steal the car. Could be he tried to shoot you with the pistol he kept in a holster strapped to his Harley, but which has gone missing. But you moved faster and popped him with the tire iron. That could be."

"Plead guilty," I said.

The day of the hearing, Ramos said, "That biker gang packed up and split."

"Who chased them out?" I asked. "The law or the hippies? Or did they just give up?"

Ramos shook his head. "They're gone all the same."

The marshall who came from Eureka and drove me to my hearing looked too old to be employed. All the way, he talked about fly fishing the Klamath River. Besides the marshall, the judge, and the prosecutor, only Ramos and I attended the hearing.

The charge was voluntary manslaughter. I let Ramos do the talking. Both he and the prosecutor failed to mention that Vic was already down and half dead when I bashed him with the tire iron. The judge went out for coffee or something and returned to deliver a sentence of three to six years. Ramos convinced him that a guy as educated as me could best pay my debt to society on a road crew and tutoring illiterate felons in a certain program he knew.

Before I got sent to the Siskiyou Honor Camp near Yreka, Steph the waitress visited. She said Paul McNees had talked Ava and her sister into a trip to Hawaii. He was paying the bill. Nobody knew when or if they would return.

Chapter Twenty-seven

In fall, along I-5 in the shadow of Mount Shasta, we repaired potholes, pouring, raking, and tamping hot tar. Evenings I tutored. I didn't sleep well, only a few hours each night before I woke and brooded, often trying to understand how my life would proceed from here on.

I couldn't imagine a future. A felon can't practice law. And my passion for music had cooled as I saw I had no gift for composing. After all I had experienced in Evergreen, if I had a gift, songs should've come to me. They didn't.

I tried to make some kind of peace with the killing I'd done, like Alvaro and other veterans of a war they suspected was futile and perhaps wicked. Only most of the veterans had killed in self defense, not mashed a tiny fallen man with a tire iron.

That Pop had gunned down Danny Katoulis and gone on to become a far more than decent man gave me some hope. But he had Mama to help him.

I had nobody. Not Pop or Alvaro. Their highest motive was justice, like mine had proved to be. Besides, they couldn't forgive me because they never blamed me. They blamed Little Vic. Mama would've blamed us both, and forgiven us both.

Forgiveness had to come from someone merciful. An angel like Mama who could see my evil heart and love me anyway. Mama could forgive anybody, because she knew by heart something that came to me like a message delivered by a phantom who woke me late one night. The message was, we all are part

God, part devil. Because like God is love, the devil is pride. And pride, nothing else, had turned Vic and me into killers.

For all of us who hadn't tried to flee or assaulted any guards or prisoners, Thanksgiving was a holiday. A Calvary church from Mount Shasta brought us turkeys, yams, biscuits, and canned creamed corn.

But what made me almost glad to be alive was, we got to eat with our families. Because the mess hall wouldn't hold everybody, we ate outside in an icy wind, on frozen benches with our feet in snow.

I saw Pop at the gate. But when they let him enter, he didn't hustle over to me like he had every weekly visit before. He loitered just inside, chatting with other visitors, while a woman all bundled in a ski cap and full length down coat walked toward me. Until she came so close I could see her frosty breath, I didn't even hope she could be Ava.

She wore no makeup, but her lips and cheeks were rosier than ever, from the cold. Her hair was braided. She looked a few years older than she had three months ago. She was too tan for a hippie girl in winter. And she looked so happy I stood waiting for her to announce her engagement to some Honolulu surfing legend or brain surgeon.

"I asked your dad where Alvaro is," she said. "He told me to ask you."

So we sat on the frozen bench, and I told her the story of my brother's journey. I told her Alvaro wrote me a letter most every day, and that he phoned Pop often and promised he'd come home as soon as he helped the Van Dykes get settled.

"Where are they going to settle?" she asked.

"He doesn't say. Pop doesn't ask."

"You're sure about that?"

"Yeah. Why?"

"Clifford, I love you, and your family. Do you think I would turn in your brother?"

"Maybe you'd turn in Roy. He killed your boyfriend."

"You're my only boyfriend," she said. And though she had read the rules that forbade prisoners and guests from making any physical contact, her hand crept and folded over mine.

"Maybe Costa Rica," I mumbled. My heart swelled. But I looked around and saw three to six more years. Then my heart broke open.

Ava let me weep on her breast, even after a guard shouted at us. He was a decent guy. When I waved at him, he turned and walked away.

To receive a free catalog of Poisoned Pen Press titles, please contact us in one of the following ways:

Phone: 1-800-421-3976
Facsimile: 1-480-949-1707
Email: info@poisonedpenpress.com
Website: www.poisonedpenpress.com

Poisoned Pen Press
6962 E. First Ave. Ste. 103
Scottsdale, AZ 85251